img_1

I0445521

FINALLY HOME

Alpine Valleys – Book 3

L. Simpson

www.BOROUGHSPUBLISHINGGROUP.com

FINALLY HOME
Copyright © 2019 L. Simpson

ISBN 978-1-951055-02-8

For Nanna. You would have loved this.

FINALLY HOME

Chapter One

Whoever coined the phrase that "nothing is certain in life except for death and taxes" forgot to add that people will disappoint you and that life is relentless. I'd been hanging on by a thread for years now, and I didn't see any relief ahead. But despite how much I didn't want to leave, now was the time if I was going to make it to my new *home sweet home* by nightfall. I did what my mother had taught me: put my head down and got on with it.

I didn't want to move at all, let alone with a horrendous hangover and after having my confidence broken by so-called friends. But destiny, the fickle creature, had other plans for me— tortuous, evil plans. I had a choice: I could either wallow and be consumed, or get angry and use that anger to fuel my action. Today, I was taking door number two. I often gave myself pep talks as I drifted towards despair. When my world had fallen apart five years ago after my parents had died, I'd stood on the precipice of oblivion. That time, I'd opted to shatter and become a sad, pathetic mess until I'd almost lost myself. Since then, I'd decided to skip the shattering part. It was too messy.

I would move to the country to look after a grandmother I didn't know and who my mum hadn't spoken to in decades, and get on with it. When bad things happened to me, they happened in a major way. Go big or go home, right? Moving to Harrietville, population 338, had come at me like a slow-motion sledgehammer. I should have prepared, but I hadn't. I'd been anxious in a way that made my feelings on the subject fuzzy and hard to pin down. I didn't know my grandmother at all and it was going to be painfully awkward as I moved to a new job, in the place where my mother grew up and fled at eighteen. But then I didn't love my current job or my apartment, and after last night, I found out I didn't really have friends either. As lightning bolts of booze-fuelled pain struck my brain, I was even more muddled. The only thing I was sure about was that I was alone.

As I moved my worldly belongings into my car, it felt like one of those nightmares where you need to hurry but you deliberately dawdle. At least I didn't have to move furniture; I'd given all of it to charity. I felt guilty because it was Mum's stuff, but I was already carrying enough emotional baggage when it came to my parents. I had no room for couches and dinner sets. When I put the last bag in the boot, I stepped back and looked at the '93 spearmint-green hatchback. It was ugly as sin and the tinted windows and pearl paint finish didn't make up for the fact it had a lawnmower engine and sounded like a jet-powered shit box. I'd been so proud when I'd bought it because I'd saved for it myself, and Mum and Dad had been impressed. Now I hated it, because like me, it didn't belong here, in this upscale inner-city suburb. I also wasn't sure it would even get me to Harrietville.

I looked in the backseat to see my twenty-five years represented by an old car full of overpriced, baggy black clothing, a hair straightener, a box of celebrity slim meal replacements and some tampons. What did that say about me? Clearly I wasn't ready for a zombie apocalypse, but maybe a casting call for *The Bachelor*. With nothing keeping me, I drove away from my home for the last five years. The map application on my phone had me taking a windier route than I remembered, but I had more faith in Google than I did in the memory of my only visit to Nan when I was eight.

As I watched the city shrink in my rearview, it started to rain heavily. My thoughts plummeted as the day and my outlook on life got more and more grey. Needing a distraction, I fiddled with my playlists, bringing up my 'Menstrual Mix.' The road started to wind up and over a small mountain range that had been burnt by a bushfire years ago, but the charred black trunks still remained beneath the green leaves. I began to wonder if I would ever sprout new leaves.

I gave myself thirty minutes to cry about how shitty life was, then I knuckled down and began to prepare mentally for what was coming. Because my mum and my grandmother hadn't spoken in years, I really only knew three things about her. One: Alma was a great cook. My mum had protected the handwritten recipe book that Alma had given her like a family grimoire. I now kept it safe by not using it. Eating? No problem. Cooking? No way. Two: Alma liked to garden, and her lawyer had included looking after her garden as part of my duties. This was another strike for me; I struggled to even keep *myself* alive, and that should've been instinctual. Third: Alma liked a drink. This was based on Mum's hatred of the stuff and reference to it reminding her of home. At least we could get drunk on sherry at five o'clock as she recuperated from major surgery in the nursing home.

The only other thing I knew was that before whatever happened that split them apart, Mum had loved growing up in the country. Interestingly, she hadn't talked about my grandfather much, although they must've been close because she had a photo of him beside the bed. But as all things with my mother, she avoided talking about anything personal.

A few hours into my trek to the arse end of the earth, I needed to feed my hangover with comfort food. I stopped in the next town, which was called Yarck. It would've been more fitting if it was called Farck. Seeing cars parked out the front of a strange place called the Giddy Goat, I pulled up next to a truck the size of a shipping container and a very shiny, sexy-looking motorbike. While I waited for my sausage roll and bucket of Diet Coke, I noticed one of the best-looking men I'd ever seen beside me in the queue. It was unexpected, and my overloaded brain focused in on him. He was tall with a big barrel chest, filling out his grey Henley under a killer, worn-leather jacket. He had dark auburn hair that was a bit too long, the waves framing his handsome face. His denim-blue eyes that were looking at me speculatively were beautiful and rimmed in thick lashes. Wait. Looking at *me*. Shit. Embarrassed, I gave him an awkward smile, which he returned with a full-blown one, his pearly whites on show. I blushed hard. This was seriously one sexy ginger.

Then I remembered what I looked like—black striped leggings that may have been a little sheer across my generous bottom, designer runners that were covered in mud and an oversized black woolen sweater that dropped off one shoulder. My dark hair was tied in a knot on my head, my fringe was all over the shop and I knew I had panda eyes. My blush deepened, but thankfully the server called my order, giving me a reason to get away from his attention. But my reprieve was short lived.

I'd like to say that what happened next was because the world was conspiring against me. But that wasn't true. I was an idiot, plain and simple. When I got my sausage roll I was desperate to leave after drooling over the Sexy Ginger and as a result, I grabbed the tomato sauce with too much gusto because PLOP! I had squeezed the plastic bottle so hard, it squirted sauce up in the air, landing on my forehead. I was stunned for a moment, wondering how I'd managed such a humiliating feat. I mean really, I deserved a medal in how to be ridiculous. I stood still, hoping it was a dream, but alas, the cold, viscous substance was in my hair and running towards my temple.

I chanced a look around to see if others had seen. Everyone was looking at me in astonishment. Well, everyone except for the Sexy Ginger. His hand was over his mouth as he tried not to laugh. He was losing the battle because his hot as hell, burly body was shaking. With laughter. At me. Dear God.

Desperately needing to leave so I could finish dying of mortification by slamming my head in my car door, I grabbed the sausage roll out of the bag, and ran it up my head where the sauce was running down towards my ear. Then with a smile aimed at *him*, I said, "Waste not, want not," before strolling out the door like I wasn't a complete moron. No one said anything but I could hear one person who I knew was tall and sexy, boom with laughter.

***

Wow. I mean seriously. WOW. I'd seen the most brilliant thing in my life and no one would believe me when I told them. On this dreary winter's day in Yarck of all places, the most beautiful woman I'd ever seen waltzed into the Giddy Goat, took her time checking me out, then did something that belonged in a *Three Stooges* movie. She'd managed to coat her head in tomato sauce before wiping it off back on her food. She had a will of iron to not buckle under everyone's stares, and when she'd played it off like it was on purpose? Comedic genius. Shit, I'd been half in love with her already, but when she sauntered out, her sexy ass swaying in leggings that showed me she liked stripes, I was done for.

Little did she know that I was following her now, not because I was a creeper, but because it appeared we were headed in the same direction. That was interesting. What was more interesting was the fact that for the first time in a long time, a woman intrigued me. Sure, I wanted to bang her. She was sexy—all curves and big grey eyes, and loads of gorgeous dark hair that I wanted splayed over my pillow, or chest, or, let's face it, both.

But I didn't *only* want to bang her; I wanted to know about her. The way she looked at me was unguarded and honest. She liked the way I looked, and her blush was cute as hell. All that wouldn't matter though, because if our paths ever crossed again, one of two things would inevitably happen. We would either have one night of amazing sex, or she would tell me about her hopes, dreams and disappointments and want my friendship—nothing more. I liked that people were comfortable sharing with me, but it happened too often. I was a man who could hold a conversation and the word *feeling* didn't make me break out in a rash. This was my lot in life: women either used my body, or cried on my shoulder. But this woman? Something about her old-beyond-her-years grey eyes and full, pouty lips made me hope I'd get both.

At least she gave me something good to think about, as opposed to the consulting gig in Melbourne I was returning from. I needed money to get my farm up and running, but my consulting job was sucking my will to live. I'd started fulfilling my dream: a farm that grew a range of boutique crops, had accommodation on site and a sustainable home to raise a family in. But it was slow going, and every cent counted. Occasionally travelling the four hours to Melbourne for work was necessary.

As I approached the turnoff for the Snow Road, I was surprised that she was slowing down, and indicating. I followed her as she drove cautiously off the highway. I kept my distance, not wanting her to think I was a stalker, and it seemed smart because her god-awful green car was blowing smoke. I hoped it made it to wherever she was headed.

As Mt Buffalo came into sight, I smiled. I was getting close to home. I'd been abroad for ten years, during which time the prospect of coming home had elicited mixed emotions. I'd loved growing up here. It was beautiful, there was always something to do and I was part of the community. I got to be close to my mum and two sisters, despite the latter being continual pains in my arse. I had good friends too, especially Erik, my best mate since kindergarten. All that was reason enough to want to be in the Alpine Valleys. But home reminded me of my father. He'd died almost twenty years ago of cancer, and I still missed him. Then there was Sheridan, and all that had gone down between us. She was the reason I'd left like an overly sensitive school boy. While I was happy to be back, I was regularly reminded of things I hadn't been able to fix.

My phone in my pocket buzzed and while I contemplated not pulling over to check it so I could keep following the mystery woman in her deathtrap on wheels, it may've been important. After reading the text from my sister, telling me she had, '*serious Erik-related shit to talk about,*' I still wasn't sure. Erik had recently met the love of his life but was fighting it. I'd given him advice that he didn't want to hear and he was risking losing her forever. He didn't listen because he'd never understood why I wanted to settle down. Until now. I hoped this *shit* was positive, because my man was in deep and didn't know how to hang onto his Annie. I promised myself, again, that if I ever found *the one*, there is nothing I wouldn't do to keep her with me.

Chapter Two

Turning off the freeway, I'd discovered the valley floor was lush green, dotted by little towns. Impressive mountains rose up around me the closer I got to Bright, reminding me of my mother's stories about hiking here. I'd wondered if she was lying at the time, because we never did anything like that when I was a kid. Snow now capped the mountains, and the river snaked its way along beside the road and houses with home fires burning. I couldn't deny it was far prettier than the city.

I arrived in Bright to pick up groceries. Surprisingly the town was pretty big. I wasn't sure what I had been expecting, but it certainly wasn't two roundabouts, two supermarkets, fifteen coffee shops and thirty hairdressers. I walked down the street to the community hub where I started work next Monday. All the lights were on inside, despite it being close to five p.m. I hoped the people at work would be professional and let me get on with my job. I had no interest in making friends and being social; I'd learned my lesson.

Heading into the supermarket, I picked up enough supplies for a few days: Panadol, milk, bread, peanut butter, baked beans, dark chocolate and an apple. That right there was the diet of champions. I considered going to see Alma at the nursing home before heading to her house, but I was too terrified. I had only one vague childhood memory of seeing her and a brief conversation at the funeral; that was it. She had called me often since, but I had ignored her until the lawyer called and told me she was recovering from a fall that had almost killed her, and that I had to come and help. So now, here I was. But how on earth was I supposed to do that when we were strangers?

I needed more time, even if it was only a few hours, before I had to face an old woman I didn't know. I left Bright and continued along the valley floor, towards the alpine mountains where people skied in winter and mountain biked in summer. Dusk had not fully set in, and the warm golden glow of sunlight hit the top of Mount Feathertop, making the white peak look a brilliant pink. It was beautiful, but I felt like a visitor, with no connection to my mother's childhood home. Gone was the concrete, the sound of trams rattling up Chapel Street, and the smell of coffee, exhaust smoke and restaurants was replaced by green fields, pollen and wood smoke.

I peered at the tall mountains through my windshield, overwhelmed by their size. Mum had often talked about walking the Bungalow Spur Track and I wondered if I was looking at the summit she'd walked to. We weren't close before she died. She loved and cared for me, but we weren't like those best-friend mother-daughter duos. Maybe retracing her steps would bring her closer to me. Unfortunately, I was overweight and utterly unfit for hiking.

As houses became more frequent, and large, leafless oak trees lined the road, I paid closer attention. Alma lived on the edge of town. I pulled into her overgrown driveway; it had a rambling, wild sort of appeal. It was a weatherboard house painted soft pink, with white framing the windows and a corrugated iron roof. I drove down the driveway, past the narrow veranda that led to the front door and into the backyard to the shed to park my car. I hadn't left myself much room to get out, and squeezing into the darkness, I imagined spiders lurking there. I brushed past the side wall, and something soft and sticky rubbed against my skin. I whimpered, rushing out of the shed, my key at the ready. If a possum came near, I would gouge its eyes out. Urgently needing to be somewhere with the lights on, I ran to the front door, but as I stood trying to get the key in the lock, I heard a rustle in the bushes behind me and I froze.

"SHIT," I yelped when I heard a strange growl. Was that a dingo? My hands shook as I frantically opened the door and fell in, landing on my stomach on top of my handbag. Scooting forward, I managed to sit up and slap blindly at the wall in hope of finding a light switch. With luck I did and when my eyes flew to the door, I found the wild beast. Then I laughed. Sitting in the open doorway was a cute little orange dog wagging its tail. It looked at me in the eye, then trotted over my legs and towards the back of the house like I hadn't made a complete spectacle of myself for the second time that day.

Working hard to control my breathing, I stood and took in the lounge room. I was assaulted by an extraordinary amount of knickknacks, doilies and framed photos. This was nothing like the home I grew up in. At least there were two redeeming features that made up for the OTT old lady-ness: a wood fire glowing red, and a large flat-screen television with an Apple TV sitting proudly on a table with the sides folded down. I almost deflated on the spot with relief.

My perusal moved from the entry to a server window into the kitchen where someone had placed fresh flowers. Above were three enlarged photos: one of Mum and Uncle Luca when they were little, a family photo of Alma, Granddad, Mum and Luca and another black and white one of Alma, with some other women taken what must be fifty years ago in front of old tobacco sheds. Based on my mum's dislike of her own mother, I was surprised to see her in pictures that clearly had pride of place.

The dog barked, making me jump, and I walked through to the kitchen where it sat in front of a microwave. There, I found a note explaining Marmalade belonged to a neighbor who had left me dinner in the fridge, and Marmalade had treats in the tin on top of the microwave. I frowned; people didn't just do things like that, nice things, the right things. In my experience, people did what was right for them, and didn't think about anyone else. I got a biscuit from the tin, and gave it to Marmalade who had been patiently waiting. She scarfed the biscuit quicker than I could eat KFC popcorn chicken, then sniffed the air, looked me up and down then trotted back out the front door like she owned the place. Even the dog recognised an imposter.

Now completely alone, I explored the rest of the house. My mother had started from humble beginnings but the house was lived-in and full of character. None of this spilled over into the home she built for my father and me. Our home had taken minimalism to the extreme. I found Alma's bedroom, with an old wrought-iron frame bed covered in a patchwork quilt, and you guessed it, potpourri and lacework on the bedside table. I sat on the bed, feeling like I was trespassing because I didn't know her at all but here I was, making myself at home in her house.

After eating lasagna and reading one of Alma's racy Mills and Boon romance novels—something else my mother hated, *frivolity*—I went to bed early. The worn white sheets smelled good, and the bed was soft, but when my head hit the pillow, sleep did not come. Anxiety about meeting Alma simmered away in the background, but it was the painful memories of the night before when my friends had showed how little they thought of me that kept me awake.

***

I'd headed straight to Mum's for a family dinner, only to be bombarded by my sister Melanie who had seen Erik's girl demonstrating quite clearly that she still loved him in front of the whole shire council. I needed to talk to Erik. While he claimed to be a commitment-phobe, he was in love with Annie and needed to stop fucking about. He didn't realise how lucky he was.

"Give him some space," Mum said, coming in on the end of Melanie's retelling of events.

"Why? He loves us," Evie said, attempting to put me in a headlock. Melanie was sort of normal, where Evie was batshit crazy. But she was also correct.

"Now that's out of the way, there's something else you should know," Mum said as we sat down for dinner. We all regularly ate together at home, partly because since I lived in a shed on my farm, cooking was limited, but also because we were tight. Meal times were important growing up, and we continued that tradition now we were all older.

"What's that?" I asked as I dug into her beef, mushroom and red wine casserole. This was a favourite, and I could easily finagle leftovers.

"It's about Sheridan," she said and I paused, fork mid-air, cursing Sheridan for interrupting my happiness.

"What about her?" I asked, forcing myself to eat.

"She's engaged," Mel said, and they all watched me, worried about how I might react. But I didn't need to be coddled.

"That's good, right?" I asked as though it didn't matter. And it didn't, or least not in the way they thought.

"I think so," Mel hedged.

"You think so? Is the guy no good for her?" I asked.

"Trust you to ask that," Evie said rolling her eyes.

"What's that supposed to mean?" I asked my youngest sister.

"Evie," Mum reprimanded, but as usual, Evie kept on coming.

"What? The girl who broke his heart, kept his engagement ring and is a raging bitch is getting married, and he is worried about the man she is going to marry?" Evie was incredulous.

"Evie, it's not like I still want her, and it's normal for people to want exes to be happy," I said.

"There's nothing normal about you. You're like some sort of relationship expert to everyone else, but you can't see yourself, or how hung up you are on Sheridan bloody McCauley."

I sighed. It wasn't the first time we'd had this conversation. The girls were convinced my unhappiness, which I had thought was hidden, stemmed from unrequited love for my former fiancée. They had reason; I'd left after I'd called the wedding off because I'd been heartbroken, and I'd kept away because I hadn't wanted to be reminded of what had happened. But now? I couldn't care less about her romantically.

"I'm not hung up on her," I said honestly.

"Then why are you sad and shit."

"Evie!" Mum tsked.

"Sad and shit? How old are you?" Mel asked and Evie poked out her tongue.

"I'm not sad," I lied. "I'm focused on the farm."

"Of course you are dear," Mum said disbelievingly and I shot her a look before changing the subject to something that would occupy my sisters—town gossip.

I called Erik on the way to the farm to fill him in on what Mel had learned about his girl. He was hurting, so to cheer him up I told him about the woman I'd seen in Yarck and it made us both smile. I was glad for it, because the discussion about Sheridan, the glacial pace my farm was moving at, and the shit-storm Erik was facing were a surefire way to put me in a hole.

It wasn't easy hearing that despite being a bitch, Sheridan had found someone, and Erik, who had never wanted a relationship, met Annie. It had always been me who wanted to get married, and who had done right by everyone, but was still alone. I'd given up on the prospect of love for ten years, only partaking in sex or friendship—never both—but it left me empty. I wasn't built like that. I loved having someone to talk to, share my day with. I wanted a wedding, honeymoon, kids and a dog. Shit, I would even drive a minivan if I needed to. I wanted all that, but no one wanted me in that way. In coming home, I'd thought I'd settle down on my farm and live the life. Instead, I was spinning my wheels.

I arrived at home to find a tree branch had fallen on part of the chicken run. I grabbed a flashlight and checked the structure, relieved it was only minor damage and all the girls were fine, tucked up in the roosts for the night. I couldn't afford major works but I would need to do some fixing to keep the chooks in and the foxes out. Smoko Farm only produced forty dozen eggs a week, but it was income that I needed.

I checked on the handful of pigs and sheep I had before going inside the small shed I lived in and lighting the fire. I'd saved for the farm while working abroad, but aid work isn't exactly lucrative, and I'd also made sure Mum had a little extra as she was raising two daughters who had no fucking clue where money came from. I had the acreage I wanted, the views of the snow, access to the river, a shed to live in, a work shed and some basic fencing, but that was pretty much it. I was covering my mortgage repayments, and slowly reinvesting in the land, but I hadn't been able to progress anything else.

Desperate for sleep, I took a shower, then crawled into my king-size bed, which took up the majority of the small room, and tried to clear my mind of problems that needed fixing. I loved to problem solve, and to make sure the people I cared about were okay, but there were times when it did my head in. At least tonight was different. Tonight, I would think about the girl from Yarck, her sexy body and her sassy attitude. She was fascinating in a way that pushed all my buttons. Maybe my luck would change and I would find her again.

Chapter Three

When I woke up, I was still groggy from the hangover, but the brilliant sunshine streaming in reminded me that even though my life was a shambles, and I was a friendless, family-less sauce-misfiring lunatic, life still went on. My mother and father, among other things, had raised me to be resourceful, responsible and determined. I'd faltered for twelve months after their death, and since then I'd done my best to make my own way regardless of the obstacles I faced. Rolling over, I looked at my suitcase spilling clothing on the floor, seeing the outfit I'd worn out two nights ago and my positivity wavered.

My watch said nine a.m., which meant I'd slept for at least twelve hours. My body was rested but my mind and soul were still whirring. I could approach my predicament one of two ways. I could wallow in my newfound misery. This was appealing; I'd been hiding my misery for a long time and I was dying to let that monster loose. Or, I could put my head down, bum up and create the life I wanted. It would be lonely, but I could have a career, get healthy and maybe even build a relationship with my grandmother.

Feeling better with a plan, I got myself some breakfast and sat on the back veranda, taking in the winter sun on Alma's garden. I knew that this was a beautiful place, but I struggled with the idea of *me* living here. I was alone in a small town where people came as tourists, and the scant permanent population consisted of farmers and a few old fogeys. My resolve was faltering but I couldn't put it off any longer. I got up, showered and got ready to meet Alma. Well, re-meet.

I left the house and headed to the local bakery, which was full of people, amazing smells and ski memorabilia. Seeing the cabinet full of delicious pastries, I knew this would be a hurdle for my weight-loss journey. I bought vanilla slice for Alma, hoping it would be an icebreaker. She couldn't hate me too much if I brought pastry, could she? I walked out not sure of anything and drove into Bright.

I pulled up at Rosella Lodge aged care facility, which was attached to the hospital, and was surprised at how beautiful the setting was, with easy sloping hills looking down over the river that was edged with silvery gum trees. I'd been expecting something akin to an institution—*Alias Grace* style. At reception I was met by the strange smell of naphthalene flakes and the school canteen. I rang the bell then sat in one of the two faded floral arm chairs, noting the largest bunch of fake gladiolas I'd ever seen. I'm no green thumb, but I was pretty sure that flowers didn't come in rainbow.

"You must be Kate Bloomington, Alma's granddaughter," said a short lady with a tight perm, shorts hot off the elna press and a matching apricot shirt showcasing applique doves. Now the gladiolas made sense.

"Um, yes. That's right, is Alma available?" I said, secretly hoping the answer was no.

"Of course, we've all been waiting for you," she said handing me the sign-in sheet.

"Really?"

"Yes dear, I know all the *good* people in town, including your mother and your grandmother, although Alma *does* keep is on our toes," she said, laughing conspiratorially.

"Could you show me..." I started to ask but she kept talking, waving for me to follow her.

"I volunteer around town, as well as work here. It's all about doing your part. Maybe I'll see you when you're working at the Hub. I'd be happy to share a sandwich, tell you who is who. Sound good?" she paused momentarily as she rounded a corner, then continued.

"This Hub, well, they have unusual ideas about imports and help people who *should* help themselves but you can't stop change, and people who think they can are *divusional*," she said. I looked up to clarify what I'd heard, but she was already meters ahead. I hurried to catch up. "Charity starts in the home, I tell my husband all the time. Although, I wish he would not be at home all the time. If he eats any more Iced Vovos, he'll be obeast—but he doesn't listen no matter how many times I tell him." She kept prattling as we took more turns and I struggled to make sense of her rambling. *Divusional? Imports? Obeast?*

"The Vollies will all tell you city folk don't understand how we do things. Druggies and layabouts? Well, they need our guidance," she continued as she looked over her shoulder at me. I blinked and tried on a smile. "You must be tired, you look it."

"Well," I managed to get out, but was interrupted because we came to a stop and she knocked on the door.

"Alma, it's Barbara, and I have a special guest for you all the way from Melbourne," she sung patronizingly. There was no answer and I was about to turn when she pushed the door open.

"Alma," she called shrilly as we stepped in.

"Piss off," an old, cranky voice boomed. I swallowed hard.

Barbara laughed nervously, "That's no way to greet a visitor who has brought you morning tea."

I looked anywhere but at my grandmother, not ready to find out how much she disliked me. The large room had a big window with a view down to the river, and the décor was exactly what you would expect in a nursing home: pastel everything. She had a small table and chairs, a TV with rabbit-ear antennas and a bed that rested against the wall, covered in a hand-knitted blanket. The silence clung to the air uncomfortably as I looked around, and Barbara busied herself, snatching the vanilla slice out of my hand and putting it on the table with a plate and a knife. Finally, I looked at Alma, who sat in a big armchair, glaring at me.

"I said, piss off, Barbara," she said quietly but no less irritably, keeping her gaze fixed on me.

"Oh, aren't you a trick. Nice to meet you, Kate," Barbara said laughing nervously as she hurried away. I looked at the door, wishing I could follow.

"Sit down, Kate."

I sat down like a child in trouble doing my best to hold her gaze, seeing the family resemblance. She didn't look ancient as I'd expected, just weary. We sat a moment longer, staring, before she broke the tension.

"I need to talk to you." Those words sounded ominous. I stared down at my feet for a beat, gathering my courage, then I slowly looked up. "So…it takes your mother dying and me to have one foot in to get you up here?"

Wow. Just like that. She slayed me. I wondered how long she'd been waiting to say that as I sat on the bed, with no answer. I hadn't seen her since the funeral. I could have, but I didn't. She'd reached out, but I'd not responded. Now I couldn't speak as tears of anger welled up; she didn't need to be cruel.

"Well, it's not like you came to visit me either," I spat. Her eyebrows raised, and her eyes danced a little.

"I wasn't invited or welcomed," she replied.

"You were welcome to help me at the funeral, or were *you* waiting for a formal invite?" I bit back, cattily. She examined me and I shifted uncomfortably, my heart racing.

"I suppose we were both grieving," she said on a sigh, giving me a sad, conciliatory smile. Guilt replaced my anger and my face must have communicated my heartache. "Well, at least we can finally battle it out," she said tiredly and I huffed a laugh. She was a strange bird. "I need you to care for my house. It's my only possession and it holds all my memories."

"I will, although I can't garden," I said quietly.

"Didn't your mother teach you?"

"She didn't garden," I responded, confused. Our backyard had consisted of grass, a fence and a washing line.

"How did you manage in your own place?" It was Alma's turn to be confused.

"It was an apartment." At this, she rolled her eyes like apartments were disgusting.

"I could never live without green around me. It's why hate being in here so much."

"I can," I said but this displeased her and she cleared her throat, then picked up a piece of the vanilla slice and pushed the plate towards me. With nothing for it, I took some, glad to have something to do. It wasn't a hardship; it was creamy with divine, flaky pastry. I was so absorbed in the sugar rush that her words startled me.

"You can come back tomorrow at 1 p.m. and bring me something decent to eat for lunch," she said, dismissing me.

"Oh-kay" I muttered as I stood, licking my fingers ungracefully. "Any preferences?"

"Something that requires teeth. Go now, I'm in so much pain I could rip the arm off this chair."

I said an awkward goodbye then left her room, both relieved and exhausted. I eventually made it back to reception and signed out as Barbara prattled at me, until a young, handsome, well-dressed man walked through the front door. He had dark hair and eyes, with olive skin and perfect, full lips. He was no sexy ginger, but when he smiled at me, I fumbled a smile back.

"Kate, did you hear me?"

"I'm sorry?" I asked, distracted by the man approaching me.

"Are you feeding her? Alma doesn't eat our food, despite it being top notch," she said, frustrated.

"Do I need to be?" I heard myself ask.

"You're family; it's your duty," she said getting riled up again, but the Italian Stallion saved my bacon.

"Mrs. Schafer, you look lovely as always. I'm here to see Nonna. How is she today?" he cooed then smiled at Barbara, leaving her mouth hanging open but with no words coming out. Hallelujah.

"She'll be happy to see you," Barbara tittered and I fought hard not to roll my eyes.

"Thanks," he said and then turned to me and smiled. "Sorry to interrupt your conversation." His chocolate eyes twinkled at me and I blushed. "I'm Frank. You must be Kate, Alma's granddaughter."

"Yeah, um, hi," I stammered.

"Don't worry, the whole town has been waiting for you; haven't we, Mrs. Schafer?" he said with a small grin.

"Oh now, Frank, I wouldn't say that," she said, giggling.

"I guess your little green car out there will be a permanent fixture around here." Ugh, the green limousine was at it again, making me stand out when I only wanted to fit in.

"Sure...I mean, thanks." I sounded ridiculous, but I was nervous under his attentive gaze. To say I was inexperienced with men was an understatement.

"I better go, but swing by our bakery and say hi," he said, tilting his head and treating me to a crooked grin. I continued to impersonate a lamppost as he walked past and gently put his hand on my shoulder. I jumped, startled at his friendliness.

"Cool," I finally said.

Cool? COOL? No, not cool.

"He is quite the catch around here," Barbara said as we watched him walk away. Finally, I was interested in what she had to say.

"Very wealthy family, they own the bakery, the biggest fruit farm and lots of holiday accommodations. Good people too. Frank is the only son, and much loved by the family and the town."

"Good to know," I said as I walked out, needing some fresh air and dignity.

I headed back to Alma's restless and uneasy. Our conversation had been intense, and then there was Frank, who couldn't compete with the Sexy Ginger, but was the first man to pay me attention in, well, forever. Not that anything would happen. My last and only boyfriend was with me as I drank and smoked my way through my inheritance and when I cleaned myself up, he'd left with my *True Blood* DVDs.

Needing to clear my head, I donned my runners, deciding now was the perfect time to attempt the Bungalow Spur track. I walked from Alma's but was puffing by the time I got to the end of her street. My confidence took another hit when I arrived at the track; it was like being back in the city with thin, healthy people in matchy-matchy outfits exercising in public, on the weekend. I'd hoped to huff and puff on my own, but as two athletic women strode past, my hopes were dashed. I was unfit and unhealthy, and people were going to notice. Taking a deep breath, I started walking, but before long, there was a sharp incline that would actually kill me. I'd been trying to keep up with the women in front of me, but my lungs wanted to burst and the air felt like razor blades in my throat. Thank God for the music blaring in my ears, helping me forget the pain in my legs.

I finally got to a flattened-off area and stopped; breathing was more than hard. I should have looked at the view, but not vomiting was more important. I was focused on drawing breath when a hand gently touched my back, and I jumped. Spinning around, I could not believe my luck. The sexy ginger who witnessed my sauce-capades the day before stood there, saying something I couldn't hear.

"What?" I huffed but he just smiled. I stared at him, struck again by how handsome he was, and how his smile was genuine and bright. He was more rugged than Frank, his muscular frame hewn from work outdoors on display under his sweat drenched shirt. Activity had his dark auburn hair looking even more mussed, but those eyes that had twinkled yesterday started to show concern. He kept moving his mouth but I couldn't hear a thing. Then he pulled out my earphones and the outside world came crashing back into focus. I'd forgotten they were in.

"Do you need an asthma pump?" he asked, brows drawn.

"What?" I blinked, trying to figure out what was going on.

"Do you need an asthma pump?" he repeated slowly, like I was simple.

"Why would I?" I was still confused when it dawned on me. Now he was fighting a grin, that twinkle back. It was too humiliating; instead of laughing it off, I went on the defensive.

"I always do that when I work out," I said, straightening my back.

"Struggle to breathe?" he asked, a little taken aback by my defensiveness.

"I wasn't struggling," I said, sounding overly adamant.

"Of course. Would you like me to walk you back down? You don't look okay," he asked, humour gone as he assessed me. He was close enough that I could smell him, and damn it, he smelled good. But he was a douche and I'd had enough.

"What's that supposed to mean?" I snapped.

"You look a bit exhausted, that's all," he said softly and I almost fell for it when I saw the two lovely looking women I'd been chasing, waiting for the Sexy Ginger Douche.

"Is that code for you look a bit like a beetroot?" I asked.

"No. But I think you look a bit whacked. That said, you did look tired yesterday too," he said, going for a cute grin which I wasn't chummy about. He knew full well that yesterday was humiliating.

"Thanks for reminding me." I laid the sarcasm on thick and he sighed.

"Look, I meant it as a joke," he said.

"You do stand-up?"

"Listen, I—" he started, but I cut him off.

"Thanks for the health check," I muttered before I turned and walked back down, ready to wallow in some misery.

***

"Finally, a woman impervious to your charm," Evie said as we finished our hike. I did this track regularly, and on occasion, my sisters came with me.

"I don't know what you're on about." I tried to pass it off but they were right. I'd seen my dream girl again, and instead of getting her onside, I had practically pushed her off the damned mountain. She was defensive, and I hadn't been able to put a foot right. I'd embarrassed her and I hated that. I was not in the business of making anyone, let alone a young woman out walking, feel bad about themselves. I needed to make amends.

I had no excuse, other than being caught off guard. I'd been completely absorbed as my eyes had greedily taken her in. There was something about her that did it for me. I wanted to tangle my hands in that thick mane of hair, and feel those soft, beautiful curves against me. I wouldn't say love at first sight, but thanks to that soft round bottom and generous cleavage that was, dare I say it, heaving, my dick had twitched to life.

She was all woman and made no bones about being herself. She wasn't wearing makeup or putting on a show. She was just out for a walk. My concern had been genuine; she was wheezing and looked pale, but as soon as I'd spoken, I could see my mistake. She didn't want attention drawn to her and I had done that. My skill as a charmer had failed, miserably.

"You like her," Mel teased, snapping me out of my sexy if not disappointing memory. I scoffed like she was crazy.

"Who is she?" Evie asked, clearly not believing me.

"I don't know, our paths crossed at a café on the way back from Melbourne."

"Well, if she's a tourist, you better move quickly," Mel said. I sighed. I didn't think it would lead to anything. Especially not after embarrassing her.

I parted ways with the girls, not wanting a drink at the pub. Instead I went home to brood. It had not been a good day, starting with the damage to the chook run that was more extensive than I'd thought. I had to run up my tab at the hardware store. Then the highland cattle stud I was looking at called with their pricing. My reserves were so depleted that I couldn't afford one cow, let alone the four I wanted to start my herd. I wanted my land to be more productive, but it took money to make money and I didn't have it.

And now I had humiliated a young woman who I wanted to like me. My gut hurt. I did not want to be an arsehole like I had been with Sheridan. She had deliberately pushed me—picking fights, going out of her way to be hurt by something I had done and clearly not intended to, giving me the silent treatment. And like a damned fool, I'd bitten at her bait. I never really got angry, rarely raised my voice, but Sheridan brought out the worst in me and then some. And I'd let her.

We'd broken up and I'd left for years, putting off my dream of having a family and a farm, leaving my mum to raise my sisters on her own, not being there when she'd found a lump on her breast. This is why I wanted to laugh when people asked if I was okay about Sheridan getting engaged. I had no love for the woman.

Needing to keep busy, I headed outside into the winter's afternoon to start work on vegetable patches that wouldn't cost me much to set up. I'd been working solidly when my phone rang, forcing me to stop and think about something other than the woman I'd hurt.

"Mum, all okay?" I asked, knowing I sounded grouchy but unable to hide it as I usually did.

"Of course. I wanted to see if you needed any help with the chicken run?" she asked, again.

"I told you I'm all good. I can fix it myself," I reminded her, trying not to let my irritation show.

"I meant do you want some money. I know there are lots of expenses and—"

"I've got this. Don't worry. Just look after you," I said, cutting her off.

"Don't get your knickers in a twist, Ben. People can help you, you know," she teased and I relaxed a little. My mum never held a grudge.

"I know, but I don't need it, truly. What I do need is for Evie to dump that idiot she is going out with," I said.

"She's a grown woman, and she can date who she likes. You need to stop focusing on solving everyone else's problems and sort yourself out," she said.

"I don't have any problems," I grumbled.

"Of course you don't, honey."

Chapter Four

On Sunday morning, I tried my luck at Bungalow Spur early in the morning and was pleased to find the path empty. I did not find it any easier, though, and this time, I did vomit. I would be eternally thankful that the Sexy Ginger Douche wasn't there. I couldn't bear to be humiliated in front of that gorgeous man again. He probably wasn't looking at me that way, but that wasn't the point. After my walk, I visited Alma who was slightly less offhand as we ate pies and watched football. It felt like we both wanted to speak, but neither of us were ready to open the floodgates. Thankfully, Barbara was absent.

By later that afternoon, I'd played with Marmalade and even gone out into the garden and pulled weeds. At least I hoped they were weeds. But I was still restless. I wandered into town looking at all the historic landmarks, before heading to the Snowline Hotel for a drink. Some people had a hard time drinking alone. Me? I preferred it.

I sat at the bar and ordered a local beer, noticing a few old men grumbling as they watched sports on the TV. The bartender was...different. His name badge said *Hello, my name is Kevin.* It should have said *I'm Kevin, fuck off* because he was acting like I was inconveniencing him by ordering a drink. As the afternoon wore on, my back and leg muscles started to seize from my physical activity, so I stood gingerly to pay. Before I could leave, a newly familiar male voice sounding too close for comfort stopped me in my tracks.

Slowly, I turned to see the Sexy Ginger Douche walking towards the bar, talking to an enormous Thor-like man and a woman who looked like she could kick my arse despite being, quite literally, half the woman I was. They took stools at the opposite end. I'd hoped to escape without his notice when the surly *and* unhelpful bartender called my name.

"Kate Bloomington, your card," he grumbled, holding up my credit card.

The old bar flies barely lifted their heads, but *Ginger* and his friends turned to face me. Under their scrutiny my cheeks flushed. Last time I'd spoken to him, he'd tried to joke, albeit poorly, about my inadequacies, and I'd responded defensively. Seeing him now, looking at me with apology, made me question my reaction to him. When he walked over, I knew he was going to say how sorry he was, but I didn't want to hear it because *I* didn't want to acknowledge my mistake, or the fact I was now admiring his gorgeous blue eyes and square jaw.

He stopped two feet away and I had to arch my neck to look up at him. He was wearing a green and grey check shirt today with another pair of sexily worn-out jeans and boots. I hated to admit it, but he was more than handsome; he was utterly beautiful with eyes that were expressive and a smile that made me warm with desire.

"Kate, is it?" he asked and I lowered my eyes to his broad, muscular chest.

"Yep," I said, hitching my bag up my arm.

"Look, I'm really sorry if I embarrassed you the other day. I was genuinely worried and I figured given how you handled yourself in Yarck, that you would be okay with a joke." His words seemed genuine and I was finding it difficult to be mean.

"It's fine," I said begrudgingly.

"Can I buy you a drink to apologise?" he asked, giving me an arrestingly sexy smile. I wanted to say yes, but I'd enjoy it too much. He was being friendly, while I was being lascivious, and given I was awkward and ridiculous, he'd no doubt regret it.

"No thanks," I said, giving him a tight smile before I stepped around him and walked out. I could feel his friends watching me but I kept my head high and eyes ahead. Later, at home on the couch with toast for dinner, I was glad to have my new job to worry about, so I would stop wondering what it would be like to have a drink with the sexy ginger.

I had no idea what to expect at the Hub. Alma had put me forward for the role, and I'd done a phone interview with a woman named Carol. She'd seemed impressed and had offered me the job. But, there was something strange about this community hub. Everyone talked about it being so different, but if it was cutting edge, what was it doing in Bright of all places and why did they hire me? I didn't know much about welfare services or volunteers, but I had the feeling I was about to get a rude shock.

Monday morning, I'd dressed in my usual work attire: black and shapeless. I'd had to purchase a whole new wardrobe for my last job to fit in with the girls I worked with. I dreamt of wearing colours, but they'd told me that I should stick to black which was more slimming. Now I had a wardrobe Morticia Addams would be proud of. I knew I could wear colours, but at the time I'd desperately wanted to fit in, so I'd listened to them. Now it was a habit. I arrived at the Hub before it opened, so I strolled down the street, which was busy with people on the way to work and kids trudging to school in the cold. I walked past the bakery like I was just meandering while surreptitiously looking inside, unable to stop myself. Frank had been kind and attentive, and I was curious.

"Kate, how are you?" I heard from behind me and I turned to find the man in question, standing out the front with a coffee in hand. He looked handsome in a crisp white shirt, dark jeans and a sports coat. His thick, black hair was expertly brushed back and his aftershave smelled spicy.

"Frank, hey. I'm good. Is this the bakery you mentioned?"

"Yeah, it is. I'd say join me for a coffee but I have a meeting and you look like you have somewhere important to be," he said, openly checking me out. He smiled while he did and my body reacted.

"It's my first day of work at the Hub," I muttered, trying to control the warmth spreading from my chest. At least he didn't ask me if I needed an asthma pump.

"It's a great place. I can't wait to work with the new team," he said and I shook my head.

"You work with them?"

"My family has foster kids and some of them use the services offered there. We helped get the funding to set it up," he said and I smiled at him.

"That's amazing," I said.

"I love this community," he said. I nodded as though I knew what it was like to belong. "I have to run, but don't be a stranger Kate, I'd like to get to know you." He gave my upper arm a squeeze.

"I won't be strange—I mean *a* stranger," I muttered ridiculously.

"You're cute, Kate, you know that?" he said chuckling as he gave me another, hotter look then walked away. I stood like a stunned mullet until someone brushed past me and I blinked. Looking at my watch, I freaked. It was one minute to nine, and I could not be late on my first day, I turned and ran to the Hub, vaguely noticing the sexy ginger douche on my way but I did not have time for any more weird conversations.

"Not now, Ginger," I said as I bustled past, catching a glimpse of his surprise and confusion.

I flew through the doors and walked to the reception desk. "Good morning, I'm here to meet Carol," I said. The girl standing behind the counter was around my age, eying me speculatively. I inwardly groaned. I hated being the new girl.

"Of course. You must be Kate," she said, holding out her hand. "I'm Mia."

"Nice to meet you," I said. We shook hands and she smiled at me. We were awkwardly quiet for a moment before she spoke.

"You're the last one to join the crazies here. I'll take you to Carol," she said grinning as she came around the desk and led me through a security door. She was being friendly, but I couldn't get close to anyone again. I looked around as I followed her, seeing four large offices around the edge of an open plan area, a kitchen and a large meeting room. It was a lot smaller compared to my past job, and seemed a lot more close-knit.

"Yo, Viv," Mia yelled out across the space.

"Hey," said another young woman. While Mia was tanned with light brown hair, hazel eyes, and a round open face, Viv had long, light auburn hair, pale skin and green eyes that looked at me with interest. Viv shared my affliction for black clothing although I doubted it was to hide her overabundance of curves. We walked to one of the offices and the sign on the door said, 'Carol Buckley, Manager Community Programs.' Mia knocked despite the door being open because we could hear a woman on the phone.

"Yes, I understand your concern... No, we do not teach our drivers to flip the bird... Of course, it's very rude... No, I can't revoke his welfare payments."

I couldn't help but listen to this strange conversation as we waited for her to get off the phone.

"Transport again?" Mia asked when the call was done. Carol stood as she nodded, looking frustrated.

"Sorry about that. Welcome, Kate," she said, shaking my hand. "Take a seat." Mia left as Carol sat back down and silenced her mobile phone, which had started to ring. She turned her assessing eyes to me.

"Welcome to the Hub. As you can see, we're a little busy. I want you to enjoy working here, but I won't lie—it's still new and not without…challenges. You'll do your induction this week, spending time with the team and some volunteers and reading our process manuals. After that, you'll start doing the administration for the Aged Care programs with me. Most of your learning will be on the job, okay?"

"Sounds good," I lied as I smiled awkwardly.

"Great—come and meet the team," she said with a grin. She wasn't concerned that I was shitting myself. We walked to the main area and I was formally introduced to Viv and Mia, who were my counterparts in administration. Both girls were friendly, but I wasn't interested in BFFs, not again.

Next I met Leslie who managed the youth programs. She was friendly and genuine as she welcomed me aboard. Later, Carol informed me that Leslie was her partner. She'd seemed a little apprehensive, but I shrugged; I had no issues with same-sex relationships, but if people like Barbara were anything to go by, I could see why she was wary. Both she and Leslie were older than I was, and Hannah, the last manager I met, was closer to me in age. She had asked me questions like she was interested in my answers, which made me put my guard up.

Unlike Carol and Leslie who wore crisp shirts and well-fitting slacks, Hannah wore a fifties-style teal dress with a thick belt, and cute suede pumps. When she noticed I was staring at her outfit, she told me, "Leona Edminston on sale—can't beat it." I was surprised by her instant friendliness and I pulled at my black sack uncomfortably. After meeting everyone, I sat down to start reading the manuals when Mia came up and perched on my desk, with Viv behind her holding a cup of tea.

"Where are you from?" Mia asked. I tried not to sigh.

"I lived in Windsor but now I live in Harrietville," I told them, as I returned my attention to the enormous Health and Safety folder, and turned the page.

"Why on earth did you leave?" Vivienne asked, ignoring my frostiness.

"I have to look after my grandmother. I don't have parents, so I really had no choice," I said bluntly. This approach worked like a charm and people left me alone. Usually.

"Wow, really, you don't have parents?" Mia asked with a look of sympathy. I didn't hide my sigh this time.

"My parents got meningitis while on holiday in Italy five years ago. I'm an only child; Dad was born in the States and had no ties with family. My mum's brother died and all that's left is me and my grandmother, who, until this week, I didn't know."

"Right," Mia said like she wasn't sure if I was joking.

"Fuck," Viv muttered. Both girls looked uncomfortable, and while we didn't have to be best friends, I could be nicer.

"There wasn't much I could do about it," I said, gentling my voice.

"Do you hate having to be here?" Mia asked, surprising me with that question.

"Nowhere is perfect," I said.

"I moved here to escape the city dating scene, and Viv moved home to be inspired to write music. I haven't met a dude yet who isn't a cockhead, and she hasn't finished an album, so the jury is still out for us too," Mia said. I found myself smiling at her frankness despite my desire to be left alone.

"You haven't met a dude because you keep making a fool of yourself," Viv said and Mia laughed. The banter seemed easy between them, and they would be disappointed when they realised I wouldn't be able to give them that.

"Whatever," Mia said, leaning towards me conspiratorially. "Bitch-face is talking about a recent night out at the pub. We were sitting outside, drinking plenty when this chick on the table next to us was bragging that she was flexible, she could do really high kicks. I'd rolled my eyes, but she'd gotten her knickers in a twist, stood up and done one. I'm blind but I think, fuck yeah I can do that." Mia stood up, talking animatedly. "I stand up and stretch like a dickhead. Viv holds her hand out at shoulder height and I draw my leg back, then light it fly, realizing too late that both legs have left ground. I'm in the air for a bit then thud, I crash to the ground."

I couldn't help laughing with them. "Did that hurt?" I asked.

"No but good thing because this knucklehead was too busy laughing to check," Mia said punching Viv in the arm in jest. It was a nice moment, and I thought about sharing my sauce incident, but quickly dismissed it. After story time with Mia, I returned to reading policies and procedures, which was incredibly boring, so my mind drifted. It landed on the Sexy Ginger Douche, who I'd seen that morning. I'd yelled at him as I'd booked up the street. He must think I was completely nutty. Luckily Frank, who made me feel good in a way I wasn't used to, hadn't seen that or my sauce-capades.

Side by side the two men were night and day. Ginger was more casual, wearing clothing that was more functional than fashionable, but he seemed like a mature man who was worldly and experienced. Frank was a snazzy dresser, no doubt, but he was younger and more obviously confident. He wasn't as handsome but not ugly by any stretch. I wanted to laugh at the direction of my thoughts—as if I was going to let anything happen with either of them. I supposed it didn't mean I couldn't at least appreciate the view.

***

"The woman-whisperer got shut down!" Erik said laughing as we sat at The Snowline, eating dinner on Sunday night.

"Fuck off," I said, then shot an apologetic look at Annie.

"Don't mind your manners on my account," she said as she leaned into Erik. They were back together and so loved up my heart ached. I wanted that feeling, that connection with someone who was just yours, and you were just theirs. "Who is she and what on earth did you say to her to get that sort of reaction?" Annie asked.

"She was the girl with the sauce," I muttered and she looked at me with interest. I told her what I'd seen, including how sexy I thought Kate was. Annie and Erik laughed at the story, but when I told them what I'd said on Bungalow Spur, Annie shook her head and Erik gave me *you're fucked* eyes.

"What? I really thought she had asthma," I said but it was futile. I should've kept my mouth shut but I'd wanted to talk to her.

"Hey Big Kev, you said her name was Kate Bloomington?" Erik called out to the old miser who had pulled beers here since 1960. Scowling, he nodded once. "Ben, do you think she's Alma's granddaughter?"

"Shit! I'd heard she was back to look after her place, I hadn't put two and two together. Well, she certainly has her grandmother's attitude," I said.

"Wait until she tells Alma what you said. You are going to get an earful!" Erik said smugly. I sighed because this was likely the truth and would no doubt dash any chances I had at redeeming myself. I smiled like it was all the same to me, while my heart sank. Seeing her tonight in tight jeans and a turtleneck had made my dick hard and my chest warm. I needed to get a grip; I didn't know her but for some reason, I desperately wanted to.

A while later and after plenty more ribbing from Erik, I headed home to check the animals and take stock of what I had to do the next day. I was going into town early meet a saffron grower. I wanted to add the spice to my farm, along with truffles, garlic and olives. After that, I needed to finish expanding the chicken run then do some consulting work so I could afford to keep the lights on.

I was in a holding pattern that made me feel like every hour of every day was occupied but not productive. If I wasn't tending to the farm, I was helping Mum or checking in on my sisters, writing reports for NGOs or researching ways to make more money. I wanted my life here to start, but wherever I turned, something was stalling me.

On Monday morning I headed into Bright to grab a coffee before my meeting, and as I walked down the street I was knocked for a six when I saw Kate, rushing towards me at a clip. She was dressed in a black baggy dress, black stockings and boots. If I hadn't seen the evidence of her glorious curves, I would have assumed she didn't have any under the tent she was wearing. Her beautiful face was done up with makeup, including sexy red lips, and her thick brown hair was out and glossy, her fringe framing her face and making her grey eyes look bigger and brighter. I sucked in a breath as our eyes locked, then she spoke as she kept hurrying past.

"Not now, Ginger."

Ginger. I was used to people mentioning my hair. It was like they couldn't help it. It was just fucking hair. People said we had a fiery temper because we had red hair. The real reason was because people kept on bringing up our fucking hair colour! Hair-ism aside, I smiled as I turned to watch her hustle to the Hub. I liked that she had given me a nickname of sorts. Perhaps all was not lost?

My good mood ended right there; at the coffee shop I ran into Sheridan's mother. She'd always liked me and didn't blame me for being so harsh. In fact, Sheridan's nonsense had embarrassed her. Now she was ecstatic that Sheridan was engaged again and wasn't concerned about me in the slightest.

"Such a nice man, and wealthy too. They are building the most lovely home," she'd said before she realised who she was talking to. I gave her an easy smile, told her how happy I was and kissed her on the cheek while my stomach churned. Thankfully the saffron grower came and I had an excuse to end the conversation. Not that *that* went any better. He talked through the prices, and the work entailed to grow it. More and more, it seemed out of my reach so I thanked him for coming to see me then headed back to the damned hardware store. I was finishing adding more to my account, when Evie called.

"Yo, bro," she said in a fake, thug-life voice.

"Young Evelyn. How are you?"

"I'm bored, hungry and need your help."

"With being bored and hungry?" I asked.

"Yes, and setting up my new tablet. I can't make it connect to the WiFi. Will you help me, please?"

I sighed. I had work to do at home, but it wouldn't take long and I needed to eat anyway. I headed to the supermarket to get food for lunch, and bread, milk and fruit for Evie because she probably needed it, then headed to her place. She made lunch while I fixed her I.T. problems, a leaking tap and refitted the wire to her security door.

"How long has the door been broken?" I asked.

"A few weeks," she called from the kitchen.

"It doesn't work if people can reach inside."

"Who is going to try to get in?" she asked, coming out. Evie was a stunner, and it had been a problem for me my whole life. She had wild, curly red hair, and big green eyes. Guys loved her, and she loved them back until she was bored with them. This is where the problems came in. Most of these arseholes wanted more and didn't like being kicked to the curb. Erik and I had to sort them out.

"How about the next guy whose heart you break? What's the new one's name? Brent, Brad?"

"Brent, Brad? It's Blaine," she huffed.

"As in Chill Blaine?" I asked and she rolled her eyes. "I actually don't give a shit. I want to make sure he is going to do right by you, and from what I've heard, he has a new girl every minute, drinks like a high school lush and grows his own pot."

"When did you get such a big stick up your arse?" she asked.

"Since always. You're beautiful Evie, but you're a magnet for dickheads. I don't want any of them to think he doesn't have to listen when you tell them to leave," I said seriously and she smiled.

"I love that you want to protect me, but I'm fine," she said, patting my arm and not taking me seriously.

"I'm sure you are, but you're also my little sister. I'll never stop giving a shit."

"I'll be careful."

"Promise?"

"Pinky promise."

"Good. And don't smoke pot, it'll stunt your growth," I said and she laughed. Evie was six-foot-one.

Chapter Five

This was no normal administration job. The people I worked with were certainly not normal. To be honest, the paid employees and many volunteers were the right kind of not normal; interesting if not unusual. But, there were some real oddballs on our roster too. Every volunteer I spoke to mentioned Alma's outspoken nature, without fail. Most liked her but some clearly did not.

There were a few standout characters who left me scratching my head. One was a lady called Jean Bean. Yes, that was her name, I shit you not. She told me she was flat out with her huge team of telephone volunteers and that she would need my help to meet demand and not *drop the slippery sucker*. When she showed me the roster of five people she had to call and seven volunteers she had to manage I said her request for more assistance was doubtful. The next volunteer I met managed to use the words *cheers*, *mate* and *onya* in every sentence. He opened our conversation with "Good onya mate, you look professional, keeping all us blokes on our toes and cheers to that because we bloody need it." I'd blinked, unable to respond, so he continued. "My name is Bruce, but me mates call me Bucket. I'm in charge of the Local Emergency Response Team or LERT as those in the game call it. If there is an emergency like a bushfire or even a terrorist attack, my crew are ready."

"You must be very important," I'd said, taking in his handmade uniform that included epaulets and a tool belt.

"Cheers mate, just doing my duty. Anyway love, gotta go, an emergency is always lurking. Good onya for coming aboard," he'd said before calling a rendezvous at the takeaway shop on his walkie-talkie. As he walked out I gave him a salute, unable to help it but he nodded approvingly. These people were more than a little nutso, but as I spent more time with my grandmother, I began to see that it was a widespread phenomenon.

I hadn't seen Alma on Monday. I was too mentally tired for that level of uncomfortable. Instead I'd decided to tackle Bungalow Spur again. I was becoming obsessed, needing to defeat it after the Sexy Ginger Douche's comments. But it was more than that; my mother had walked this path. We had been close, or as close as I could get to her growing up, but days before she passed she'd rejected me, tinging my grief with bitterness. I loved her and somehow walking this track made me feel connected.

Despite the cold incoming night, I pulled on leggings and thick fleece and started up the hill again. I huffed and puffed my way up, forcing my body to do it even with the pain and the lack of oxygen. I wasn't about to let it beat me. I was a long way from reaching the summit. When it started to drizzle I began to regret my determination. It was getting dark and the dusty rocks were now slick. On the next incline, I slipped. Pain shot thorough my hands and knees as I landed, jolting my joints and grazing my hands. Blood welled up on my hands, and a wave of dizziness rushed over me. Any enthusiasm I had evaporated as I sat on my arse, cold stone biting through my leggings, cursing the fact that I was far out of my depth. Feeling a desperate urge to go home and cry, I stood and slowly started my descent when my shitty luck took a turn for the worse.

"Kate, are you OK?" the Sexy Ginger Douche said as he blocked my path, holding my arms as he inspected the blood running down my shin. Why did I have to see him everywhere? And why was I always the center of some sort of spectacle? He had the two lithe women with him again, and my confidence took another hit. He was looking at me, his face blank, no doubt trying to hide his enjoyment.

"I'M FINE," I snapped.

"Are you sure?" he asked quietly, moving close, taking my hand to inspect it. This was too embarrassing, and everything started to really hurt. I needed to not be here, especially not with him in my space.

"Are you deaf?" I asked sarcastically before I snatched my hands back and stormed off, doing my best to get down the mountain with blurred vision. When I made it to the bottom, I rushed to my car and jangled the keys as I tried to unlock it. I dropped them three times before I managed to open the green limousine. I got in and looked back at the path ready to curse it when I saw Ginger's retreating back going up again. Had he followed me to make sure I was okay? The thought he'd done that made my throat tighten. He was being kind, and I'd been such a bitch. The floodgates chose that moment to break, and all the tired, frustrated and pain-driven tears came. I sat in the car for ten minutes sobbing uncontrollably, then I went home, showered and went to bed. The day needed to be over.

I went into work the following day doing my best to hide my injuries and my low spirits. Viv and Mia greeted me warmly as usual, but I didn't engage in any conversation outside simple pleasantries. They didn't seem hurt, but they were suspicious. I clearly didn't know how to be friendly, or how to accept friendship without thinking it was going to turn out for the worse. At morning tea, they got me a coffee and again my back straightened as I prepared to protect myself. I managed a smile and thanked them, then returned to my desk to keep working. It didn't seem to bother them, although when I saw them looking at my grazed palms, I could tell they wanted to ask if I was okay. But they didn't, and while that was what I wanted, it made everything worse.

The afternoon had dragged by as I started to mentally prepare for my visit with Alma. We had barely spoken and I knew she had things to say; I was terrified to hear them. My anxiety wasn't eased when I met more volunteers I'd be working with. Some had seemed happy that the Hub was now involved, and the work they did visiting older people in nursing homes or helping older people live at home seemed worthwhile. Then I met Patsy Fatmanical, whose first words after introducing herself were, "So, you're Alma's granddaughter. This will be interesting," Her words were true, and an accusation. Clearly my Nan had ruffled feathers, and not everyone appreciated it. My mother was the dead opposite, never causing a fuss, doing whatever had to be done. What had happened to her?

As I prepared to leave, Carol checked in with me. She was pleased with my progress, and I tried to hide my pleasure at her praise. I wanted to do a good job, but I didn't want to be included. She told me not to worry about the volunteers because people would get used to the changes soon enough. I smiled and said goodbye, but as I walked out and everyone called out their farewells, I was again faced with the fact everyone I'd met here—Mia and Viv, Frank, Carol and perhaps even the Sexy Ginger Douche—were friendly and nice. I still felt like the world was against me as I walked to my car in the cold dark night. I was on my way to see a grandmother who didn't like me but made me move, a few days after having my friends betray me and a few years after my mother rejected me from her deathbed. Not to mention my sauce-capades and hissy fits on Bungalow Spur. Sure, I'd asked for some of it with my lack of coordination and prickly attitude, but overall I'd tried to be a good person to no avail. But there was something about this place and the people I'd met that had me wondering, did my pity party need to stop?

When I walked into Rosella Court to visit Alma, I sighed as Barbara assaulted me with questions. "Hi there, back so soon? Fantastic. How are you coping at the Hub, not too strange? Are people okay with you even though Alma is your grandmother? She has some strong leftie opinions that are not always welcome."

"Well…" I said, not sure if I wanted to answer as I signed in and started walking to Alma's room. Thankfully the call button rang and she bustled off. I knocked on Alma's door, nervous, as usual.

"Kate, come in." Her voice was marginally less frosty. Maybe today would be better.

"Hi, Alma," I said, coming in, starting to lay out the antipasto platter we were going to share as our dinner.

"You need to call me Nanna; Alma doesn't seem right," she said and I nodded. I knew what she meant, but that was a term of endearment earned from childhood and we didn't have that.

"How is work?" she asked when I didn't comment.

"It's interesting," I muttered, my thoughts dark as I laid out salami.

"How so?" she asked and I turned to look at her.

"Well, some of the volunteers are a little unusual," I said. This was an easy topic.

"Any in particular?"

"Jean, Patsy and Bruce," I hedged.

Nan's lips turned up, as she smiled slyly. "I hope they're behaving. I've volunteered with them for years, and they were none too happy about the new Hub. But, I've been a supporter all along. We needed to be more professional, and with all the paperwork, why wouldn't we want help? They're like Barbara, unsure about change," she said and I nodded.

"Barbara mentioned that, amongst other things like *Imports* and *layabouts*," I said. Alma scoffed.

"That woman is insufferable and a bigot. She tries to help people but is as narrow-minded as she is misguided. She's a sticky-beak. Always has been, ever since we worked together picking tobacco for the Mancinis."

"You worked together at Frank's grandfather's farm?" I asked, not sure why I was interested.

"Frank?" she asked, giving me a stern look.

"I've met him a few times. He seems nice," I said, trying to sound disinterested. It didn't work.

"Of course he does. He's a charmer, like his father and grandfather."

"He's done a lot for the Hub," I said, feeling the need to defend the man.

She nodded like it wasn't necessarily a good thing. "I haven't figured out what angle he's working, but believe me, there'll be one."

"Maybe they're just good people," I said.

"You sound like Barbara now," she said, laughing. I couldn't help but smile. "Kate, I know you're new to town, and I doubt your mother told you much about growing up here. But let me assure you, I know the Mancinis, and they're snakes in the grass. Do what you will; you're sensible and have a brain in your head, but be careful."

I didn't know how to take that. On one hand she had paid me a compliment, and on the other she had assumed I was going to chase Frank. He may be handsome and make me feel attractive but I wasn't about to jump into bed with him. I didn't respond and we returned to awkward silence.

"Open the wine," Alma demanded. I set about my task, but the movement hurt the grazes on my hands and I winced, catching her eye. "What happened?" she asked, taking my hands in her weathered ones. She was gentle as she touched me for the first time in my memory. I looked into her pale blue eyes, seeing nothing but genuine concern, so I decided to 'fess up.

"I fell walking the Bungalow Spur track," I said as she returned to inspecting my injuries.

"Your mother used to walk that track when she was in high school. The first part is the worst," she said, and my chest warmed.

"I haven't made it past the first part yet."

"You'll get there. It's popular now," she noted, putting my hand down and digging into the food.

"I know, I've already had people witness me puffing so hard they thought I had an asthma attack."

"They must have been tourists. Locals would have helped you out."

"I think he was a local. A big guy, longish red hair, lots of muscles, dark blue eyes. I've run into him a few times, actually. He can't help but make fun of me whenever I'm at my worst," I muttered, taking a big sip of wine as the image of the burly, sexy, infuriating man came into mind. It was true; he'd seen me with sauce on my head, a face like a beetroot and with blood pouring out of my hands and knees while I had only ever seen him looking sexy. It wasn't fair.

"It sounds like you're describing Ben McTavish, but it can't be. He would never treat *you* like that," she said and I looked at her.

"I don't know who he is, but our conversations have been less than pleasant."

"Nope, can't have been him. Ben is a gentleman. His friend Erik is a bit of a larrikin, but Ben is made of the right stuff. The way he looks after everyone, especially his mother and sisters? There's a reason I call him Saint McT."

I stewed on this information for a while. It was possible we weren't talking about the same Sexy Ginger Douche. But then, we might be.

"What does his friend look like?" I asked, hesitantly.

"Erik? Big, blond and handsome. He has had a rough time of life lately, but I hear he has a woman now who is sorting him out."

Shit.

"And Ben's sisters? What do they look like?"

"Well, they're athletic-looking, I suppose. Melanie is older than you but Evie would be your age. They're both tall and red-headed. They'll all make glorious ginger babies. The McTavishes are from Harrietville, although Ben's bought land in Smoko. His mother played netball with your mother for a time." She was almost absentminded as she described the McTavishes, but my mind was racing. The man who featured in my daydreams was called Saint McT.

***

I was irritable and I didn't know what to do about it. However I looked at it, saffron was out of my price range. I'd been wracking my brain because I needed to do something or I would be stuck driving to Melbourne during the week to make ends meet. I was not one for being patient. I needed action, to keep moving forward and solving problems, not sitting on them. But I hadn't done any of those things recently. I'd thought when I'd returned I would be able to create the life I'd been wanting. In fact, I'd been looking forward to the hard work it would take. But reality had been very different. Instead of racing forward, I was inching.

My irritation didn't stem from that alone. There was Erik. I loved that man, but now he'd met Annie, I was left to my own devices even more. This was not good when I couldn't make anything damned well happen. Then there was Kate. For all my so-called skill with the ladies, and being the most befriended man in the history of the universe, I was failing miserably. Seeing her hurt on the walking track, her beautiful eyes filled with tears, her mouth drawn tight with pain and humiliation had almost killed me. And to think I was adding to her agony? It was a nightmare for me. I'd tried to offer help but yet again, it was the wrong thing to do. I was having a hard time reading her but she was constantly on my mind. It was more than her beauty—it was the brittle vulnerability I saw behind her defensive, abrasive attitude that had me wanting to know her.

I knew bits and pieces about her family—we all did. Alma was a character but was fun, generous and non-judgmental. I'd done some gardening work for her growing up, and now I still mowed her lawns when she asked me to. Her husband had been a strange, bitter old man who had died years ago, not long before her son Luca had died in a dirtbike accident. Then her daughter had up and left. Alma had been devastated, but the whole town rallied around her, helping her cope. When her daughter died, we all wondered how she would react, and now she was in a nursing home as she recovered from an operation after a fall of some sort and Kate was here to look after her. The woman had had a lifetime of heartache.

Perhaps that was the reason Kate was distant. I'd lost my dad and it had almost killed me, but to lose your whole family? I couldn't wrap my head around that. I wanted to apologise again for making her uncomfortable, but after seeing her practically run to her car, desperate to get away from me, I had to let it be. I would bide my time but it was not my strong suit.

On Tuesday afternoon, I dropped into Mum's to chop some firewood for her, knowing she would be getting low. She said she could do it herself, but I'd seen her with an axe and I wanted my mum to keep all her limbs.

"Hey, Ben, I can do that, you know," she said, bringing me out a coffee.

"Sure you can. You help me with the eggs when I'm away," I reminded her as I took my cup and we sat on the edge of the deck in the cold afternoon.

"It's no hardship," she said and we were quiet, my mind returning to Kate. "What's on your mind, love?" she asked and I turned to see her watching me, her bullshit radar scanning me. I'd often fancied I could fool her, but deep down, I knew that was impossible.

"Kate Bloomington," I told her, seeing no need to lie.

"Who?"

"Alma's granddaughter. I've seen her around," I said looking back at the garden, not wanting to give anything more away.

"I've been meaning to drop in to Alma. What's Kate like?"

"I don't really know her, but she seems… strong and brittle."

"Strong and brittle?" she asked. Her curiosity would kill this cat, especially if my sisters got wind.

"She has a backbone made of steel and such strong resolve, but behind her defenses, I think she's hurting," I said, sighing as I remembered once again that I contributed to that.

"Hmm."

"Hmm?" I asked my mother. She was about to say something I didn't want to hear.

"Maybe you should get to know her and not make her a project, Ben."

"Make her a project?" Yup. I didn't want to hear that.

"Settle Gretel. Maybe she has reason to feel how she does. Her parents died, she's now with her grandmother, and while I love Alma, she isn't the easiest person to get to know. That doesn't mean you need to intervene."

"I never said I was," I murmured.

"I know, but I can see your mind working. You want to help," she said. I huffed a laugh. I wanted to do a whole lot more than help her, but that was not anything I wanted to discuss with my mother. "Maybe you should start by being her friend."

At this, I laughed out loud.

"Mum, I have more than enough friends." It was the truth. I was everyone's bloody friend, especially when they needed something. I wanted someone to just need *me.*

I left Mum's after chopping and stacking her wood for the week, going home to re-heat leftovers and check my emails. At the very top was an offer for a few weeks' work in Melbourne. I deflated; I had to do it. Then again, maybe some distance from the farm, Kate and people talking to me about Sheridan would be a good thing. I emailed back confirming I would take it and accepted the fact I would see out winter spending half my time in cold, wet and miserable bloody Melbourne.

Chapter Six

The next month moved consistently slow, and that wasn't necessarily bad. It was—predictable. Lonely and predictable. I'd taken to walking the first part of Bungalow Spur a few times a week. The ritual of walking the path my mother had taken was calming and becoming easier as I got fitter. Retracing her footsteps made me think of my mother in a way I hadn't since she died. I still felt guilty that I hadn't pushed and been there for her, but instead of channeling that feeling into anger at her, I had a deep-seated sadness that I didn't think would ever go away.

The month had seen the weather get slightly warmer. I still had to light the fire every night, and rug up to do my walk, but the blossoms were starting to burst free, transforming the valley floor into a sea of green teeming with life. The birds were loud as they inundated Alma's garden—as did the weeds. I found myself out there every Saturday weeding and even mowing the lawns. If I'd thought I would be doing this a few months ago I would have signed up for psychiatric testing. The sun was out longer, and this was a godsend as I drove the Green Limousine to Bright and back at dawn and dusk, and I'd almost hit two deer and three kangaroos. I headed to Albury to buy new clothes for work. I'd chanced a few colours in the mix, and a Leona Edmiston dress. This exercise regimen and not having uber-eats meant I was losing weight without even trying.

Work was great, but it was becoming increasingly harder to keep myself separate. I envied the camaraderie between Mia and Viv, and between the managers. They often gave me expectant looks as they included me when something funny happened at work, or they had done something interesting on the weekend. On my birthday, Hannah had made the most amazing chocolate cake I'd ever eaten and we'd had morning tea together. I'd been respectful, and thanked everyone, but I couldn't let myself join in on the happy. But on my way home, the leftover cake on the front seat, I'd cried like a baby.

Frank and I often crossed paths, and he would take a moment to tell me how good I looked because I'd lost weight, or how great it was that I was working at the Hub. I'd fumbled my way through each interaction, unsure how to take his comments. It made me feel good and terrified in equal measure. I'd always been a bigger girl, especially after my year of binging, but he didn't seem to mind. In fact, he noticed my body and liked what he saw. It was hard not to bask in male appreciation. He vindicated me after my two friends had shredded my self-confidence before I'd moved.

I'd seen Ben only once, but he'd looked at me in surprise as he took me in. He had looked particularly handsome in jeans and a thick green woolen jumper. I was still embarrassed at how I'd treated him, but I was too much of a coward to apologise. Instead, I'd given him a tentative smile. Despite our brief meeting, he had been constantly infiltrating my dreams. I wasn't a sexual person. I hadn't any real experience other than a few drunken one-night stands, but I wasn't into it. My mother and father were cold, rarely showing emotion or physical affection. I'd thought all the hype about sex was a myth, until Ben started appearing in my dreams. It started with me meeting him on walks, then he was in my house, and after that, he progressively wore less clothing. I imagined he had a big, beautiful man's body, with chest hair and muscles that pointed south. They'd gotten so vivid that I'd awoken on the verge of an orgasm. I was an idiot; I'd been mean to him, and he probably wanted to be friends. But then again, I was asleep, sue me.

Getting to know Alma was going slowly too, but she'd noticed my weight loss, asking me if I was starving myself because I was losing the meat off my bones. She'd said that I needed to make sure I didn't lose my boobs or my bum because they made me look good. I'd been taken back by this strange compliment. I'd not been told *not* to lose weight before. When we spent time together, we focused on current events and my work at the Hub. I was surprised that Alma was active on Twitter, and she would tell me about stoushes she got into with politicians she didn't like. I cracked up; it was another chip in the icy wall between us. I'd started paying attention to politics too, realising there were bigger issues in the world than my anger at how my life had turned out, and guilt that I hadn't been there for my parents. We shared political views, along with a dedication to pastry, wine and big bottoms.

We ate dinner together every Tuesday and Thursday night, watching the five o'clock news, the six o'clock local news, then the main network news at six-thirty followed by the ABC news and if we were lucky, ending with a current affairs program. We saw the same stories rehashed and commented on the different bias each station had. Before long, I found myself looking forward to sitting with her, craving the company.

It was Tuesday evening, six weeks after I'd moved and we'd finished our roast chicken and chips for dinner when Alma turned the TV off. It was only six-thirty. I looked at her expectantly to see her eyes guarded.

"Kate. We need to talk," she said lightly but I knew what was coming would be anything but.

"Okay," I said hesitantly.

"Are you happy here?" she asked, surprising me.

"I'm happy enough," I said, deciding to be honest.

"Happy enough—what does that mean?"

"Well, I haven't been happy for a long time. Not since before… you know."

"Were you close to them?" she asked, and it felt strange she didn't know.

"They made sure I was always safe, and cared for, and gave me lots of opportunities. They scrimped and saved so I could go to a private school and I'd always made sure I did right by them," I said and she gave me an odd look.

"It must be hard not having them. My own mother died when I was young and I'd missed her terribly." We were silent for a beat, and I didn't know how to fill the void. "Did you have many friends that you left behind, to come here and help me?" she asked, her wrinkled face frowning as she asked this, but I shook my head. She didn't need to feel guilty.

"No, Alma. I don't have any friends."

"What? None?" She was shocked but clearly she didn't know me very well.

"I had two friends at work but it turned out they didn't think very highly of me." My throat threatened to close as I desperately tried to keep the humiliation at bay.

"What about from school?" She was not able to comprehend that I was a loner.

"After Mum and Dad didn't come home from Italy, I didn't cope," I said, sick at the memory. Then I looked at her; there was no judgment in her eyes, I decided to share my burden with her. No one knew and it had been a great heaviness I'd been carrying around. "I started to drink. A lot. I never left my apartment. I stayed home and ate, drank and smoked like a machine. Mum and Dad didn't have a lot of money, but they left me a little and with the help of a few deadbeats who were happy to join me as I pulled away from everyone I knew, I spent most of my inheritance in a year. It wasn't until one of Mum's friends and her lawyer told me I'd wasted an extraordinary sum of money and my parents would have been disappointed, that I stopped and looked around. The moment I realised what I'd done, the grief and shame felt like it was going to crush me. I'd been physically sick, but I'd promised myself that I would make it right. I've been saving ever since and have barely earned back all the money I wasted being pathetic. I was so hurt and upset, that I'd shut out anyone who meant me well, and befriended people who did not care for me. I have no old friends, and the only two I've let in since, didn't deserve it," I said. I was equal parts bitter and sad, lost in the painful memories.

"Kate, I'm sorry you faced that alone. I should have come to you. I wasn't sure what your mother had told you about me, and if you would even want to see me. But that's an excuse and I should have done better by you," she said grabbing my hand and squeezing. When I looked at her, her eyes were full of tears. Tears for me and tears of guilt. My heart raced as my own tears formed. I didn't want her to feel bad; I'd made my mistakes on my own, and I had to wear the consequences.

"No one would have gotten through to me," I said, giving the hand she was gripping a squeeze. She sighed.

"That doesn't mean I shouldn't have tried," she said, her voice shaking. We were quiet again and I drew a breath to steady myself. Given we had crossed some sort of threshold, I decided to ask questions of my own.

"Mum never said much about you. I don't mean to be hurtful, but I have no idea what happened between you."

Alma chewed on her lip as she deliberated what to tell me.

"A lot has happened in my life that I am not proud about, and losing my daughter before clearing the air will haunt me until the day I die," she said and I nodded, understanding this well.

"Will you tell me what happened?" I asked. She sighed, then took a drink of wine that was almost half the glass. If I didn't have to drive I would've done the same.

"It's a long, sad story, I will tell you a little now. I don't have the energy to do all of it in one sitting, but I promise I'll get to it. Okay?" she asked, leaning back in her chair looking exhausted.

"Okay."

"Well, Tulio Mancini was your Uncle Luca's father."

***

It was early spring, but I hadn't been able to ride my bike in weeks. I'd been stuck driving to and from the city in my truck because I had to wear a suit, and had too much luggage for my bike. I hated being between two places, especially when I spent the lion's share stuck behind a desk, while Mum and my sisters handled the work at my farm. Battling the guilt made my head hurt and my gut ache. I'd done my best to make sure I wasn't a burden for my family. It had been tough after dad died, and his parting words were, *I love you; look after our family*. I'd done my best, but now, I was forced to lean on them.

When I was home on the weekends, I was busy making sure my animals had what they needed, adding fences, mowing grass, making sure Mum had enough firewood and catching up with friends and family. I wasn't necessarily unhappy, but something about the monotony made me start to dread each day. It was made worse because I hadn't been paid yet, and my bills were overdue.

I'd seen Kate only once, and I still struggled to cope with the fact that I'd made her unhappy. I wanted to apologise, but I didn't know how. She had probably moved on, and didn't care. But I hadn't. Seeing her again after a few weeks hit me like a freight train. She was as beautiful as ever, her big grey eyes guarded as they communicated her unhappiness. But she had changed and lost a little weight—enough to surprise me, and I hoped she didn't lose too much. She was sexy and curvy in all the right ways. I wanted her still, and seeing that gorgeous body in a fitted purple dress had become a permanent fixture in my fantasies. We didn't speak, but she looked at me with a hint of curiosity that hadn't been there before. When I smiled at her, she'd blushed, but returned it. No doubt she still thought I was an arsehole, but perhaps I she didn't *hate* me.

I'd managed to spend time with Erik, even though he was busy with the end of the football season and Annie. I was a little envious. I hated being in Melbourne, but maybe the distance was secretly helping me while I got my head out of my arse. I was trying not to be a shitty friend, but this holding pattern kept me in a perpetually foul mood.

I was now home for a few days before having to go back to Melbourne one last time, and Erik had asked me to come to dinner to with some of Annie's—and now his—friends. They were all good people. The girls were friendly and a riot, and the guys were easy to get along with. I liked Dave who owned a winery—a handy profession especially for Annie and her crew, and the quietly spoken Howard who was some sort of construction mogul was interesting to talk to. We were an odd bunch but I liked that, and it was always good to meet people who I hadn't known my whole life.

I should've been enjoying myself, but I was the only uncoupled person besides Fleur and too frustrated with myself and my lack of progress at the farm to really enjoy myself. I was being a dick. These people meant well, but I couldn't get over this shit in my head. I'd been making moves to leave early because I was floundering in all the togetherness when the topic turned to Hannah and Carol's place of work, and their new staff member who was none other than Kate Bloomington.

At the mention of her name, I'd sat back down and taken Hannah up on another (my third) piece of banoffee pie. The women were discussing that they wanted to invite her out socially, but they weren't sure it would be well received. Carol, who was Kate's boss, noted that something was off with Kate and that she was worried. At this, I became fully engaged in the conversation and I realised my mistake too late. Erik noticed, and gave me a smug look.

"Benny boy, you know Kate, don't you? Why don't you try to use your woman voodoo and get her to open up?" he said.

"I'm sure she'll talk when she's ready," I muttered, giving him a dirty glare.

"Woman voodoo?" Carol asked curiously.

"Erik thinks that because I can hold a conversation with a woman, *and* talk about my feelings, that I practice voodoo. He's jealous because he is a big boy with a little... brain." Erik scoffed while the women laughed.

"Well, your voodoo wasn't working that day in the pub," Annie added unhelpfully.

"When was this?" Carol asked, honing in.

"A good month or two ago now. I'd crossed paths with her a few times, and she... didn't want to be reminded," I said, not sure how to explain the sauce incident, or her almost going into cardiac arrest on Bungalow Spur.

"What he means is, he'd seen her out running, and she had evidently been puffing so hard he had asked her if she needed help with her asthma. But, she doesn't have asthma," Annie said and everyone winced. Shit. She paused for dramatic effect before continuing. "Then he tried to make a joke of it," she teased good-naturedly. Laughter erupted around the table while Erik scratched his head wondering what was wrong with that. I knew what was wrong with it: it was mean.

Thankfully, the conversation moved on to other hikes but the fact her colleagues seemed worried sat heavy in my chest. I'd seen quite clearly that she was not okay and intent on going it alone. It went against everything in me not to seek her out, but she'd drawn a line in the sand and I had to respect that. It didn't mean that I stopped thinking about her; another reminder that life was not as I wanted it to be, and another thing I was powerless to do anything about.

The rest of my time home had helped me feel more myself again. I was able to get outside and build what would be vegetable gardens. I'd seen my sisters and spent time with Mum who was exhausted from working at the cafe. I mowed her lawns and brought in firewood setting her up for the week, but she continued to watch me like she knew how unhappy I was. She didn't say anything but her looks spoke volumes. I would need to do a better job of managing my emotions.

Exhausted, I'd gone back to Melbourne for the final two days of the job. The project had been hectic, but I was the happiest I'd been in weeks knowing I was almost done. I was so eager to leave the city, I'd battled peak hour traffic instead of waiting so I could get home that night.

Spring was around the corner, but it was still cold and the night was pitch black and frigid after rain. I was tired from my long day and driving four hours, but had my eyes peeled for deer and kangaroos as I wove along the river on the way to the farm. All I wanted was to get inside, light the fire, have a shower then crash. I rubbed my eyes and rolled down the window in an effort to stay awake.

I was yawning when I caught a glimpse of something shiny ahead. Getting closer, I realised it was Kate's little green car pulled to the side of the road. I slowed as I went past but it was empty. I drove a little further and was about to turn back to see if I could fix it when I saw a figure marching ahead of me on the side of the road. Was that Kate in heels and a dark coat? I blinked in disbelief as I slowed and rolled down the passenger window. As I pulled up beside her, she glanced up, clearly freezing and no doubt shitting herself that I was a serial killer.

"Kate?" I asked but she ignored me and kept marching. "Kate, it's Ben McTavish. Are you okay?" At my name, she faltered, almost tripping and dropping her bag.

"Shittity fuckity shitballs," she muttered, bending down. I pulled up in front of her and got out.

"Kate, let me help you. I mean you no harm," I said holding my hands up in an effort not to frighten her.

"Of course you don't. But, I'm okay. It isn't that much further," she said as she angrily shoved items back into her bag. Well, at least that was something.

"It's at least ten kilometers to Alma's," I told her and her eyes snapped to mine.

"It is?" she asked, her voice barely above a whisper, a tremor letting me know she was upset. Clearly, her anger this time wasn't directed at me specifically. Thank fuck for that.

"It is; let me drive you. Please, it's dangerous, and freezing out here. I need to make sure you get home safe," I said, moving closer to her. She was gorgeous even now, illuminated in my brake lights with blue lips, chattering teeth, and her eyes full of tears. Her dark hair that I'd been fantasizing about putting my hands into was wild and I desperately wanted to brush it away from her face to see if she was really okay. I could tell she was struggling to make a decision; she needed my help but she was fighting hard not to take it. It made me sick that I'd made her even hesitate.

"I just want to make sure you're safe," I said and she nodded, still not at ease.

"A lift would be great, thanks," she said eventually and I released the breath I'd been holding. Then she surprised me completely as she stuck out her hand and said, "We haven't properly met. Hi, I'm Kate."

I couldn't stop my grin as I took her freezing hand in mine. "Hi, I'm Ben. Nice to meet you," I said and she smiled shyly.

"Likewise."

I walked to my truck and opened the door for her, holding her bag while she got in. I did my best not to be a dirty perv and admire her now-gaping shirt as she sat back and put on her seat belt. It was difficult though. I got in the driver's seat, started the engine and took off. We didn't speak at first but I could see her looking at me speculatively. She was trying not to be obvious but she clearly noticed my suit, and looked in the back to see my travel bag.

"I'm on my way back from work in Melbourne," I said into the car, hoping to get her to talk to me.

"Really? What were you doing there?" she asked.

"I've been working down there for the last month or so," I said and she nodded, like this made sense to her.

"What do you do?" she asked.

"I consult on aid projects at the moment."

"Aid?"

"International aid, welfare, that sort of thing," I said and her eyes flew to mine in shock. It was almost quizzical and I laughed.

"Believe it or not, I'm a do-gooder, despite my ability to put my foot in it," I said dryly and a smile ghosted across her lips. Her face transformed in that moment even though the smile was barely there. Gone was the lost, defensive girl, and a sexy, confident woman shone through for a moment. We said no more as we got to the outskirts of Harrietville. The silence was uncomfortable but I had a rare opportunity that I couldn't miss.

"How is the Hub?" I asked and she looked at me.

"How do you know I work there?" she said almost suspiciously.

"I had dinner with Hannah, Leslie and Carol last weekend," I said and she seemed confused by this.

"You did?"

"Yep. Their friend Annie is with my best friend," I said and she nodded. "But even if I hadn't, I would've found out anyway. It's a small town and news travels fast, especially when it's about your grandmother." I tried to infuse my voice with friendliness.

"You're right about that." She paused for a long minute. I turned off the main road towards her house. "Everyone knows Alma it seems," she said, sighing.

"Of course, she's been here forever, and an active part of the community. I remember her always having the best sponge cakes at our school fete when I was growing up. One year she caught me stealing a piece. My mother had been horrified, but Alma gave me a wink then nodded towards a box under the table that had a whole cake uneaten. I'd gutsed on it and felt sick as a dog after, but I think that was her lesson," I told her. She listened with interest, but when I pulled into her driveway and looked at her again, I could see sadness in her eyes. "Did I upset you again?" I asked as we sat in the dimly lit cab and she drew in a breath before turning to me.

"No, you haven't. I'm learning how much I missed out on because of what happened between her and my mother," she admitted. I didn't know how to respond; I didn't know what had happened.

"I think your mum used to play netball with my mum. If you like you can talk to her about your mother," I offered, unsure if this was the right thing to do.

"Thanks, I'll think about it," she said, opening the door. The interior light came on so I could really see her face. I'd expected her to continue looking at me warily but right then, her face was open and thankful. Finally, progress.

"Please, do."

"Thanks for the ride. I would've been stuck without you," she said, giving me a smile that was small, but at least it reached her eyes.

"My pleasure. Do you want me to pick you up in the morning so you can get to work?" I asked, unable to stop myself.

"It's fine, I'll catch the bus," she said adamantly, the openness passing. I sighed, knowing I should be patient but not liking the idea.

I was more than happy to drive her whenever she needed, but if I pushed, she might not speak to me again.

"Goodnight, Kate."

"Goodnight, Ben, and thanks."

Chapter Seven

It had been a strange night, starting with me opening up to Alma. It was nerve wracking, letting someone in when you haven't done that before, but I was glad for it. Me sharing how I'd handled my grief had encouraged her to talk. I was shocked that she'd had an affair, but I imagined it was why my mother hadn't coped. I'd wanted to know more, but she looked tired after our conversation and to be honest, so was I. We had a lot of ground to cover, and I knew I wouldn't like all of it. We could wait.

After I'd left her, I'd made it a part of the way home when my car started to chug, and a few minutes later, it had lost power and I'd coasted to the side of the road between Bright and Harrietville, where I was unable to restart it. Of course it broke down in a place with no phone reception. Any emotional headway towards being happy I'd made evaporated as I was plunged back into my absolute dissatisfaction with the world and my place in it.

Then Ben had come along, and as much as I didn't want to see him because I was cold, tired, my feet hurt and I'd been a bitch to him, I was relieved. Without him, my night would have been a whole lot worse and I would be forever grateful that he drove past and I didn't have to walk ten kilometers in my pumps. When he'd pulled up beside me, and I'd stopped worrying I was going to be snatched, driven into the woods and strangled, my heart started to race for a different reason. He looked incredibly handsome in his suit, the navy of the jacket in stark contrast against the white shirt open at the collar. It made his eyes look darker and his auburn hair deeper. And sexier. My initial reaction was to be defensive, but when I'd seen his hands up as though I might attack him, those defenses crumbled. He feared my reaction and it said more about me than it did about him.

The conversation in the car had been surprising; he was friendly and open, making a joke of himself, giving me a reason to smile. In fact, the more he spoke, the more I realised that my irritation with him was misguided. Perhaps he was not out to make a fool of me. Maybe he was another good person who until recently, I didn't think existed. I could tell by the way he carried himself, and managed to get me to talk despite my foul mood, that he was intelligent and mature. When I'd found myself staring into his handsome eyes, I realised that he was a man, a sexy adult. I bet his car never broke down, and I was sure he always had someone to call. Clearly, he was the knight in shining armour in this scenario, and I was a dreadful, unfriendly awkward damsel who, let's be honest, was more like the scullery maid. I'd already been having sex dreams about Ben McTavish, but seeing him again, and how he 'handled' me, I knew I needed to stem my lusty thoughts because they would not be reciprocated.

The following morning, after dreaming about Ben carrying me in the ten kilometers in those big, muscular arms, I lay in bed, unsure of myself because I think I was changing for the better. To start with, I was wearing a little colour now and not one person had said I looked terrible. In fact, I'd gotten compliments. Alma and I had started talking, *really* talking. I'd told her how low I'd fallen, and she shed tears for me. It was unexpected, and made me want to tell her everything, and for her to tell me it would all be okay. I'd been friendly with Mia and Viv and the sky hadn't fallen in. In fact, it had only made things better. I wasn't ready to host a Tupperware party or go speed dating, but perhaps being a little friendlier wouldn't kill me.

I started immediately, smiling at the bus driver when I got on the eight a.m. bus into town—and what do you know, I didn't catch fire. Maybe one day, I would stop expecting it. Floating into the office on a good vibe, people were looking at me strangely.

"I've brought morning tea," I'd blurted to Mia and Viv when I'd made it to my desk. The fact they both stared at me had me fidgeting—was I really *that bad*? Then they noticed the bag I was carrying and they swung into action.

"Are those vanilla slices from Harrietville?" Mia asked, her eyes cartoonishly large.

"They are," I said, and I smiled as she did a fist pump.

"What has you so excited, Mia?" Hannah asked as she walked in with Carol and Leslie.

"Kate brought in morning tea, and not any old bun loaf. She has the Rolls Royce: vanilla slice," Mia said pointing at the bag I was holding.

"Right, diet starts tomorrow," Hannah said holding out her hands as though there were no other option.

We dispersed after that, but my peace offering had sent of a clear signal to Mia and Viv. Mia had asked me how it was going with Alma, and I'd actually answered honestly. She hadn't judged, just laughed at our news watching. Viv had told me she had been writing some new songs. She was self-deprecating, telling me it wasn't a big deal, but when I said I wanted to hear them, the words tumbling out of my mouth of their own accord, she'd given me a big smile. At lunch time, I'd walked down the street to get a sandwich when I'd crossed paths with Frank.

"Hey Kate, how are you?"

"Good, thanks. You?" I'd said blushing as he smiled and checked me out.

"Great, actually."

"That's good. You look great. How are you doing it?"

"Oh right," I said when I realised he was referring to my weight. "Eating healthy and walking a lot."

"Where are you doing that?"

"Bungalow Spur," I said, nervous under his gaze.

"That is such a beautiful walk, I haven't done it in ages. We should do it together some time. I'd like to get to know you," he said, giving me a full smile that left me a little dazed.

"That sounds good," I heard myself saying.

"Here is my number; give me a ring and we'll set it up," he said and I blushed as I opened my phone and added his number. I'd never been given a number by a man who looked at me the way he was. This was probably because *I'd* never looked this way. Part of me still wanted protect myself, because if my life was anything to go by, it would end up being a disaster. But after last night, and my breakthrough with Alma, a little bit of optimism had snuck in. He certainly wasn't Ben McTavish, but then, no one could compete with Ben—he was too brilliant. And while Frank didn't elicit the same physical response, the fact he liked me made me feel good and Frank was handsome in a polished way, and closer to me in age. While I didn't think he was promising forever, maybe it was time to open up a little.

The next few weeks followed in much the same vein and I kept on letting my defenses fall. I started to talk more at work, bringing lunch in so I could sit with the team and laugh at their stories. I'd shared more with Alma, about the sports I played in high school, and more about my dad, and how he and Mum were together. She was surprised to learn they were both serious. Evidently, my mother hadn't been growing up. When I mentioned the cookbook Mum had entrusted to me, Alma had teared up. It had been another breakthrough, and in return, she told me how close my mother and grandfather were—like they were in their own world. It explained the photos Mum had at home.

I'd not seen Ben on Bungalow Spur, or around town for that matter, and I wondered if it was for the best. My feelings towards him, after I realised he wasn't out to get me, had taken a completely different direction. I found myself hoping I'd see him on the street, wondering if he had written me off. His handsome face and cheeky smile continued to infiltrate my dreams, and I found a need building that I knew nothing about. I hated to admit it, but this was the reason I didn't call Frank. Each time I saw him, he mentioned catching up, or how good I looked, but I never followed him up. I had misplaced loyalty to Ben, who was only kind because I was Alma's granddaughter, when I should have been taking a chance on someone who actually wanted me.

The only real thing getting me down was that I was still catching the bus. My car was so old, they needed to order specific parts in to get it fixed. I had my parents' inheritance, and could have bought a new one, but I refused to use it. Mum had always said that I needed to be able to manage on my own. I would only use my savings, which after a few shopping sprees, wasn't much. The mechanic had said it would be at least another week; I was heading into yet another weekend stuck in Harrietville. But when Mia and Viv asked me to drinks on Friday night, I agreed, deciding the splurge on the taxi home was worth it. I was even looking forward to being social.

***

I'd thought my time commuting to Melbourne for work was done for a while. But this week, it was worse: I had to go to Sydney. That said, it would cover my loan repayment on the farm. So to Sydney I went. When I finished, I delved in farm work. Spring had arrived and the garden needed serious attention. I'd been able to finish my vegetable gardens, clear blackberries and burn off debris. I'd painted Mum's living room and managed to get Evie and Mel to help.

I hadn't seen Kate since I'd driven her home, which wasn't surprising because I'd either been in Sydney or focused on getting ahead. I thought of her often. Too often. In fact, it wasn't merely thinking about her; it was more along the lines of fantasising. She was beautiful, with gorgeous curves and full, dark pink lips that I wanted to kiss. I was attracted to the strength she showed when she thought she was up against the world. I was drawn to her backbone, and her vulnerability. But Mum's words, that I should be a friend, echoed in my head, and made my gut hurt. I didn't want to be her friend, and part of me knew that if I reached out, that was the likely outcome. I wasn't a big fan of self-torture, so I didn't seek her out.

By Friday night, I felt a little more in control of my life. I was still only a payment away from defaulting on my loan, but I'd made headway on the farm and kept the debt at bay with my recent earnings. It was a small win, but I needed every one I could get. I headed out for a drink with Erik, Annie and her friends. Bright was busy despite it being a cold night, and we headed to the Gin Distillery where they were grabbing a drink.

"Hey, Ben," Annie said, giving me a kiss on my cheek as I entered. I liked her, and her friends. They were all good for Erik, and if Kate ever opened up, I think they would be good for her too.

"Annie, how are you?"

"Great, starting to get antsy for the finals," she said referring to her netball final. Erik was also playing in the football final and with both teams from Bright making it, the town would be set alight with festivities.

"I bet you are."

"Are you going to come and watch?" Fleur asked.

"Wouldn't miss it, Fleur. How is Tate?" I asked, keen to check in on her son.

"He's doing well. He starts high school soon, and it terrifies me," she said.

"He'll be fine. He's a great kid, Fleur, and they don't stay feral for too long," I said. She smiled.

"It's his birthday tomorrow, and I bought him a gaming console. He's at a friend's tonight but I was wondering if you could help me set it up on your way home?" she asked tentatively. I grinned. Fleur was one person I never minded helping. She rarely asked—only when she needed it, and she never expected me to do things for her.

Drinks continued but there was no mention of Kate. I didn't know if I was disappointed or not. I wanted to see her, but after the last time, I wasn't sure where I stood. Fleur and I were getting ready to leave when I heard Erik growl.

"Fucking brilliant," he said and I turned to see him staring at the door.

I followed his gaze to find Sheridan walking in, dressed up for her hen's night. Fuck. Erik looked at me, and I could feel the others turning their attention.

"It's cool, Erik," I murmured as Fleur got closer.

"You need me to kick someone's arse?" Annie asked. She could certainly do it, I thought with a smirk.

"I'm in," Fleur muttered.

"Me too," Hannah exclaimed. I appreciated the sentiment but my feelings about Sheridan weren't that simple. She had played games, forcing me to break up with her, but I'd bitten at every piece of bait. Instead of making it better between us, and fixing what had been broken, I'd only made it worse—losing my cool, and taking it out on her.

"Thanks guys, but it wouldn't be much of a competition," I said, smiling as I turned to Fleur. "You ready?"

She linked her arm in mine and we said our goodbyes. As I walked towards the door, Sheridan caught sight of me and in that moment, with her giving me a tepid smile with all her overdone makeup and hair, I realised that it was a good thing we broke up.

"Hi, Ben," she said weakly and her friends, some of whom I knew, laughed nervously.

"Sheridan, I hear congratulations are in order," I said warmly, catching her off guard.

"Ah, yeah. They are."

"Well, all the best to you and your future husband," I said, leaning in and giving her a kiss on the cheek, astounding everyone. Sometimes being a bigger person was the best sort of revenge.

"Thanks," she said awkwardly before looking at Fleur, a hint of jealousy in her eyes. "Hey, Fleur."

"Sheridan, you're here on your hen's night. Do not look at me like that. I'm not with Ben, but you made your bed, now you can lie in it." I almost fell over and Erik burst out laughing behind me. I was very glad in that moment to be in Fleur's friend-zone.

Chapter Eight

As Mia, Viv and I walked down to the local pub on Friday night, I felt alive for the first time in ages. We sat by the open fire and Viv and Mia chatted about their plans for the weekend. I'd been out for Friday night drinks in Melbourne with my old friends Cleo and Layla, but while the activity was the same, the feeling wasn't. Here, I wasn't panicking about people looking at me, or being cornered into buying drinks. Mia had ordered a bottle of wine and fries, which we all shared as we talked, and I let go of the last of my defenses. I wanted to be present, and enjoy the moment.

We'd only had a glass or two when the conversation turned to Mia and her stories that, if I had to admit it, rivaled Sauce-Gate. Then Viv nudged Mia to tell me the story of the doctor she flashed and Mia laughed before leaning in. It felt like I was being let in on the secret, and it along with the wine, made me warm inside.

"To be fair, I was tired," she said and Viv rolled her eyes. "I was travelling overseas and I needed some immunisation shots. I went into this enormous medical clinic and the doctor who came in was this handsome as sin, young registrar. I smiled, and with nothing for it, pulled down my pants and undies, and told him to *have at it*. That was when he told me that the injections would go in my arm."

I couldn't help it, I laughed out loud—hard.

"It was embarrassing, but I couldn't stop laughing at myself. I even snorted. Yep. SNORTED," she cackled.

"What did he do?" I asked, trying not to snort myself.

"He was trying to be professional which only made me laugh harder. When I said goodbye, he'd rolled his lips in to stop himself giving in to the hilarity, but his eyes were twinkling."

"Wow, Mia. That sounds like something I would do," I said before ordering another bottle of wine off a waiter who'd walked past. When my attention returned to the group, they were looking at me strangely.

"What?" I asked, looking down to make sure I looked normal.

"Well, I can't imagine you doing something like that," Viv said.

"You seem too in control," Mia added and I smiled, but inside I died a little. I'd been putting on a show of cold indifference for weeks, not wanting them to get close. Now I was here, having a good time, letting myself be and they couldn't believe the real me because they'd never met her.

"I'm not. I try to be. Things got a little out of shape for me after my parents died, and since then I've been inwardly focused, sorry," I said.

"No need to apologise, you had good reason," Mia said softly and I smiled at her. The wine arrived and I poured everyone a glass, the effects loosening my spirits and my tongue.

"You should believe I can do ridiculous things," I said.

"Oh yeah? Like what?" Mia asked; clearly she couldn't believe it. I told her about sauce-gate and she almost fell on the floor with laughter. It was a rival to her high kicking, and bum flashing. It felt good to let it out, to laugh at myself and be laughed at in a way that left me feeling better, not devastated. We continued like this, laughing and talking, and I was free as a bird. Viv grabbed her purse to buy the next round when the waiter brought over a bottle of Bollinger.

"Ladies, compliments of the gentleman at the bar," he said as he placed it on the table. We all gave each other big eyes before whipping our heads around to see Frank, holding a beer up in salute.

"Frank Mancini?" Mia breathed.

"Whaaat?" Viv said.

Before I could speak, Frank winked at me. Both girls whipped their head back to me.

"I don't know why he did it," I stammered, flushed at the attention and Frank's heated gaze.

"I do. He wants to get into those sexy jeans you're wearing in. Go you," Mia said.

"He likes what he sees," Viv commented but I shrugged. "You don't like him? He's pretty easy on the eye."

"He is... I can't really imagine what he wants with me."

"Have you met him before?" Viv asked.

"A few times, we always talk whenever we bump into each other, and he seemed keen to catch up."

"He likes you," Mia exclaimed.

"I'm not sure about that," I hedged, trying to hide my grin.

"I am and it looks like he's done waiting," Mia said giving me a smug grin as I blushed.

We sipped the champagne, all of us feeling the effects of the alcohol. I needed to stop at this, or else I would have a raging hangover tomorrow. As we were on our last glass and sharing the opinion to call it quits, Frank walked over and took a seat.

"Ladies," he said smoothly.

"Hi, Frank, this is Mia and Viv," I said nervously. Frank looked put together as always, wearing a black shirt and dark jeans which made his chocolate eyes seem even darker. He gave a wide smile and we all blinked at its pearly white brilliance. We made small talk about the Hub and we thanked him for the Bollinger. Frank was easy and comfortable, charming all three of us.

"I'm going home—I'm wrecked," Mia said, looking at me with twinkling eyes. "Come on, Viv, walk me home?"

Viv in her buzzed state did not pick up the obvious byplay, and looked at her like she was strange, until Mia gave her the eyes.

"See you on Monday, Kate?" Viv asked as she stood and almost knocked the table over. I smiled awkwardly. At least Frank didn't seem perturbed by their slapstick obviousness. When they'd left he turned the full force of his handsomeness and charm on me, leaning in close, his eyes now hooded.

"How about another drink?" he purred, and I blinked slowly, ensnared.

"I don't think I can drink anymore."

"How about coffee then, at my place? I have an apartment in town, around the corner."

Coffee sounded perfect. With my newfound confidence and acceptance of the fact that people might actually be okay, I decided that I should want to get to know him, that it was normal. The alcohol had given me a confidence boost and then there was the fact he was handsome, and he wanted me. Yes. *Me.* Besides, Ben wasn't really an option, and Frank was no slouch, so why not?

"A coffee would be nice," I said a little shyly and we left the pub. It was cold outside, and after helping me into my coat, he held out an arm. I took it, smiling at the gesture and we walked down the street to an alley between two shops, up a narrow staircase and into a studio apartment. It wasn't flash, but it had a kitchen, a couch, a bed and an enormous TV. Looking at the bed made wonder what impression I was giving in coming here. I purposefully sat on the couch with my bag in my lap.

"You sure you just want coffee?"

"Yes, thanks," I said as he helped me slip out of my jacket before putting the kettle on. When he returned, he stood behind me and rubbed my shoulders. His touch made me tense up; it was unexpected, but as he deepened the massage I started to relax.

"How do the men fare up here, not quite as sophisticated as Prahran?"

"Ha, well they're more pleasant and approachable," I said. I wasn't sure if I was supposed to be complimentary, or answer the question.

"Really? I would have thought the boys would have been chasing you all over Chapel Street," he said, moving to sit close beside me. I laughed a little, because I certainly had not been chased.

"Not quite," I said, blushing at his blatant flirting.

"Their loss, because you are stunning," he said, taking my hand in his. I couldn't help but smile; he was intense but he seemed comfortable. Clearly I was doing something right. "Did you ever have a boyfriend in Prahran?" He asked one of the questions I usually dreaded.

"No, not really."

"Something else I find hard to believe." He seemed almost pleased by my inexperience. Before I could thank him for his compliment, he put one hand on my shoulder and pushed me back on the couch so I was lying down. I squeaked in surprise, but then he was kissing me. Hard.

Shocked by his sudden and ardent movement, I had to remember to kiss back, not just lie there. I could feel him move his full weight on me, but I was uncomfortable, my legs bent at an unusual angle. There was no way I could stay in this position.

Frank intuitively knew this, and with one hand by my head, he held himself up, and with the other, moved my legs, so that when he lay down, his crotch was against mine, my knees at his sides. Again, it took me a minute to realise what had happened—we had gone from flirting to physical contact. My breathing quickened. Frank was kissing me passionately, and I didn't know what to do next. Was this normal? It wasn't entirely unpleasant, so I lay there and let it wash over me, trying to get into it.

His right hand made its way under my top to my bra without me even noticing. I tried to relax, and the contact felt good, until it didn't. He'd gone from caressing to squeezing in a way that wasn't about my pleasure, but his. He was thrusting against me, and it was good for a little while, then it too started to hurt. Frank looked up and must have seen my discomfort. He stood, removed his shirt and then took me by the hand and did the same to me. He smiled warmly and again I was lulled into going with the flow, although kept trying to cover myself. He shook his head as he moved my hands away, his eyes glued to my chest, showing a feral sort of desire. Something about it wasn't right and I was trying to take stock of what was happening, when he kissed me again, slower this time.

I sensed it took him effort to slow down, but I appreciated it. I didn't want to sleep with him, but I was okay with more of this, so I relaxed. He pulled me back to the couch, and returned me to my back, and he lay atop me, but this time his legs straddled mine, pinning my arms at my side.

We kissed for a brief moment before he was restless again, his hands going to my fly, but I didn't want more.

"Frank, maybe we should take a moment,"

"Why? You know you want this," he said, not slowing down at all.

"Well, I do, but…"

"See, that's all you need to say," he said and then something changed. He pinned me down with his weight as he tried to unzip his fly. I struggled, asking him to wait, but then he shoved me into the couch with his hand right below my throat. I realised what was actually happening and I started to panic.

"Wait, we need to wait," I said breathlessly, desperate to extricate myself.

"For what?" he said as I heard his fly lower.

"I don't feel ready, Frank." I struggled in earnest, panicking at having my hands pinned.

"Of course you are, I can feel it," he said as he crudely pinched my stiff nipple through my bra.

"Get off me. I don't want this." I started to rock back and forth trying to get my hands free. He was too strong, and he knew it as he smiled at me.

"Don't fight, Kate, you know you want this." He was no longer charming; that smooth, crafted mask had frayed, revealing a man who got off on having me struggle beneath him.

"Don't, please don't." I was frantic, and he was getting rougher and rougher as he tried to unzip my pants. I kicked my legs, trying to get purchase with my foot to roll him off me. Then there was a searing pain as he bit my shoulder. My scream died in my throat as he looked down at me smiling, my blood on his teeth.

"I told you not to fight," he said coldly and I knew, down to my bones, that I had to get out of here. I needed to think, so I stopped fighting for a second. He mistook me needing to clear my head as giving in and he chuckled, returning to my fly. I let him fumble as I relaxed a little, keeping him focused on getting my jeans undone. It was all I needed to get a hand free and he didn't see my fist coming to the side of his head. I hit him in the ear and he howled with the pain and reared back. This allowed me to do my best to punch him in his crotch with my other arm. I made contact and he fell back awkwardly onto the floor. I didn't waste a second, I got up, grabbed my shirt and bag and ran, leaving Frank and my coat behind.

"Bitch," he roared but I was down the steps, and into the alley as I pulled my shirt on. There was no way he could chase me without being seen now. Adrenaline rushing through my veins, I ran until I came to a stop in front of the Hub. It was shut for the night. I tucked myself around a corner and tried to catch my breath. I didn't know what to do, so I stayed put and tried to breathe. Eventually, the cold started to penetrate my panic and I had an intense desire to get home. I rubbed my face to find blood on my hands, so I rummaged through my bag to find a tissue and get it off me. It was my blood, but he had put it there. Once I thought I wouldn't draw attention despite not having a coat, I headed to the taxi rank outside one of the pubs and called the number. It was busy, so I hung up and called again. I would keep calling until someone picked up.

***

"Ben, I appreciate it. Thanks."

"No problem, Fleur; it should be all sorted now," I said as I stood from the couch.

"Is this how you thought you'd spend the rest of your Friday night?" she asked giving me a wry smile.

"Having a crumpet and tea with you while I set up your gaming console? Sure. Listening to you lay Sheridan out? Not at all, but I fucking loved it," I grinned at her and she rolled her eyes.

"She had it coming," Fleur muttered as she gave my forearm a squeeze.

"People are going to think we're an item," I told her and she grinned.

"At least it will get people off my back." She sounded sad. I looked at her worryingly. We'd been friends since high school, and Erik and I'd always checked in on her since one of our old friends left her pregnant at seventeen.

"How are you really?" I asked her, noticing that her smile was only partially genuine.

"I'm good."

"Has something happened? Is it Reece?"

"No, Ben, I haven't seen Reece in years."

"Can I do anything?" I asked, not liking the dimness in her eyes.

"You already do too much. You should look after yourself more."

"Don't worry about me," I said.

"I'll worry about you if I want. You should be out on the town or on a date, Ben, not having crumpets with me. Any woman would be lucky to have you," she said, smiling warmly, and I knew she was trying to be kind, but instead it made me feel worse. I was single and not because I wanted to be.

"Good night, Fleur," I said before heading to my truck. I was ready to crash after my overloaded week. I started to head out of town when I saw her and I almost stopped in the middle of the road. Kate was waiting at the taxi rank, no coat, her hair disheveled, her eyes black with mascara, holding herself protectively. I pulled up beside her and got out, moving to her quickly but she didn't register I was there. She kept pressing buttons on her phone.

"Kate?" I breathed. She faced me with wide, unseeing eyes.

"Ben?" she asked.

"Yeah, that's right. Are you okay?"

"I'm good, thanks. Just waiting for a taxi."

"I'll take you home," I told her, taking her elbow to help her stand. When she flinched I stopped and looked at her. Her eyes were red and puffy from crying.

"I'll be okay on my own," she whispered, more to herself than to me.

"Please. I want to make sure you get home safe," I told her quietly and she nodded.

"Alma calls you Saint McT, did you know that?" she said absentmindedly.

"I've heard that before. Kate, do you trust Alma?" I asked her gently.

"Yes."

"Well she trusts me, and you can too. Let me get you home," I implored and eventually she looked less panicked, but weary and sad. Immensely sad. She didn't answer, only nodded and walked to my truck. I opened the door and she climbed in, sitting in the seat with her eyes shut tight. I felt sick. What had happened? We didn't speak as I drove. I cranked the heat and put the radio on in the background. It was ten minutes before she broke the silence.

"Thanks."

"Of course," I told her. "Are you okay?" She was quiet a long moment before she spoke.

"I will be."

We said no more but she seemed to come back to herself as we headed further down the road. At Alma's I walked her to her door. Her hand shook as she tried to unlock it. I took the keys from her, and opened the door.

"Do you want me to sleep on the couch?" I asked, feeling that was the right thing to do.

"You would do that?" she asked, quietly incredulous.

"Yeah, I would."

"Why?" she breathed, giving me a hopeful, but confused look.

"Because you look frightened and I want you to feel safe," I answered honestly and her beautiful grey eyes turned bleak as she assessed me. Something she saw in my face let her know I could be trusted, because she nodded and walked inside. I followed, trying to hide my concern as I headed straight for her fire to light it.

"I need to shower," she said, walking down the hall; I brought in some firewood and put the kettle on. It wasn't long before she came out and handed me a blanket and a pillow. With her face clean of makeup and her wet hair tied back, she looked as beautiful as ever and I ached to hold her. But I didn't. Something told me not to and while it was killing me, I needed to trust my gut.

"Do you want to talk about it?" I asked and she shook her head. Instead she wrapped her arms around my waist and lay her head against my chest. Instinctively, I put my arms around her, feeling her warm and soft against me as I held her close.

"You're safe, Kate. Go to bed," I murmured against the top of her hair.

"Will you be all right?" she asked looking up at me, her chin resting against my chest.

"Of course. I need to go early tomorrow morning. Will that be okay?"

"Yes, thank you for doing this. I don't know what to say," she said, sounding lost.

"You've said all you need to. Go to sleep," I said giving her a smile, and reluctantly she withdrew her arms and walked towards the bedroom. I lay down on the couch, my legs hanging off the end, and pulled the blanket over me. It was so uncomfortable that there was no chance of sleep. Instead, I listened to her cry herself to sleep as my heart broke.

Chapter Nine

When I stumbled into the kitchen on Saturday morning groggy with a headache, I found a note on the bench sitting on top of the blanket I'd given Ben. Shit. Ben. Memories of last night came rushing back along with tears, and I wished he was still here. I wanted to be in his arms again, but as he'd said he would, he'd left early. I opened the note to find his masculine scrawl: *Kate. Call me to let me know you are okay. Ben* and then he listed his number. I took in a deep breath then I put my phone on charge. I wanted him, but taking that step, reaching out seemed too hard. I didn't want to be a mess in front of him again. I would wait because I was not okay.

Making a coffee and wrapping myself in the blanked he'd used, I walked out onto the back deck to sit in the morning sunshine. It was still cold and I pulled the blanket close around me. I focused on Alma's garden and the wattle that was in flower and the birds that were in her bird bath chattering. I found myself staring into space, the world going on around me, but I was back to being stuck. Stuck and in pain. I sobbed, emptied my tears into the blanket as I relived last night. Frank had lured me, that was the only way I could put it. He somehow knew I was a target, that I was looking for attention and he gave me enough to get me where he wanted me. I kicked myself for being so stupid. Sure, the alcohol had impacted my inhibitions, but I'd wanted to go with him, and I wasn't impaired when I realised what he was doing. It was too late then, I was under him, and he was strong.

The look in his eyes as he assaulted me… *assaulted* me—I still couldn't believe it. That feral look had scared me. I'd gone from taking a chance to get to know a guy who seemingly liked me to him doing his best to violate me. And he succeeded. He did violate me. He bit me, held me down and tried to unzip my pants when I said no.

I rubbed my shoulder, which was tender, a reminder of the mess I'd found myself in. I'd taken a picture of the marks last night, knowing I should go to the police and have him charged. But I was afraid of what he'd said. He'd asked me if I'd wanted it and I'd answered yes. It was out of context but I knew now what he was doing. He was setting me up. Then there was the drinking, and us leaving the pub together arm in arm. That, along with telling Mia and Viv that we'd been friendly, made it look very consensual. That wasn't the complete truth, but what would people think? Would they believe me? I was new in town, and I had a flighty mother and crazy grandmother. I wasn't sure who would win when it was his word against mine.

The idea of sharing made me sick and my skin clammy. What did it say about me? People didn't know me. No one did, and for them to see me for the first time, and me tell them I was drunk and went home with a guy who I decided I didn't want to be with? What would that mean for the rest of my life? I knew I didn't ask for him to do that, but others? Would they be understanding? I doubted it. Then there was Frank. He was terrifying and calculating, and I knew if I made moves against him, there would be retribution, and I would be defenseless.

Being powerless made me physically sick, and I ran to the bathroom to expel the meagre contents of my stomach. I couldn't tell anyone; there was no way I could do that. I was too humiliated. Even after opening up a little and making friends, I wasn't ready for that level of exposure. I doubted I would ever be.

I spent the whole day around the house, unable to manage going outside. I thought about calling Ben. I'd picked up my phone dozens of times but I didn't have the guts. While I'd originally thought he was an arsehole, he'd proven he wasn't. Instead, he'd been kind and thoughtful. It was me who was mean and a user. He probably only helped me because my hopelessness must pull at his heart strings. I was someone who was broken and needed saving. Or maybe he was a grown man who always did the right thing and never found himself in situations like this. Not Saint McT.

He was out of my league and now out of my reach. But I still wanted to call him. I wanted him here, holding me again. I wanted his strong arms around me, his heart beating under my cheek, his brilliant blue eyes looking at me. But I resisted. I stayed indoors all day, watching television with the blinds drawn. I battled the need to call him on Sunday as well, as I did my best to bury the incident with

Frank. I completely believed he was at fault. I had done nothing wrong. But I was not ready to take on the system, and my own humiliation. The mental torture was exhausting, so when I was napping in the afternoon I almost missed the call from Rosella Lodge.

"Kate, dear, it's your grandmother's nurse. She's had a fall and we with think it might be good for you to come and see her."

Hearing that Alma was hurt and needed me, I panicked. My tired, fractured mind went to memories of my mother's last phone call, and I felt lightheaded, my cheeks flushing. I did not want to be too late. Ever again.

"I'll be there," I heard myself say before I hung up. I hoped that this wouldn't happen again, but after last night, any optimism I had was waning. At least this time, I would be able to say goodbye. I took the paper with Ben's number out of my pocket and with shaking hands, dialed him.

"Hello?" his strong, steady voice came across the line.

"Ben," I breathed.

"Kate, are you okay?" I could hear the concern in his voice, and the people in the background recede. Shit. He was out with people.

"Sorry, you're busy. I wouldn't have called but it's—Alma—and I need a ride."

"I'm on my way," he said and hung up. Just like that. He was coming for me, and I breathed a sigh of relief.

I quickly had a shower and got dressed, having been in my PJs all weekend. I didn't bother with makeup; nothing I could do would impress him now. He arrived as I was looking for a coat, given Frank had my everyday one. I opened the door and stepped out to meet Ben as I slipped my enormous puffer jacket on.

"Everything okay?" he asked, taking in my no doubt pale face.

"Alma had a fall. They've asked me to come in and I have to get there. I'm sorry to be a pain, but I can't have it happen again," I said as I let him lead me to his truck. As we headed down the road, my panic slipped out of my control as I looked at my phone and then back at the road, then at my phone again.

"Did they say if she was going to hospital?" he asked calmly.

"No, only that I needed to come in. I have to get there."

"You said again. What can't happen again?"

"I can't be too late. I can't miss the moment," I whispered, my throat getting thick.

"What moment?" he asked and I drew in a deep breath, unable to stop my mouth.

"My parents. I knew they were sick when they were in Italy. I was going to come but Mum told me that I needed to stay home. I did. Then they died. Ben, they didn't want me to come, and I missed out on telling them goodbye. I could have helped. I should have fought to be there," I said, a tear escaping. It was strange to say it aloud; he was the first person I'd ever told.

"I'm sorry," he said and he leant across to squeeze my hand. I smiled, looking down at his large weathered hand covering mine, the image watery.

"I've never told anyone that before. Alma doesn't even know."

"Can I ask why?" he sounded unsure, like he didn't know if he was overstepping. His kindness made my heart hurt—how had I thought he was an arsehole?

"I'm hurt and ashamed. They didn't want me there. I loved them and they were supposed to love me, but they didn't want to see me. My mother knew she was dying, the report from the hospital clearly said that they had a severe case of meningitis and that soon, they wouldn't be able to speak. But instead of letting me come and be there, see them, they told me not to. I should have fought to be there, not given up," I said, my voice a whisper now as we came into Bright.

"Beautiful, I'm sorry you had to go through that, and that you've been managing on your own. But don't worry about Alma. I'm sure she is fine; if she wasn't she would already be in an ambulance." I took in a deep breath and thought about this.

"You're probably right, but I can't bear the thought of it happening again. It's no secret I'm alone in the world, and she is the only person I have left," I said as my knee bounced. I fiddled with my phone. "You have memories with her. I don't."

Ben was quiet as we turned off the main road and I wondered if I'd offended him. I stole a glance in his direction to see his face calm and focused.

"You're not alone," he said as we pulled into Rosella Lodge and I looked at him. He wasn't angry, upset or patronizing me. He said it like it was fact. I didn't know what to say because I wasn't quite sure what it meant. Did he mean himself or Alma? He parked the car and we both got out.

"I can make my own way home if you have something to do," I said as we walked in.

"It's fine. I'll wait."

"I might be a while," I said as I signed in, relieved Barbara wasn't here. I had no capacity for her bigotry.

"Kate, see Alma. I'm fine." I looked at him. He gave my shoulder a comforting squeeze, and I couldn't hide my wince. He'd touched me right where Frank had marked my skin. He gave me a concerned look but I did my best to smile before I raced off down the hall. Alma's door was open and I surged in, needing to see her.

"Kate? What's wrong?" she asked, looking at me around one of the nurses who was arranging the blankets on her bed.

"Are you okay?" I asked, needing to know that she was okay. She stared at me a beat then asked the nurse to come back later, before patting the bed. Woodenly, I moved and sat on her bed, looking her body over for signs of injury.

"Kate, talk to me. What's going on?" she asked, taking my hands in hers.

"I was worried, that you were... you know... and I wasn't going to be able to say goodbye again. I—" I didn't have words, only tears, and she pulled me into a hug, patting my hair as I cried, telling me she was going to be fine, that we were going to be fine. With the dam broken, more pent-up tears came out and she held me all the way through it. When I'd emptied my reserves, I pulled back and she smiled at me.

"What is really going on with you, Kate?" she asked me, and seeing nothing but openness and—was that love?—I told her what happened with my parents. Her weary face crumpled, tears running into the wrinkles around her eyes.

"I'm hurt Mum didn't let me come to her, not letting me get close to her growing up, for not giving me you. But I still love her, and I'm ashamed that I didn't fight and go to her. I never got to tell her and Dad that I loved them," I said as Alma sniffed into a hankie.

"I know a bit about that feeling. I was hurt by Jennifer too, but I will always love her. She was my only daughter, and she brought me more joy than anything else," Alma said and I smiled, in awe of her ability to love despite her loss.

"Are you all right?" I asked and she nodded.

"A slight fall with the physio. I think they thought I was in a bad mood, which is why they called you. I was in a bad mood, and let's be honest, I'm always as cranky as I am crazy. I just didn't want my recovery to take any longer. I want to be home," she said.

"I think I may have jumped to conclusions."

"I can see why, Kate, but don't worry. I'm not about to cark it," she said, chuckling.

"Good to know," I murmured, a small smile on my face.

"Is everything else okay? Work?" she asked, looking at me closely. I thought about telling her what happened with Frank. We had crossed a line and it felt good, but as with Ben I didn't want her to know. I knew that everything would be better if it never happened, so I pretended it didn't.

"I'm good, really," I said. It wasn't a complete lie.

"Is your car fixed?" she asked.

"Not yet."

"How did you get here?"

"Ben drove me," I said hesitantly but I need not have worried because she gave me a huge smile.

"That's the best news I've heard all bloody year."

***

Waiting was not my strong point in any way, shape or form. I sat in the uncomfortable peach and lavender chair in reception trying to focus on the *National Geographic* in my hand. But I couldn't get Kate's face out of my mind. I would switch between remembering her tear-soaked face on Friday when I found her waiting in the cold, to how she looked at me when I said I would stay over, to right before, in my truck as she shared her heartache. I didn't know what had happened to her on Friday, but it must have been serious. I wanted to ask her but the haunted look in her eyes made it clear that I would have to wait. But perhaps I wouldn't have to wait long; she'd opened up in the car, flooring me with her strength despite the trauma she'd experienced. There was that backbone.

An hour after she ran down the hall, she came back out looking exhausted but emotionally lighter. She gave me a shy, tired smile and I was struck again how beautiful and genuine she was. There was nothing insincere about her. She didn't play games, and she didn't manipulate. She protected herself because she felt alone, but that was about to change, starting now.

"All okay?" I asked as I stood and walked to her.

"Ah, yeah. I might've overreacted. She had a small fall and was cranky so they called me to see if I could put her in a good mood." She was embarrassed, blushing as she bit her lip nervously, and it was too cute and too damned sexy. I was a little surprised when my dick twitched given we were in the least sexy place on earth, but she had that kind of pull on me.

"Don't stress; you had a right to be worried, especially after a rough weekend," I said as we headed outside again. "It's nearly six, did you have plans for dinner?" It was cold and clear, the sky still a little pink as we held onto daylight.

"Yeah, I had plans. I was going to eat my feelings by way of ice cream and watch *Fifty Shades of Grey*," she said but sucked in a breath when she realised what she'd said. I waggled my brows at her.

"I love that movie," I told her.

"What?" she asked, assuming I was joking.

"The book was better, and I think they could have found a character who actually had red hair. I mean, they got someone for *Outlander*, didn't they?" I said as I opened her door and helped her in. When I got in the driver's seat, she was still staring at me.

"What?" Now it was my turn to be confused.

"You've read and watched *Fifty Shades*?"

"Uh-huh. This will surprise you too then. I read and watched *Twilight*."

"Really?" She couldn't hide her smile, and it made her even more gorgeous.

"Really. I like to know what all the fuss is about."

"Wow," she muttered and I smiled.

"Real men don't need to act hyper-masculine all the time. The ones that do are compensating," I told her as we pulled out. "Would you mind postponing eating your feelings and try the Wandi Pub instead?" I asked, hoping she would say yes.

"You want to eat dinner with me?" she asked like it was unusual and I grinned at her. Feeling brave, I responded.

"As long as you don't have tomato sauce on your chips." At this she laughed naturally and I relaxed. We walked into the pub to see Annie and Erik there. I hadn't expected it but given how close by they lived, I wasn't surprised. Kate stiffened when she saw Erik stand and smile at me.

"We don't have to sit with them," I whispered in her ear and she moved close to my side.

"Ben, how's it going?" he asked as he came over and slapped me on the shoulder.

"Erik, Annie," I said over his shoulder, and Annie smiled and raised her glass.

"Who's this?" Erik asked, giving me a big grin. This was not the time for him to rib me about her, but telling him that would only encourage the prick.

"This is Kate, Alma's granddaughter. She's been for a visit," I said.

"Nice to meet you, he said, holding out a hand. "I'm Erik." Kate looked at me shyly before taking his hand.

"Nice to meet you. Alma has mentioned you, although she doesn't call *you* Saint McT," she said. Erik chuckled.

"She wouldn't. I'm nowhere near as nice as Ben." He grinned and she blinked a little at all his Nordic handsomeness. I was about to intervene when Annie walked over.

"Isn't that the truth. I'm Annie," she said, holding out a hand. Kate seemed overwhelmed but right when I thought it was too much, Annie saved the day. "I'm close with Hannah, Leslie and Carol. They mentioned you've started working there. Tell me, is it as mad as it seems?" Annie asked, using the woman voodoo that I'd been lacking of late, drawing Kate to a table and ordering her a glass of wine.

"At least she wants to talk to you now. Is your fuck-up forgiven?" Erik asked as we headed to the bar. I rolled my eyes.

"A misunderstanding," I said as I ordered a beer.

"I see. And now what? Are you friends?" he asked, teasing.

"I think so," I sighed.

"And you want more than that, clearly," he said. I looked at him flatly.

"What makes you say that?" Shit. Now he *was* really interested.

"Well you walked in, keeping her so close you were practically attached, and then you hovered so protectively you'd think you were her bodyguard. I can see she is important to you," he said honestly.

"She is."

"That's good. I hope she does right by you," he said. It was a nice thing to say but I could not let it stand.

"That subscription I got you to *Feelings Weekly* is paying off," I teased.

"Piss off, you idiot."

"I can see that you've been working on your emotional intelligence."

"What?" he asked, dumbfounded.

"At least some part of you is getting smarter," I said and Erik laughed hard.

We joined the table, and I was happy to see Kate relaxed and talking to Annie. Kate sat close to me as we continued to discuss everything and nothing, and ate dinner. While it was a good distraction from the heaviness of her thoughts clearly weighing her down, it felt good for me to be out and not be the third wheel. As we finished our last drinks, Kate tried to hide a yawn.

"Take the girl home, Ben, she's tired of your blathering," Erik said. Instinctively, I put my arm around her, and she stiffened at first. I wanted to curse my error, but then I felt her relax and lean into me. I didn't know what this meant, but I wasn't going to complain. Annie was watching us speculatively, and I had no doubt this would be reported back to her two lieutenants, Molly and Hannah. As we drove out of town, it started to rain softly.

"What time do you start work?" I asked as I fiddled with the radio.

"Eight-thirty, so I can walk after work," she said, yawning again.

"I'll pick you up at eight then," I told her.

"I can catch the bus; I've already inconvenienced you enough," she said, sounding sleepy and cute.

"It's no problem. Be ready at eight," I said, but there was no answer. I looked over to see her angled towards me, fast asleep. I glanced at her often as I drove her home, admiring the length of her lashes and the way she slept with a small smile on her face. I was glad to see it and hoped this meant I would see more of those smiles in the future.

Chapter Ten

True to his word, Ben was at my door right before eight in the morning. I was running a little late because I was struggling to focus. My emotions were a tumble, and while I was unable to deny my excitement at seeing Ben despite the fact he was Saint McT and I was a hot mess, I was still trying to bury the events of Friday night. Images of Frank would pop up, and I questioned my decision to do nothing. But the system wasn't fair; I needed to move on. I had just started to get my life back, to feel like I belonged, and after being alone for so long, I simply couldn't go back. It wasn't right, but I couldn't see any other option.

"Do we have time for coffee?" he asked as I got into his truck.

"Of course," I said trying not to turn into mush as I took him in. He was dressed casually again, and while I missed the suit I'd caught a glimpse of, his navy woolen jumper and fitted, faded jeans had my mouth watering.

"Great," he said and drove us straight to the bakery. While we ordered coffees, every local in the place stared at us. Their gazes sharpened when Ben put his hand on the small of my back as we walked out. I wanted to tell them all he was just being Saint McT, but it was hard to concentrate because my body came alive at his touch and I was within smelling distance. Yes. That's right. The pastries held no sway now; I was all about Ben and his sexy, fresh soap smell. This trip was going to be a nightmare; would it be easier or harder on the back of his bike?

"Do you not ride your bike often?" I found myself asking, trying not to sound hopeful.

"Not as often as I'd like. I didn't think you'd appreciate it in that skirt," he said grinning wickedly at me. I blushed.

"Have you ever been on one?"

"No way, my mother forbade them."

"Well, anytime you want a ride…" he trailed off and I laughed, blushing. "So, much on today?" he asked after I'd almost burned myself on my coffee, spilling it on my scarf.

"We're having a drill with the emergency response volunteers today, to see how fast they can set up a command post. Bruce is quite excited."

"I bet he is. He used to be friends with my father, but Dad was never as intense he was."

"I'm sorry," I said.

"For what?"

"About your dad. It's hard," I said.

"It is. But unlike you, I had a chance to speak to him," he said warmly.

"What did he say?" I asked before I could stop myself, but Ben only smiled.

"He told me he loved me and that I needed to look after Mum and my sisters. I've been trying to do that ever since." At this, my heart melted a little more.

"I wonder sometimes what Mum would have said to me, if I'd made it," I said, finding it easier to talk about with Ben.

"She would have said she loved you," he said simply, like it was obvious.

"I want to believe that. I wish she could have let me come and hear it," I said, feeling the hurt and guilt come back.

"You'll get there," he said and gave my leg a squeeze. I wasn't sure if that was a friendly gesture or not, but I wished he would keep doing it. It made me feel warm and supported, my grief less isolating. He dropped me off at work, and I gave him an awkward wave as I got out of his truck. I'd wanted to kiss him on the cheek even but I didn't want to make a fool of myself. So, awkward it was. When I arrived at my desk, Mia, Viv, Carol, Leslie and Hannah swamped me.

"Well…?" Mia asked suggestively.

"How was dinner Sunday?" Hannah asked coyly.

"Sunday? You saw Frank on Sunday?" Mia asked in surprise.

"Frank?" Carol asked and everyone turned to me.

"Well…" I started, not sure what to say. A lot had happened and I had to think on the spot what to tell them about Frank.

"Mia, well… Frank didn't work out. I don't think he's for me," I said, trying to smile and failing. Carol zeroed in on my apprehension and Mia and Viv's confusion. Luckily Hannah distracted them.

"Frank Schmank. I want to know about Ben McTavish, our resident Ginger Hottie who you had dinner with on Sunday at the Wandi Pub," she said. "I'm not spying on you, not really. Annie is a very close friend of mine," she said looking at me excitedly, and I nodded, remembering. Now I was dreading responding for a different reason: I didn't want to give away that I'd been fantasising over Ben McTavish for months. But again, I didn't need to respond.

"Ben? Ben McTavish of the ginger locks and square jaw?" Mia asked, disbelieving. I tried that awkward smile again but I probably looked constipated.

"We're friends," I said, but none of them were listening, except for Carol. The others were too busy talking about how Ben had done aid work overseas. Then Mia said he has the best eggs in town.

"Eggs?" I asked, not sure if she was referring to his… you know… eggs.

"Get your mind off his gingery goods. He has chickens, and sells eggs," she said, giving me a wicked grin that made me smile back, genuinely this time.

"Of course he does," I muttered, thinking I knew nothing about Ben in his everyday life. I wanted more information. I was desperate for it, but if I asked now, it would draw attention to my feelings for him. Eventually, they stopped badgering me for more information and the crowd dispersed.

Surprisingly, work flew by, and I found myself relaxing despite the flashbacks of Frank and his feral grin. They would come when I was sitting quietly, my mind idle enough to drift. But I tried to remain focused, and this time when people spoke around me, I listened and tried to participate. Ben's message confirming my pickup time had me grinning stupidly, but luckily it was only Carol who saw and gave me a look like she knew something was up with me. I hurried as I left because if any of them saw Ben picking me up, they would think there was something really going on. Sadly, my plan failed.

"Hey, Kate," he said as he stood up from leaning on his truck as I bustled towards him. He looked sexy, all manly and rugged, and my body tingled at the thought of him touching me again. I'd never been sexual, but when it came to him, I found myself constantly noticing his body, and wondering how it would feel pressed against mine.

"Let's go," I said as I raced to the car door, looking ridiculous. I had no place running without a sports bra on.

"You in a hurry?" he asked as he unlocked it, but it was too late.

"Bye, Kate," Viv said as she walked out the front door and I could hear her interest.

"We'll talk tomorrow," Mia added, almost singing her threat.

"Ladies," Ben said as he smiled at them.

"Ben," they giggled. "Take care of our girl," Mia said and I couldn't fight the blush as I turned to glare at them.

"Of course," he said as he got in his truck and took me home. On the way, I peppered him with questions, not wanting to dwell on Mia and Viv's innuendo. I learned that yes, he had chickens, and sold eggs. He told me about his farm, and how he wanted to grow boutique crops and build accommodation on site, as well as a family home. Family home. The thought of Ben with a wife and children had my blood pumping because I didn't like the idea that he would inevitably end up with a Nobel Peace Prize winner, but also because the thought of him with children might make my ovaries explode.

"Are you walking Bungalow Spur tonight?" he asked as we neared Alma's.

"Yep. It's become a thing I have to do. I keep trying to get as far as I can in forty minutes, and one day when I'm ready, I'll walk all the way to the top."

"Can I join you tonight?" he asked hesitantly. Part of me wondered if he was a masochist because twice on that path I'd been a shrew to him.

"As long as you bring your asthma pump," I said dryly and he laughed, shaking his head.

"Fair enough. I have my running gear with me."

We got changed at Alma's and I tried not to think about him in any state of undress, only one room away. Then we set out and I focused on the path ahead.

"Why do you want to get to the top of this one so badly? There are lots of walks around here," he said before we started the steep incline.

"My mother did it, and I... want to feel close to her again. I don't know if that makes sense," I said, pleased I was finding it easier to breathe.

"It makes perfect sense. What was she like?"

We kept walking, and I proceeded to tell him about my mum and dad. They were simple stories from growing up: where we went on holidays, what we ate for Christmas, how I learned to ride a bike. We made it back down without me having a heart attack or falling over the edge, and when he said he was picking me up in the morning, I found no reason was good enough to say no.

For the rest of the week, we kept a similar pattern. He would pick me up in the morning and take me to work. If I was visiting Alma, he would get me after that; otherwise we would go home and walk the Bungalow Spur. We talked more about my mum and dad, Alma and my work. I offered him money for taking me, but he refused so adamantly, I was fearful to offer again.

As I walked in to see Alma on Thursday evening, I was amazed that almost two months ago when I'd arrived, I'd been hurt by my friends, nervous about my new job, afraid of how Alma would receive me and having been humiliated in front of Ben. I hadn't thought happiness was possible, but since then, despite the fact I was assaulted by Frank, I was infinitely happier.

"You have a spring in your step," Alma said as I walked in and sat down. "Ben picking you up again?" she asked, her brows raised speculatively.

"He's insisting," I told her, and she nodded as though she expected it.

"That's how he is. Always helping everyone else. Maybe he needs someone to look after him?" she asked looking at me like I was that person. I wanted to be, but therein lay the issue. I had nothing to offer.

"I'm sure they do."

"He might be able to help you with something else. Even when your car is fixed, I'm not sure it will make it to Melbourne."

"Why am I going to Melbourne?"

"Because you need to find out about your inheritance from your grandfather." I looked at her confused. My grandfather had been dead for decades.

"I'm not following."

"Your grandfather died a long time ago, not long before your Uncle Luca did. At the time I didn't realise it, but he must have had his own money hidden away. Now his partner has died, they have found the paperwork."

"Why didn't he leave it to you?"

"We parted on poor terms," she said, not elaborating, and I sighed. Neither of us was ready to open up completely. "Your grandfather's partner's family found an envelope as they were cleaning the house. It included a letter from a law firm in Melbourne addressed to your mother. I called the firm but they will only speak to you, and they want to verify who you are. I think this will be an in-person thing, not over the phone. You should go to Melbourne and find out," she said, leaning back in her chair, looking utterly exhausted.

"Are you okay?" I asked.

"Tired," she said, nodding, giving me a tight smile. I wanted to know what she wasn't telling me, but I didn't know how to push. Instead, we ate dinner and talked about the news, needing to be off the heavy topics. When Ben picked me up, he knew something was on my mind, but I didn't know what to tell him. Instead, I told him about Melbourne. Without hesitation, he said he would take me. I reminded him my car would be ready the following day, and he gave me a look that told me exactly what he thought about that idea. I shared his concern for the green limousine making the trip, but that wasn't why I let it go.

***

Driving Kate around meant I'd had to get up earlier than usual to sort the animals and stay up later to do my consulting work, but it was worth every ounce of effort. It had distracted me from my financial situation, which had steadied a little. Now her car was fixed, I was going to miss spending time with her. She wore her emotions on her sleeve, and since whatever happened that night I picked her up and she was upset, she had been open with me. Now, she seemed to be freer, and let her personality—including her dry sense of humour—show. She was still guarded about some topics, like her mother and boyfriends, but that aside, she'd let me in. I was completely enamored with her.

However, I was unsure how she felt about me. I knew she wanted to be around me, and I wasn't complaining. A large part of that was me making her feel safe, and while that made me feel like I could hang the moon, I didn't know if it was anything more than that. I wanted her in every way, to keep her safe but also to love her. She was sexy without trying, all curves with the prettiest face I'd ever seen. Her lips were dark pink and pouty, making me want to kiss them all the time. She had clear grey eyes that were ringed with thick dark lashes, and when she looked up at me, her amazing hair framing her face, I was done for. It had been a struggle not to let her see how much I wanted her when we were together. My dick had been at half-mast for a good week, and that was no fun in running shorts. On Friday evening when she hadn't needed a ride home, I'd felt lost. It made me feel like there was something else I should be doing. Instead, I was at Mum's.

"Will you sit down?" Mum asked.

"You don't need me to do anything else?" I asked, keen to be busy. I'd been there all afternoon, pruning her hedges.

"I need you to sit down and talk to me," she said. I sighed, taking a seat at the worn kitchen table. "Are you going to the game tomorrow?" she asked, referring to the netball and football grand finals.

"Of course. Annie and Erik are both playing, it's going to be the event of the century," I said dryly. I loved country sport, but I didn't obsess over it. I'd played football, but preferred to mountain bike and hike.

"Look after your sisters, will you? I know there will be much celebrating after," she said, handing me a beer and a chopping board, knife and onions. I still helped Mum cook; my part-time work as a kitchen hand had left me with knife skills to be rivalled only by *Masterchef*.

"They can look after themselves," I muttered irritably, and my mother's gaze sharpened.

"What's gotten into you lately?" she asked.

"Nothing."

"It's not about Kate Bloomington, is it?" she asked, and now I narrowed my gaze on her. My irritation with my sisters had nothing to do with Kate. "Don't think I haven't been informed that you're seeing her all the time," Mum said flatly.

"Her car broke down; I gave her a ride," I said focusing back on the onions.

"And you are the only person to help her?"

"She doesn't have a lot of friends, and Alma is great."

"Of course," she said smiling.

"What?"

"She's beautiful," Mum said, going to the stove.

"That helps too," I said and she laughed.

Driving home after dinner, I thought about texting Kate, inviting her to the game with me tomorrow. I'd asked what her plans were for the weekend, and she told me she intended to hike and visit Alma. I wasn't sure if she was telling me that so I didn't ask her out, or to demonstrate she had time.

At home, I lit the fire and checked my emails. Seeing another loan rejection from the bank made my mood plummet. I needed the money to get my herd started so I could make more money. But getting that up and running with most of my capital tied up in the farm was proving difficult. I poured a whisky and headed outside in to the cold, clear night. The moonlight lit up the fields, making them look silver. I could see Mount Feathertop in the distance, snow still clinging to the peak. It was beautiful, and I knew once I had my house built, life would be good here. Getting there, however, was like banging my head against a brick wall. I was normally positive, ready for a challenge, but in that moment, I wanted something to be easy for once. My phone buzzing in my pocket interrupted my self-pity and I pulled it out. There was a text from Kate.

Hey, Ben. I hope you are well. I was wondering, are you going to the netball finals tomorrow by chance? I am thinking about going but I don't know where to go.

I smiled; I saw through what she was saying. She could find out the location in any number of ways, but instead she asked me.

I'll pick you up at eleven.

I can drive.

I want to make sure we arrive. See you at eleven.

You should really give the green limousine a chance.

I'm not ready to make that leap of faith yet.

Lying in bed, I thought about Kate as usual. Tonight, just remembering her in her new work attire from yesterday—a slinky green dress and black heels—had my dick hardening. Before I took care of myself, I grabbed my phone and texted her.

Wear jeans.

Why?

We're taking the bike.

When I arrived at Alma's, Kate was out the front looking adorable and sexy in a bright blue puffer vest, skin-tight jeans that clung to her sweet arse, with her hair wild and free. I desperately wanted to kiss her, then take her inside and do a whole lot more. She had said go to the game, not go down on her, so I would wait until I knew it was what she wanted.

"Team colours, right?" she asked, fidgeting under my appraisal.

"You got it," I said, grinning, and she relaxed, gifting me with a wide, unguarded smile.

"I see you continue to pay homage to your heritage. How many tartan shirts have you got?" she asked, taking the helmet from me.

"One for every day of the week," I said.

"Cute," she said then realised what she was calling me and she blushed. Now that *was* cute. What was even cuter was her trying to sit behind me on the bike. I started the engine and she let out a yelp before clinging to the seat under her thighs.

"Kate, hold on to me," I said over the rumble.

"You?"

"Yeah, me."

"Where?" At this, I laughed.

"My waist, Kate. Hold on to my waist," I said as I chuckled.

"Right, gotcha." Then she wrapped her arms around me tight. I wasn't prepared for the feel of her behind me, her breasts pushed into my back, her hands perilously close to what would soon be my hard-on, her soft thighs against mine. I loved having her there, but it would make being only a friend even harder if that was where we were heading. We took off down the street, and after a little while, she relaxed, turned her head to the side, and we enjoyed our ride in the spring sunshine.

"What time is your appointment with the lawyer on Friday?" I asked when we stopped for coffee, which she insisted on paying for. I never understood why women fought me on this. It wasn't because I was a man and I should pay; I did it because I wanted to, because it was a nice thing to do. Me having a dick didn't have a damned thing to do with it. I didn't argue, however, because she had agreed to let me drive her to Melbourne, but only when I told her I had meeting for a new consulting job on Thursday afternoon.

"Friday at ten in the city. Carol said I can leave work at eleven on Thursday. Will that give you enough time to get to your meeting?"

"I'll pick you up from work. You can check in to the hotel and chill while I'm at my meeting. I'll be busy from four to six p.m."

"Sounds like a plan. Are you sure I can't pay for the hotel?" she asked, but we had been over this.

"I had some free nights banked up, so I booked two rooms," I said and she rolled her eyes.

"Saint McT," she muttered. I knew it was in jest, but it was a good reminder for me. She might see me as most women did, a nice guy who would lend a hand when you needed it, even if it was to talk about your ex. With Kate, I desperately didn't want that to be the case. I wanted to be with her but I didn't know where I stood and it made me nervous. When we arrived at the game, we earned some looks from locals who were there, but I didn't care. I was proud to be there with the most beautiful girl in the North East.

Kate had seemed apprehensive, like she didn't know what to do with herself, no doubt finding her way after her self-enforced loneliness. I sat by her, and I don't think she realised how often she leaned into me, or touched me, making sure I was there. When she felt comfortable she got drinks and talked to her girls, leaving me to talk to all the people I knew. We kept tabs on each other in a way that garnered attention from her colleagues and our friends. But when they inferred something was going on between us, she referred to me as just a friend. In fact, she was adamant and it felt like a hit to the gut. It was true, we'd been spending time together, but my feelings for her were not friendly in the slightest.

The netball team narrowly lost, and Annie was furious. I couldn't blame her; the umpiring was appalling and Annie and Fleur had played their hearts out. Erik's team had won, with Erik getting Best on Ground. Given the convincing score line, there would be some serious celebration when the team made it back to Bright.

When I asked Kate if she was ready to get back, she looked at the bike, then back at me and grinned. I loved that she wanted to ride with me, so we took the long way back to Bright, before heading to the brewery to celebrate the end of the season with half the town.

The band started playing, and people got to drinking seriously. I was driving, but I encouraged Kate to let loose. She'd had a few glasses, but she'd seemed almost afraid to let go. The wary look on her face made me think of the Friday night I picked her up. I'd smelt alcohol on her then, and I could tell she'd been drinking but something had happened and I feared the worst. Even though she wasn't drinking didn't mean she wasn't loosening up. She was smiling, laughing with the girls and dropping the odd wisecrack that had them in stitches. I gave her space, but watching her come out of her shell was a beautiful sight. I found myself relaxing too, and the celebration was contagious. I loved being social: parties, drinks, meeting people down the street. I loved a chat, and these were people I'd known for a long time. Before long, I was being urged onto the dance floor.

"You dance?" Kate asked, seeming shocked.

"You bet, especially to 'Uptown Funk.' You?" I asked her, grinning at the bemusement on her face.

"Not really," she murmured looking at the packed floor.

"You do now," I said, grabbing her hand.

Hannah, Annie, Molly, Dave and Fleur were already dancing, and we joined them. Clearly enthusiastic about more people joining the group, they made space for us. Hannah called to Howard to join but he shook his head, giving a rueful smile. Erik was nowhere to be seen, as usual when it came to dancing. As the floor became crowded, Kate was forced into my space. Seeing she was unsure, I pulled her close, and she put her hands at my sides and kept rhythm with me. This brought her lush, soft body close, and I had to force myself not to hold her flush against me. That would certainly communicate my more-than-friendly intentions.

Soon enough, she started to smile too and I wanted to howl in victory. She laughed at me as I pulled out all my best maneuvers, including the lawnmower, and when "You're the Voice" came on, I even managed some highland dancing when the bagpipes played. This had her in hysterics, and that made me so happy, I even contemplated doing the worm. Luckily, I was nowhere near drunk enough. Eventually, the last call came, and after the team song, people started to say their goodbyes.

"I'm ready to go when you are," Kate said, placing a hand on my chest, leaning in to speak into my ear. Her hair fell around us and I could smell her rose-scented shampoo and feel her breath on my skin. We'd never been this close, or intimate, but I edged closer, our hips almost touching, and for a moment, she looked at me like she wanted me to kiss her, her eyes going hazy. I was leaning in, about to put my mouth on hers when Mia called out to Kate, clearly not reading the situation until too late.

"Hey Kate, did you see Frank? He is with some other—oops."

Kate froze, her eyes going wide before her face went blank.

"No, but good for him," she said almost vacantly.

"Sorry, didn't mean to cock-block," Mia added, clearly enjoying herself, and I smiled.

"Frank who?" I asked Mia, but Kate spoke:

"I'm ready to go home."

Chapter Eleven

After having one of the best days of my life on Saturday, I was devastated it had ended with finding out that Frank and I were at the same place. I should have expected it in a town this small, but I hadn't been prepared. Being so close to Ben's big, muscular body, looking into his brilliant eyes, wanting him to kiss me, I'd begun to hope that maybe I wasn't just a friend. It was clear that everyone loved him, and I could see why. I was right there with them. Then I heard *that* name, and I'd felt like an imposter. It reminded me that he was Saint McT with good reason, and I was still a mess. Deep down, I knew Ben would only want to be friends if he knew what had happened. I'd hidden at home on Sunday, not even walking my track, trying to rein in my feelings.

It was a foolhardy mission because I wanted Ben with every cell in my body. Being near him made my skin too hot, and being on the back of his bike, holding his big, barrel chest, smelling him and feeling him hot and hard against my cheek had made me edgy and needy. I constantly remembered how it felt to touch him, and my body still craved the contact. By Thursday, I was a wreck. I hadn't given the visit with lawyer any thought, because all my energy was focused on anticipating seeing Ben, and trying to find a way to not throw myself at him.

"When is the Ben of the Ginger Locks and Square jaw—" Mia started to say when Viv interrupted.

"And killer dance moves," Viv interrupted to add.

"Yes, that too—when is he coming to take you to Melbourne?" Mia finished with a dramatic flourish as I started to clean up my desk. She had relentlessly asked me about Ben, and if we were together. I'd flat-out denied it, because it was the truth. We were just friends, and a strong, respectable grown man like that did not dally with the likes of me. While Mia and Viv were frustrated with my response, Carol and Hannah had given me wry smiles. Hannah, who headed to Melbourne with Howard for work the day before, had told me to call her if we wanted to catch up for a drink, but it sounded like a double date, and that made me wary.

I'd been so lost in my nervous energy, when my phone buzzed on my desk I'd yelped, startled. Mia laughed as I read the text from Ben, then turned my computer off.

"Have fun with your *friend*," Mia sung as I walked out, and I gave her a flat look, which only served to make her smile wider.

"Thanks for this," I said nervously when Ben took my bag and we walked to his truck. I hadn't seen him since Saturday night and my eyes eagerly devoured him. Looking at him had a flush spreading over my body, and an ache starting down low. Beautiful body aside, I'd missed his steady, positive presence. I'd tried to concoct reasons to see him but since my car was in perfect working order, and on the nights when I usually walked the trail it had been pouring with rain, I'd not had any options that didn't make me look desperate. Just because he was treating me as a friend, did not mean I could keep my thoughts the same.

Then there were the sexy daydreams. From the moment I saw him I was attracted to him. It had probably exaggerated my hurt feelings when he'd made a joke at my expense. Now, however, after brushing against his hard body on Saturday, I was ready to combust. Not that I'd know where to start with a man like Ben. If I were to guess, though, I'd take off his shirt and get my hands on that flat stomach I felt when we were on his bike, and then lower them to the top of his jeans.

"All okay?" Ben asked, snapping me out of my impromptu sexual fantasy.

"Ah, yeah. Right. I'm okay. A-Okay in fact. You?" I stammered, my cheeks flushing. He gave me a strange smile, then nodded.

"I'm good. Any musical preferences?" he asked as he started to press buttons on his phone.

"Not really," I said, and to my surprise, Taylor Swift's "End Game" came on. I couldn't help but laugh.

"What? Just because it's popular doesn't mean it isn't any good."

"Is there any music you don't like?" I asked in return.

"Not really. I'll give anything a go."

"That sounds like your personal motto," I said and he nodded.

"It is; everyone and everything deserves a chance or two. I didn't love cross stitch in the beginning, but I gave it a second chance," he said.

My mouth dropped open. He didn't leave me hanging long and burst into laughter.

"I'm kidding. I don't cross stitch."

"That's a relief, because I prefer macramé," I said and he chuckled.

"I do think everyone deserves a chance or two though," he said. I smiled, glad I'd dropped my defenses and gotten to know him.

From that moment, I smiled for rest of the trip. Ben told hilarious stories of his aid work overseas, and growing up with younger, outrageous and unruly sisters. Not only was he a talented storyteller, he had a protective and righteous streak that made me respect him even more. Alma was right. He was a saint.

When we arrived in Melbourne, I was almost disappointed, because I'd wanted to stay cooped up with him in close confines. But he'd had to go to a meeting, so he encouraged me to rest then grab a drink and let him know where I was so he could meet me after. I'd gone to my room and tried to rest, but I was too energised. Ben's enthusiasm for life was contagious. I'd been thinking about what he'd said about chances, and decided that I would reach out to my old friends Cleo and Layla. I wanted to see them, to clear the air and give them a chance to apologise. I wasn't the fat, sad pushover anymore and I wanted them to see that.

I was a little surprised that they agreed to meet me for a drink after work, so I set about getting ready. I'd packed a few outfit possibilities, not knowing where Ben and I would get dinner. Wanting to look good given we were going to a bar in the city that would be full of suits, I went for a black, high-waisted pencil skirt and low-cut red long sleeve top that was tight. It showed a lot of cleavage, but now instead of hiding my body, I wanted to show it off. I had boobs; people would have to manage. I wore black pumps to give me some height because Ben was tall. I curled my hair at the ends, added smoky eyes and red lips and looked in the mirror. I wasn't vain, but I knew I looked good and it wasn't because I'd lost weight. I felt like myself, and I liked what I saw.

I texted Ben where I would be, and walked down the alley to the trendy bar we'd often hit after work. I passed a gift shop on the way, seeing a throw pillow with a giant highland cow on the front. Ben had explained he wanted these in his herd, and seeing it made me think of him. It could be a great decoration when he finally built his house on his farm. I bought it, then made my way into the bar to wait. Ben had texted back, confirming he knew where I would be, but that he might be late. I tried not to be disappointed, but I couldn't help it. I wanted to see him.

My newfound confidence took a hit when Cleo and Layla walked in right after five thirty. I'd forgotten how beautiful they were. Cleo was tall and willowy, with a platinum pixie haircut, enhanced breasts and the longest legs you had ever seen. Her tanned skin was accentuated by the dusky pink long-sleeve jumpsuit she wore. It was daring and she looked like a supermodel. Layla was the same, with long brown hair and a body and look that rivaled Kim Kardashian. I'd always wondered why she'd suggested I wear clothing that hid my shape, because looking at her now, I realized we were a similar size.

"Kate! You're so thin now. You look much better," Cleo said, air-kissing me. I tried not to flinch at the un-compliment.

"You look... different," Layla said as she eyed me suspiciously. I tried to remember Ben's words, and give them a chance.

"Drink?" I asked, and at this, they smiled smugly.

"Of course, Goose and cranberry," Cleo ordered.

"Sapphire and tonic," Layla added. I hated that they both used brand names to make sure I ordered top shelf when they knew I was paying. But I didn't want to be petty, so I placed the order, getting myself a red wine.

"How are things in the arse end of the earth?" Layla asked as we took a stool at a high-top table. I didn't like her insinuation, but before I got a chance to correct her, Cleo jumped in.

"It must be bad if you're back here wanting to see us. Last time we saw each other, you had some not-very-nice things to say," she said, looking down her nose at me.

"Well, I didn't say them for no reason," I started but Cleo interrupted me again.

"You made such a fool of yourself, all because you heard a few home truths. I'm sorry, Kate, but you are overweight, and you do really embarrassing things because you are clumsy. It's not my fault you are how you are, but you took it out on me. I thought we were friends," she said. I started to feel sick as I clammed up. That wasn't how it had happened.

"You should be nicer to us," Layla chimed in. "We're your only friends, and have been for years. We put up with your shitty, poor-me attitude because God knows no one else would. We took you under our wing, introduced you to our friends, I even let you sleep with my brother's friend, and you still embarrassed us. There's good reason you're alone, Kate." I could feel the tears start to form. They were twisting everything. I hadn't expected this, and I couldn't get my thoughts together.

"But she's not alone."

Hearing his voice, I froze.

***

I knew something was up the minute I locked eyes on her. Well, after I'd gotten over her profile in that sexy-as-fuck skirt. Holy shit, she was gorgeous. But then I'd seen her face, and she had that same look when I'd seen her hiking, after she'd fallen. It was a look of desolation, hurt and sadness. She was trying to get words out, but coming up empty because whatever the two women had said had stolen her breath.

"And you are?" one with short, blonde hair asked, blinking slowly at me. She was assessing me like some women did when they were considering how you could be of use to them.

"I'm Ben. I'm with Kate," I said and she looked confused.

"You're… with Kate," the shorter one said, looking between us as though it was impossible. Kate sucked in a breath, not yet able to respond. I put my arm around her and pulled her to me, leant down and kissed her on the cheek.

"Sorry I'm late," I said for them to hear, and then I whispered, "You okay, beautiful?"

At this, she relaxed a little, and let go of the breath she'd been holding. She didn't answer, only wrapped an arm around my back under my suit jacket and squeezed. Turning my attention back to the women who Kate had clearly thought were friends, I took them in. They were primped to within an inch of their lives, nothing out of place and nothing that seemed genuine. They were here to be seen and were looking at Kate like they had underestimated her because

I'd arrived. It pissed me off; Kate was brilliant irrespective of whether or not she had a man. They introduced themselves as Cleo, the taller one, and Layla, the shorter one with angry eyes.

"Another drink, ladies?" I asked, and Kate stiffened. Both women smiled and nodded.

"Kate, give me a hand, will you?" I asked and led her away.

"Don't buy them drinks, they're leeches," she hissed more to herself than to me.

"What's going on?" I asked as we stood at the bar, waiting to order.

"These were my only two friends in Melbourne, and the short of it is, the night before I left I found out what they really thought of me. It had hurt at the time, but now I'm feeling more... me... I took your advice and decided to give them a chance. It was a mistake. They still think I'm nothing but an embarrassment," she said, swallowing hard in an effort to not cry. It broke my heart, and I needed to put the smile I'd enjoyed all the way to Melbourne back on her face.

"What are we going to do?" I asked and she looked at me, confused.

"We?"

"Yeah, I'm your wingman. What's the play here?"

"Um, let's leave and I'll eat my body weight in dumplings?" she asked almost seriously, but I couldn't hold back my laughter.

"You crack me up, Kate," I said as I ordered another round of drinks.

"I do?" she asked hesitantly, looking up at me like she wasn't sure I was telling the truth.

"You do," I told her and she smiled at me, some of the pain gone.

"I want them to see me, the real me, and realise it's them who is missing out on my friendship. It may be petty, but I want to win," she whispered and I gave her a squeeze.

"Well, let's do it." I quickly sent a text to Hannah, explaining what I needed, then we rejoined the group. I leant on a stool and pulled Kate into me so she was almost sitting on my lap. It made me a dirt bag because she thought we were pretending to be an item, but I'd do anything to have her close like this, even for an hour.

"Ben, what do you do?"

"I'm a farmer," I said. Cleo frowned.

"A farmer."

"Yep, I'm a farmer, and you're a good listener," I said, smiling, and she wasn't sure if it was a joke or not. Perfect.

"You don't look like a farmer," Layla said almost cattily looking at Kate as though she thought it was a farce.

"He's a farmer now and is working on a paddock-to-plate operation with accommodation and sustainable crops. But he used to be an aid worker, helping the poor and impoverished around the world. He's helped feed refugees, distribute medical supplies and set up an orphanage for babies with AIDS. Now, he consults while he sets up his agri-business. That's why he's in a suit," Kate said, stepping in. Cleo nodded like it made sense to her now, but Layla's mouth flattened. I had to fight a grin; Kate had said it with pride, and that made my heart give a big, heavy thud.

"And how did you meet?" Layla asked, and Kate stiffened slightly.

"Well, we actually crossed paths when she was driving to Harrietville. I was drawn to her right away, and you know her, it's obvious why," I said.

"Obvious?" Cleo asked, showcasing she was a few slices short.

"Well, she's saucy," I said, giving Kate a nudge. She almost spat her wine everywhere, then she leaned back into me and I could feel her move with laughter. The girls continued to pepper me with questions, which was no good, because I wanted them to talk about Kate, not me. But then Hannah arrived.

"Kate, Ben, great to see you," she said giving us a kiss on the cheek in a whirlwind of movement. Kate whipped her head around to me, giving me big eyes, but I merely winked at her. "Go with it," I murmured. She nodded slowly, and we focused back on Hannah who was introducing herself and Howard to Cleo and Layla. Both the young women were in awe of Hannah and Howard. They looked as they always did: Hannah a fifties bombshell and Howard a *GQ* model.

"How do you know Kate?" Layla asked cautiously.

"We work together. We are very lucky she came to us, she is brilliant."

"What do you do again?" Cleo asked. This was a green light for Hannah to tell them in detail, about the community Hub and how

Kate played a key role in making sure local people who were doing it tough got what they needed. Kate had made a comment about Hannah exaggerating her skills, but Hannah had looked her dead in the eye, and told her she was telling the truth. After that, Kate took over asking questions of the girls about her former workplace and what they did on the weekend. At their banal answers, she told them about the Hub, her other colleagues, hiking and me. I chanced a look at Hannah, who was smiling, then stood to get more drinks, accompanied by Howard.

"Thanks," I told him.

"Don't mention it. We wanted to come, and besides, smack-downs are Hannah's specialty. Do we get drinks for those two?" he asked quietly frowning.

"Nope, between Hannah and Kate, this will be wrapped up soon enough."

"Good, this place doesn't do it for me. I might sell it," he said and I barked out a laugh before we ordered drinks and returned to the group. Layla, clearly furious that her plan to hate on Kate had been derailed, homed in on Howard.

"Howard, what do you do? Another farmer?" she asked sarcastically. Hannah drew in a breath, ready to lay waste, but Kate stepped in.

"Don't you know who he is? This is Howard Ambrose, as in Ambrose Constructions. He owns the building you work in. Geez, no wonder you two are single. Your attention to what is right in front of you is terrible," she said, delivering the death knell.

Howard smiled at them, but Hannah and I beamed as they stared at Kate open-mouthed. Needless to say, they finished their drinks quickly and left.

"Wow, I'm sorry you all had to witness that, but thanks," Kate said giving us a nervous smile.

"It was a pleasure. You're one of us now, Kate, and this is how we roll. We have Ben to thank for giving us the heads up, and it was perfect because I was here for work and Howard works around the corner."

"I really appreciate it," she said quietly, her words heartfelt.

"Anytime. Now, you two have a nice evening," Hannah said pulling Kate into a hug and whispering something in her ear that made her look at her in shock and confusion.

"What was that about?" I asked when they were gone and she'd stood to put her coat on. She looked at me with wide eyes, as though I'd startled her. She collected herself and smiled at me. Then she moved into me and wrapped her arms around my waist and hugged me. Instinctively, I returned her embrace.

"What's this for?" I asked, peering down at the top of her head. She looked up, those beautiful grey eyes clear and bright.

"You're right."

"About what?"

"You're an awesome wingman." She smiled huge and kissed me on the cheek, while my heart sank in my chest. It was happening. Again.

Kate couldn't help but be cute, telling me she was ready for those dumplings, and I tried to smile, even while I was dying inside. I'd begun to think maybe, just maybe, Kate was into me. I could read women, and Kate had shown the signs, although I didn't think she was fully aware she was doing it. Now, I was second guessing all that. She liked that I was her wingman, and next, I knew she was going to tell me all about how Cleo and Layla had hurt her. Don't get me wrong, I wanted to hear it, but it would also seal my fate.

As we sat at a tiny table in a dumpling house that was doing a roaring trade, she ordered more dumplings than even I could eat, but I couldn't stop her; she was too happy with overcoming whatever battle she'd had with those girls. When our food arrived, she looked at me like she had something serious to say, and I braced.

"Ben, I don't know how to thank you for tonight. I couldn't have done it without you."

"What are friends for?" I said trying to keep bitterness from my tone. I wanted to be her friend. But I wanted to be more.

"That was above and beyond. I want to tell you about how they hurt me, because I don't want to keep things from you, but I'm worried what you'll think," she said looking at me, fear evident in her eyes. It wasn't what I expected her to say, and I never wanted her to worry about telling me anything.

"I promise I won't judge," I said and she kept looking at me, fighting an internal battle.

"When my parents died, I didn't cope. I was lost and alone, and I withdrew from everyone I knew. I also picked up a few bad habits, and with my inheritance, I spent a year drinking, eating, smoking and hanging with deadbeats who wanted to mooch off me. After a year or so, a family friend pointed out how far I'd taken it. It was enough to scare me and so I pulled it together, found a job and started to lose weight. I never went out because I had to save money to make up all I'd wasted. After a few years, Cleo and Layla started where I worked. They were hopeless, and because I knew my way around, they hung close to me. It was to use me, but at the time, after being alone for so long, I'd loved having people interested in me. We'd started to hang out, and they would invite me to drinks and parties that a girl like me would never have been invited to. I was often paying for drinks and cab fares, but I didn't care, because I was lonely. So, during the week, I was even tighter, going without to make sure I had enough to cover the weekends and put the money back in the bank. Then they started commenting about my weight, and what I should wear, and foolishly, I listened."

She paused a moment, to drink some wine and eat. I wanted to tell her she was beautiful, and damned sexy as she was, even with sauce in her hair. But I didn't.

"I'd started to realise I was being taken for a ride, but I didn't want to acknowledge it. When the letter from Alma's lawyer came, I made a show of not wanting to go, and in many ways I was terrified, but part of me also knew I wasn't happy. When I'd told them I was leaving, they weren't upset. We'd briefly discussed going out for drinks the night before I drove up, and I'd gone home to my empty apartment to get ready and have a few drinks while I waited for one of them to tell me where. But the call never came, and I texted them both but got nothing back. Unsettled and on edge, I drank too much. Nothing ridiculous, but enough to make poor decisions, and I went to the bar I thought they would be at.

"They were there, in the VIP area, with my replacement at work who was a handsome young guy with absolutely nothing between his ears. I called them but I could see Cleo look at her phone and send me to voicemail. The guy asked who it was, and she said nobody. I was pissed. I called again, and she ignored my call, explaining that I was a lost puppy they'd taken in because I'd been wallowing in grief and bacon since my parents died. They said they felt sorry for me, but at least I'd made them laugh with all the ridiculous things I'd done and said. When they said they were only sorry I was leaving because there was no one to pick up the check, I'd felt sick. I'd considered telling them what I thought, but instead I went to leave. Sadly, as you've seen firsthand, I have a penchant for doing ridiculous things and humiliating myself, and I knocked a waitress over on my way out, slipping on wet floors.

The drinks went everywhere, and the waitress was furious, telling me to watch how I used that body of mine. I was mortified, and people all around looked, including Cleo and Layla. The tears came but they didn't help me as I got up off the floor, in front of a crowded bar that was laughing at me. I looked to Cleo and Layla, and Cleo laughed and pointed, and Layla walked a few steps towards me and hissed that I was an embarrassment, and I needed to leave." She swallowed hard as she finished talking. I wanted to find those two and rip them a new one. But it wouldn't help. The damage had been done.

"You have to know you are worth a hundred of those girls. I get it hurts, but you *have* to know that none of that is true. The fact is, you're generous, kind, honest and real and they are nothing. What you overheard says more about them than it does about you. You were preyed on because you were vulnerable, and you had every right to be that way. When Dad died, I was lost. But I had my mum to make sure I had a soft place to land. You were on your own. I'm in awe of you. Despite all the terrible things you had happen to you, you have prevailed. You are strong, you still have compassion, a sense of humour, a desire to do and be better. That is the mark of someone who has character and strength in the only way it counts. I'm sorry those vacuous wastes of space made you feel like shit, but it's only another chink in your armor that has made you who you are today, and that is someone who shines bright." My words exposed too much, let her see too much. I couldn't help it.

She looked at me with wonder and amazement. I held her gaze, even though it cut my heart to shreds. The way I approached problems, my need to make things right, meant I would seal my fate and miss out on someone who made *me* happy. We would be friends, no question. And it would be torture.

We eased out of the heavy conversation, but I could see she was still affected by all that had taken place tonight, and she looked utterly exhausted. I walked her home, and as was her way, she leant in close without knowing she was doing it. And as was my way—being a masochist—I put my arm around her and kept her close in the cool spring evening. We were quiet, and while she was lost in her thoughts, I was going down a rabbit hole, experiencing the feeling of being stuck in the same place, wheels spinning, that had dogged me since I returned to Australia. My relationship with Kate had given me a brief reprieve, let me put my head up for air and take in the world as it could be again. But that would be over soon. It was a bleak thought, and I was so focused that I didn't even realise we were at her door.

"Goodnight, and thanks again," she said, looking at me strangely. I gave her my best smile, but I knew it didn't reach my eyes.

"Anytime. Goodnight," I returned, squeezed her shoulder and walked down the hall. I was at my door when I heard her call out.

"Ben, wait." I turned to find her chewing her lip, indecision all over her face.

"Everything okay?" I asked as I started to walk towards her.

But then she said, "Not yet," and started running, directly at me. I stopped in time for her throw her arms around my neck and kiss me.

Chapter Twelve

My alarm startled me awake, and it took me a moment to remember I was in a hotel room after another one of the best days of my life. As I lay on my back, staring at the ceiling, I covered my face and grinned so hard my cheeks hurt. I still couldn't believe all that had happened. I'd gone from thinking Ben was only wanting friendship, and being prepared to take whatever he'd offer, to him helping me in a way that meant I could put another piece of my past to rest. Then, he'd told me that he thought I was brilliant. Yes, that's right. Me. ME. And after taking Hannah's advice, I took a risk and made sure he knew how I felt. Remembering that part didn't only make me smile, it made my stomach dip deliciously. Ben sure knew how to kiss.

As soon as he recovered from me literally launching myself at him, his tongue was in my mouth, kissing me so fiercely that I'd hung on for dear life. He closed his arms around my hips, pulling me against his big, beautiful hard body, and I was done for. My lack of sexual experience didn't weigh into to the equation and when he pushed me up against the wall and ground his hardness into me, I'd whimpered his name and begged for more. He'd given me more, until we were both breathing heavy and his eyes became unfocused.

Thinking about that look now had me wondering if I needed to take care of myself before we met for breakfast, for fear I'd orgasm from being within three feet of him.

Given my meeting this morning, I had no time. I got out of bed and did my best to get ready while smiling like I'd won the lottery.

When the knock sounded at my door, I jumped even though I was expecting it. Ben had put a halt to our serious necking in the hallway, promising me more soon, and as far as I was concerned, that soon was now. I checked myself in the mirror, noting I looked presentable in skinny jeans, a sheer polka dot shirt and blazer. I didn't know what to expect from my meeting today, but I thought I should look responsible. Satisfied, I slipped into my suede boots, walked to the door and opened it. My eyes devoured him and this time I let him see. Last night he'd looked like a sex god in a suit, but today he was sexy in a different way in fitted, dark jeans, a white henley and Converses.

"Hey," he said. I finally looked at his face to find him giving me a sexy, smug smile.

"Hey," I said, smiling back as his eyes dropped to my shirt, which was straining a little over my bust, before they returned to mine.

"Come here, beautiful," he said as he snagged me around the waist and pulled me into him for a quick hot kiss. I was still dazed when he pulled back and looked down at me. This made him chuckle, then he moved past me to get my bags. We stowed them in his car then headed out for breakfast. I'd kept the gift bag with his pillow in it with me, and he held my free hand like it was what we were born to do.

We meandered through the bustling streets of Melbourne as everyone rushed around us in the morning sunshine, and I was optimistic for the first time in my life. He took me to the European, and we sat outside, facing the state Parliament and ordered goat-cheese omelets, croissants and coffee.

"Are you worried about the meeting today?" he asked as he took my hand in his across the table.

"Not really. I don't know a lot about my grandfather, only that my mother loved him dearly and Alma said their relationship was complicated. He's been dead for a long time, and I have no idea why I'm being summoned," I said.

"It might be good," he said and I nodded, hoping he was right.

I looked at the pillow in the bag, nervous all of a sudden. So nervous in fact, I almost dropped my coffee on the table, the cup landing in the saucer with an indelicate thud. I was blushing hard, apologising to Ben as I reached down and pulled out the gift-wrapped present.

"This is for you," I said, thrusting it at him, causing him to almost spill his coffee.

"What is it?" he asked as he tried not to laugh at my antics. I was a complete disaster, but he'd had fair warning.

"A gift."

"For what?"

"For driving me." He looked ready to object. "Look, Saint McT, people are allowed to do nice things for you too, you know. I saw it yesterday and thought of you. Open it." He stared at me, completely still. I started to worry; did he hate presents?

"Thanks," he said quietly as he took the gift and unwrapped it. Seeing him smile as he looked at the pillow made me relax, and when he turned those twinkling blue eyes on me with gratitude, I decided that I was going to find other ways to get him to look at me like that. "It's perfect," he said standing and leaning over me to kiss me softly on the mouth.

After that, we chatted about highland cattle and garlic crops as we finished breakfast. He drove me to the law offices, offering to come with me.

"I'll be fine," I said. "Are you sure you don't mind waiting?"

"Go, do this so we can hit the road," he said, nodding. "I think we should take the long way home; it'll be fun." He gave me a quick kiss before pushing me in the direction of the building.

Reluctantly I walked inside and took the lift to the fifteenth floor. I gave my name to the receptionist sitting behind a large, intimidating mahogany desk. I didn't have to wait long before they called me through to a moderately sized meeting room where a middle-aged man in a suit stood holding out a hand to me.

"Good morning, Ms. Bloomington. I'm Mr. Griggs."

"Hi, Mr. Griggs," I said as I awkwardly shook his hand.

"Please take a seat. This won't take long." We both sat. "Your grandfather, Peter Jamieson, passed away many years ago, after a separation from your grandmother, Alma. When this happened, he moved to Sydney with his partner, Gary." My sharp intake of breath communicated my shock.

"Sorry, I thought you knew." Mr. Griggs looked startled.

"No, I didn't," I muttered.

"I see. Well, I don't have the details, nor is it my place, but I will give you the facts as they pertain to his will. Peter and Gary lived together for three years before Peter passed, and Peter was in the midst of changing his will when he died. Gary did not know, and assumed all of Peter's assets went to Alma because they were still married and she was caring for his children. However, Peter had at the time, ten thousand dollars of state bank shares. He had intended for them to go to your mother, but it was not finalised. Gary has recently passed, and amongst his belongings, this paperwork of Peter's was found. Given your mother's will clearly left everything to you, these shares are now yours."

"What?" I asked, not sure what this meant.

"Your grandfather's shares are now yours. The bank has since changed names, but the ownership of these shares is now yours. You have been receiving dividends, which are in an account with the same bank. At my estimation, your shares are now worth one-hundred-fifty-thousand dollars, and you have amassed four-hundred-thousand dollars of dividends."

My mind started to race. This was completely unexpected.

"Why didn't it go to Alma?" I stammered the first question that came to mind.

"His paperwork clearly stated that she was not to have a cent, and neither was your uncle Luca. His possessions were to be split between your mother and Gary, but the money was solely for Jennifer."

I didn't know what to say. I was excited to gain the wealth, but I couldn't help but feel for Alma. My grandfather had been gay, left her for a man to raise two children, and not shared his money with her. Did she even know? Alma had lost a child, and while it may not have been his, Luca was still Alma's son. Then she lost my mother. The whole thing, including the money, made me sad. I would have to pick the right moment to ask her about it, given all she had lost.

The lawyer verified who I was and gave me the information I needed to access the shares and dividends. I left heart-sore for Alma, and unsure what to do with that much money. Now, all I *wanted* to do was get in Ben's truck, drive home, talk about anything other than this and hopefully do more than kiss. And when the time was right, I would talk to Alma.

***

"Hi, Mum," I said, unable to hide my smile as I sat in a coffee shop checking my emails, waiting for Kate.

"Well, don't you sound chipper," she teased.

"What's that supposed to mean?" I asked.

"Well, I ran into Erik, who told me that you texted Annie asking for backup for Kate Bloomington last night. Clearly something is going on and I'm glad you're sounding happy—not like you were before," she said.

"Before?"

"Yeah, the flat, irritable and unhappy that you tried to hide," she said. I wanted to argue, but I couldn't because she was right.

"Mum—" I started but she interrupted me.

"Ben, I know you, and I know when you are putting on a show for everyone. I hope that whatever you have with Kate is what you want, not what you think she needs. You are too focused on everyone else; I want to see her do right by you."

"Geez, Mum, that's a bit deep, don't you think?" I chuckled quietly, knowing she knew I was listening.

"You're not the only person who watches *Ellen*," she said and I laughed. "Bring her over for dinner on Sunday," she continued. I hesitated.

"I'll ask her but I don't want to push it. She's had a rough time, and forcing family on her may be too much."

"It's not forcing family, Ben, it's letting her see *your* family who are important to you."

"I get that, but Evie and Mel can be… intense."

"You need to give Kate more credit. She's a big girl," she said, but I didn't want to scare her off.

"I'll mention it."

"Do that. I'll let you. I love you, Ben."

"Love you too, Mum," I said then hung up. I looked up to see Kate standing in front of me, but she was watching a couple of older women, smiling at me like I was a puppy. I rolled my eyes. Lots of men told their mothers they loved them.

"How did it go?" I stood and kissed her lightly on the mouth. She looked at me with bemused wonder. "What's that look for?" I asked, and she shook her head as we headed to my truck.

"It's going to be worse at home, isn't it?"

"What is?"

"Having everyone look at you like that. I get it, I do."

"What do you get?"

"Why women smile at you, want to be close to you. I understand completely." At her words, my insides shrunk. She was going to tell me I was such a nice guy and that everyone knew it. I hated it. I knew I was nice, but it was the right thing to do. However, I didn't want that from Kate, I didn't want her to pigeonhole me, to limit me. But she didn't. Instead, she surprised me. "I'm going to have to beat them off with a stick you're so damned hot. I mean the suit last night was, whoa, but even in this casual look? Good thing they haven't kissed you, or else it would turn into an all-out brawl."

I stopped dead and she stopped too, looking up at me with a grin and flushed cheeks. I was sure she had no idea how much it meant to me.

"You think I'm hot, do you?" I asked pulling her close, her arms instinctively going around my neck.

"Yeah," she breathed right before I kissed her hard and deep on the street, her body plastered to mine. I loved holding her, her soft breasts against my chest, her hands in my hair. The only problem was that her soft mewls made my dick so hard it was painful. Making matters worse, she was completely unguarded as she kissed me back, rubbing against me. I needed to be inside her, but I had to take my time. I wanted to be more solid before we took that step. I wanted this to be long term, and after Sheridan bailing when it got too hard, I was afraid. I got the impression Kate didn't have a lot of experience, and it didn't bother me in the slightest. I wanted to make sure she was comfortable.

We drove out of town, heading to Mansfield the very long way around, via Healesville and the Black Spur. The winding roads and lush green forests flew past as we talked about everything and nothing. The conversation was comfortable, apart from when I'd asked her about her visit to the lawyer. She'd clammed up, saying that it related to some her grandfather's belongings. The way she said it meant she wanted me to drop it. I hid my discomfort, reminding myself that she had been alone for so long, and it must be hard to trust again. She had shared some of what had haunted her, and I hoped one day she would trust me with everything. Until then, I wouldn't be able to fully believe.

Despite the easy conversation, it was becoming harder, literally, not to touch her, or pull over and kiss her. We were close, her hand in mine on my lap, and when she looked at me with unguarded lusty eyes, my decision to wait wavered.

After a lunch in Mansfield we stopped at Powers Lookout. I needed to get out of the confines of my truck because the smell of her was making me insane. It was a mild, sunny afternoon and as we stood at the railing, the sun at our backs and the breeze in our hair, things were finally falling into place. Looking at Kate, I smiled, seeing her hair being tasseled by the wind, her eyes on me, hot with sexual appreciation. I didn't know how far I should take her, but the way she was looking at me let me know she wanted me to take her somewhere.

I moved into her, gripped her hips and put my lips on hers. When Kate kissed, she fully committed and let go. Her hands drove into my hair, her grip tightening when I rubbed her against my erection. As we kissed and moved against each other, she started to make little noises that made my balls draw up. When I pulled back to look at her, her eyes fluttered open and a "please" escaped her pretty, pouty lips. And because I was such a *great* guy, I obliged.

"Beautiful, turn around, hold the railing," I directed and while she looked a little apprehensive, she did it. I stood in close behind her, pulling her lush, soft bottom into me, letting her feel what she did to my body.

"Lean back," I whispered in her ear, chuckling as she almost slammed into me. Then I let my hands roam her body. She was breathing heavily, shifting under my touch, wanting more. I kissed and bit at her earlobe as my hands slipped under her shirt, palming her soft breasts over her bra. Instinctively, she pushed into me, wanting more.

"You like that, Kate?" I whispered at her ear and she nodded. "Me too," I smiled and she shifted against my cock, making it my turn to moan. "The things you do to me, Kate, fuck." Needing more, I slipped a hand inside her bra, rolling her nipple between my thumb and forefinger, loving how her hips bucked against me.

"You wait until I get my mouth on you. You're beautiful and fucking sexy. It drives me crazy," I continued to murmur in her ear as I kept at her nipple, but moved my other hand down, over her stomach into her jeans. Over her lacy underwear that just thinking about made me want to blow, I rubbed at her folds. She started to rock forward, wanting more of my touch.

"Ben, please," she moaned low as she threw her head back against my shoulder, exposing more of her beautiful, smooth skin.

"What? What do you want?"

"More."

"More what?"

"More of you." It was a damned good answer, so I obliged and slipped my hands into her underwear to toy with her clitoris. As soon as I touched her, she sucked in a breath and pushed into my hand.

"Perfect, Kate. And so wet. Is that for me?"

"Yes."

"Say it."

"It's all for you."

"All of it?" I demanded as I moved my fingers faster.

"All of it. Everything," she breathed, putting her face to the sky as I buried my head in her neck, smelling her sweet smell all around me, tasting her skin and feeling her body quiver and shake as she approached an orgasm.

"Are you going to come for me, beautiful?" I asked as she continued to moan and ride my hand.

"I think so?"

"Your body says you are," I said as I slipped a finger inside, feeling it clench around me. "Your body is hungry for me. Do you like it when I touch you like this?" I asked, moving my finger in and out.

"Yes, I love it," she breathed moving one hand off the rail and into my hair, holding me close.

"I'm going to come," she said, on the verge of losing it.

"Do it. Come for me. Now, Kate. I have you," I said and she came apart, crying out with pleasure as her body shook with each pulse, until she became lax against me, breathing hard.

"Beautiful. So fucking beautiful," I murmured in her ear and she turned into me, burying her face in my neck as she pulled herself back together.

"I can't believe we did that," she said into my neck, sounding amused and a little shy.

"What? Sing from the mountain top?" I asked and she laughed, but wouldn't give me her face. "Kate, look at me," I said, creating enough space between us so she could see me. Her cheeks were flushed and a smile tugged at her lips. "What we did was fucking hot," I murmured. "I love how greedy your body is for me."

"I've never done anything like that before. I've been touched, like that, but not ending like that. And never with anyone who talked like you do," she said as her blush deepened.

"What? Never had anyone talk dirty in your ear?"

"Ah, no. And not, you know, finish the job either," she said and I felt a little taller.

"Sadly, I'm glad, but not for your sake. It satisfies my masculine need to provide for you," I said. She giggled then leant her head on my chest.

"What about you?" she whispered.

"What about me?"

"I need to look after you too. I don't know about... out here and—" She sounded nervous, and I squeezed her tight.

"Beautiful, I almost came from touching you, and I enjoyed every second. We'll get there, but I'm not in any rush. Besides, it's always ladies first."

After I helped Kate to the car while reciting the periodic table in an effort to shift my thoughts from laying her out on my back seat, we headed down the mountain and towards Bright as evening set in. We decided to grab a bite in town before I drove her home. She'd looked at me like she wanted to ask me to stay, but said nothing so I let it be. I would do whatever she wanted.

We sat at the bar at the Gin Distillery as she looked around, impressed by the large open space that was full of people. We sat side by side, ordered our respective gins, and Kate talked to me about how she felt after everything that happened with Cleo and Layla.

"I'm good. I've put it behind me now. It's amazing how much lighter I feel. Thanks again for helping."

"I didn't really help, I only backed you up. And of course, there was Hannah," I said and we both laughed. "What did she whisper to you?" I asked, remembering the shock in her eyes.

"She told me make sure you knew how I felt," she said, blushing.

"I have Hannah to thank for you crash-tackling me," I teased, and we both laughed before I kissed her lightly on the lips, because I could.

"I would've got there on my own. But Hannah is fierce," Kate said.

"Annie too, Erik's girl. And they both care about you," I told her.

"I don't know why—and I'm not saying that for sympathy. They're just so together. I'm a bit ordinary," she said like she had given it some thought.

"There is nothing ordinary about you."

Chapter Thirteen

Despite being exhausted, I didn't want the day to end. I craved Ben's company because he made me feel at peace with the world, and with myself. But I was tired. We'd had a big day of driving, eating, and for me, an earth-shattering orgasm. He seemed at ease, like he knew what was going to happen next, while I was completely at a loss. Should I ask him to stay? Did that make me easy? I wanted him in my bed but I didn't know how far to take it.

These questions had kept my mind occupied as we drove home. I'd been so lost in my musings that I didn't notice we'd stopped until Ben opened my door and held out a hand.

"Kate, are you okay?" he asked as he followed me, carrying my bag inside.

"Good. Great. Really great, even," I said, sounding ridiculous. Keep the sauce bottles locked up. Without delay, he lit the fire, then brought in firewood for the night. He often did things like this, thinking of what I might need. I loved it, and I was getting used to it. I shouldn't, because I didn't know where this was going. I did know, however, that I wanted as much as I could get.

"What's on your mind?" he asked after I'd been standing at the kettle long after it had boiled.

"Ah…" I muttered, caught off guard and not able to come up with a ready answer. Sensing my indecision, he turned me around then lifted me onto the kitchen bench, coming to stand between my legs. In this position, I was at his height, and I appreciated how handsome he was at this angle. His hair was even more mussed than usual, and I remembered I'd had my hands in it, holding him close as he'd made me come. His eyes looked into mine, and they were open and appreciative with a hint of a smile. He wasn't laughing at me, but I sensed he knew the direction of my thoughts.

"Tell me what you want, Kate," he said quietly as his gaze dropped to my lips.

"You. I want you. And I want you to stay, but I don't know what to do about it." The words fell out of my mouth as I looked at his lips that were now giving me a sexy smile.

"Why don't you know what to do? Ask me."

"You might think I'm easy."

"Never."

"You might think I'm going to put out, and I want to but I... maybe... don't know what I'm doing. And I think you do," I said. I didn't see the point in lying. He could be trusted with the truth.

"Well, what happens if I say yes? Do you think I'm easy and will put out?" he murmured as he rubbed my thighs.

"Of course not," I answered.

"And how do you know I know what I'm doing?"

"Because I'm on fire when you look at me, and when you touch me, I'm only seconds away from coming apart."

As I said this, he sucked in a breath, like what I said hit a target he didn't know he had.

"Will you stay with me?" I whispered right before I kissed him. It started slow and sweet, until his tongue slipped into my mouth, and tangled with mine. Then he increased the intensity. Before long I was clinging to him, needing more, desperate for contact.

"Kate, when you kiss me, especially like that, I have to fight hard not to come apart too. But tonight, why don't we sleep together, and I mean *sleep*, after a little exploring. I want to feel more of your beautiful body." He planted little kisses from my ear to my collarbone.

"I want to touch you too," I breathed as my head fell back, and my hands roamed his broad, muscular shoulders. He was hard under my fingers, and warm to the touch.

"Sounds like a plan," he said, then he secured my legs around his waist and lifted me, his hands going under my bottom.

"Ben," I said, a little startled.

"I won't let you fall," he said, and I knew he wouldn't. Ever.

He took me to the bedroom and stopped by the bed, letting my legs drop to the floor.

"Ben, I really don't know what I'm doing. You'll need to tell me what you like," I said, my hands resting on his flat stomach.

"I'm not that fussy; experiment away. I can't wait," he said then bit his full lower lip as he looked me up and down as though I were edible. But instead of taking a bite, all he did was rest his hands on my hips, waiting for me to move. With shaking hands, I undid the buttons on his shirt, then pushed it off his shoulders and onto the floor. My fantasies had been partially accurate. He was built and had a man's body, honed and defined through physical labour, not in manufactured in a gym. His skin was wasn't tanned, nor was it pale, and he had a smattering of freckles on his shoulders and forearms. I was drawn to his round, flat nipples and chest hair that lightly covered his pecs and trailed off as it went down his rock-hard abdominal muscles before disappearing into his jeans.

"Baby, you're making it hard for me, especially when you lick your lips," he said and my eyes shot to his to see them on fire.

"Maybe I want to make it hard," I said.

"It has been for days," he returned, giving me a sexy half grin. I rolled my eyes, loving that he made this fun.

"Only days?" I asked as I stroked his erection over his jeans and he hissed.

"Fine. Weeks. It's been weeks," he muttered, the smirk gone. Feeling him hot and hard under my hands made my sex quiver. Having this power, and him laying himself out for me to touch was heady. Wanting to explore, I put my hands on his bare chest and slowly moved them down, rubbing at his nipples before trailing lightly over his stomach to let them rest at his belt buckle. I was amazed as his muscles bunched and moved at my touch. Then I kissed him in the hollow of his throat, moving lower to his nipples. I took one in my mouth and grazed it with my teeth, not knowing what he liked, but when he growled, I smiled against his skin.

"Vixen, you keep that up, it'll be a quick show," he said.

"Need a break?" I asked, stepping back to undo the buttons of my shirt.

"You call that a break?" he said as his eyes were riveted to my now exposed bra.

"Hmm," he hummed as he slid his hands up my sides to my breasts, where he cupped and weighed them in his palms. "You have the best tits I have ever seen. I'm normally an arse man, and yours is outstanding, but these? Fuck... they make me crazy," he said as he pushed me back onto the bed and dragged me to the middle. Then he crawled up beside me, pulled the cup of my thankfully lacy bra down and took my nipple into his mouth. I sucked in a breath at the sensation, rubbing my legs together for relief. Being the man he was, he gave it to me, unbuttoning my jeans and slipping a finger between my now damp folds.

"Ben," I breathed, but he didn't stop, he kept at me. I was undulating under his ministrations, but before I became mindless, I needed to touch him. He was on his side, and I was on my back, which gave me enough room to unzip his jeans and slide a hand in. I groaned as I took his hard length and wrapped my fingers around it. He was long and incredibly thick. I'd never touched anything like this before, and it was glorious. I started to stroke slowly, up and down, and he let out another growl when I rubbed my thumb at his head. I moved faster, wanting him to feel as good as I did, and he let me know he liked it when he started to thrust into my hands.

His mouth left my breast, kissing his way back to meet mine. I was getting close to the edge, his fingers so attentive to my clit that when he slipped two fingers inside and pressed in, I came.

"Fucking beautiful," he murmured in my ear as I continued to stroke him, harder and faster now, not caring about my own release, only needing his.

"Kate," he groaned as he followed, coming against his chest, his body clenching and releasing.

We lay like this, hands still on each other, gently toying. We kissed softly and sweetly as our breathing returned to normal, and the world came back into focus.

"You okay?" he asked, leaning up on a shoulder to look down at me.

"More than okay. Thank you," I said.

"Don't thank me—I was there with you."

"Thank you for making me feel comfortable," I clarified, wanting him to know how important it was after what Frank had tried to do. I could never tell him what had happened; it was in my past and if he knew, he might not see *me*, when we were like this. But it was an incredible relief to know I could enjoy intimacy with Ben.

"Baby," he whispered, and kissed me again. This time, when he pulled back, he got off the bed.

"Be right back. Get under the covers."

I shucked my jeans and bra, put on a tee and got into bed, the sheets feeling soft against my skin. Ben came back and turned out the lights. I tried hard to see him in the dark but I really had to squint to make out his shape.

"What are you doing?" he asked as he pulled me into his body.

"I was trying to get a look at you in your undies," I said and he burst out laughing.

"Well, let's save something for tomorrow. I'll show you mine if you show me yours."

"Deal."

I nestled into him as I lay on my side, him curving behind me, and was surprised I could fall asleep like this. I'd never shared a bed with a man, let alone in my underwear. But as always with Ben, it was easy.

When I woke in the morning, I was disappointed to find the bed empty. I'd dreamt about him in his undies—and out of them—but he wasn't here to make that a reality. For someone without much sexual experience, I had it on the brain. All the time. He'd left a note on the pillow which read he had to go home and check his animals, and to call him when I was ready. It was only eight, and I didn't want to call now because it would make me look desperate. I reined in my need, showered, and headed to see Alma.

"Kate, you're an angel," Alma said as I gave her a coffee and a bacon and egg roll, complete with bright yellow yolk oozing out the sides.

"You're welcome," I said as I bit into mine.

"How did it go with Ben?" she asked and I was surprised.

"You don't want to know what the lawyers said?"

"Sure, but it isn't that important. My husband was a bitter, sad man. I have stopped letting his actions influence me. I want to know about what you learned, but I also want to know how it went with you and Ben. You're smiling, and you seem happier; I'm thinking it went well," she said, giving me a cheeky look. I couldn't help it. I giggled.

"Ben is…" I thought about how to describe him, but words weren't enough. "He's the best. In every sense of the word."

At this, she grinned, and I joined her. It was a nice moment, and we'd been having more of these lately, where we both connected, and time stopped a little as we enjoyed the feeling. She loved Ben, as everyone did, and I could see why. What I really liked was that she loved him for me. That she thought about me having someone as good as Ben. I considered telling her about Frank, but I didn't want to upset her. I knew it would rock her, given her feelings towards his family, and I didn't want to taint what she and I had. I wondered about bringing up the fact that my grandfather was gay, but again, I wanted to keep the good going. It was going to be bad enough telling her he'd kept money from her when she'd probably needed it.

"What did Peter leave you?" she asked, sounding only mildly interested. Sighing, I steeled myself and told her about the bank shares and dividends, but she wasn't upset at all.

"Finally, the old grouch did something right. That money will set you up, Kate, and I am glad for it. Take your time and think about what you want to do with it. I don't have much to leave you when I go. It's all yours, except my old bath. I'm giving that to Barbara," she said. I looked at her, unsure I'd heard her correctly.

"Your bath?"

"Yeah that's right. I had one plumbed on the back deck. You probably thought it was a barbeque but no, it's an old claw-footed tub," she said and I laughed.

"What does that have to do with Barbara?"

"She came to check on me once right before my surgery, but I was having a glass of wine, in the bath, admiring the view and minding my own business. She clearly couldn't do the same and she came around back to find me. She gave me a fright and I jumped up, spilled half the water out and almost fell onto the floor. She gasped, went to run away, knocked my rake over and stood on it so the handle hit her face. It was priceless," she said and I laughed so hard it hurt.

"You weren't embarrassed?" I asked.

"I've had two children—if you want to look, that's on you."

As I left Alma's, I texted Ben saying I was bringing lunch. He sent back a crude message asking if I was on the menu. It made me laugh and my tummy dip. This excited, restless feeling that was both nerve-wracking and arousing was consuming, and I didn't want it to stop.

Having picked up fresh cheese, bread and bresaola, I drove to his farm, eager to see it. It was a sunny spring day, cool but not cold and the valley was alive with blossom and wattle after a wet winter. Ben's farm was on the Great Alpine Road, in a place called Smoko. Seeing the number painted on the fence, I pulled in to what looked like a cluster of sheds with some small pens and garden beds in a big U formation. I pulled in next to Ben's truck and got out. I could see why he chose it; this place was spectacular, the fields vibrant green, stretching out towards the river, which was lined by tall, pale gum trees. There were views of both Mount Buffalo off in the distance, and Mount Feathertop, which still had a little snow on its peak. I grabbed my bags and left them on the hood of my car as I started to look for Ben. I couldn't find him, but I did find an enormous chicken run with dozens of fancy chickens roaming around.

"Hello, girls," I said at the fence, and some came towards me, making noises like they were asking who I was and what had I done with Ben. I kept wandering, seeing the pig run, which was muddy and stinky. The pigs were sunbaking by the food trough; I totally understood that. Next I ventured to the raised garden beds, full of fresh dirt. Ben had mentioned his new vegetable enterprise and I smiled at his handiwork.

"Hey, beautiful," he said and I jumped, not having heard him approach. When I turned to look at him, I jumped again because he wasn't alone. No. He had an *enormous* horse with him.

"Ah… who's your friend with the long face?" I asked, alarmed.

"This is Cora, Queen of the Corral."

"I'm sorry?"

"That's her name, and she is taking us to lunch."

***

The look on Kate's face when I brought Cora over was priceless. She was astonished and terrified.

"You know how to ride… her?" she asked, taking in the huge Clydesdale. To her credit, Cora was large.

"Of course. We all had horses growing up. My mum and sister still do. Cora belongs to my neighbor. I do horse agistment on my back paddock, but I give Cora a workout when she needs it."

Hesitantly she stepped towards me, reaching out a hand to rub Cora's nose. Cora was as placid and friendly as they came, and nudged her when she stopped.

"You're okay, aren't you?" she cooed, and on cue, Cora snickered.

"You good?" I asked as I took her hand and led her over to the fencing.

"I am," she said and leant up and kissed me. She had planned on giving me a quick peck, but I needed more of her, and I pulled her close and showed her how I was feeling. When I broke the kiss to secure Cora, she looked dazed and happy. Perfect.

I stowed the food in the saddle bags, added some wine and gave her the basics. Luckily she was in jeans and boots, so I grabbed her a woolen jumper of mine in case the breeze came up, then I mounted, and pulled her up behind me. Her arms went around my waist, gripping like her life depended on it as he had on my motorbike. I smiled as Cora shifted, eager to go.

"It's too nice a day not to enjoy it, relax, hold on and enjoy the ride."

"I'm sure I could enjoy a ride with you without the horse," she muttered sardonically and I laughed. We headed towards the river, and along a trail for a while, and eventually, she relaxed enough to look around.

"Where are we going?"

"I thought we would go up into Martin's paddock. It's a pretty view of the valley and the apple blossoms are out."

"You're romantic, you know that?" she asked and I grinned.

"Maybe I chose that spot because it's secluded and no one will hear you scream," I said.

"Promises, promises," she whispered in my ear and my hands clenched on the reins. I wanted her, desperately. Leaving her in bed this morning had been a struggle. She'd lain close to me all night, at one point holding my hand in her sleep and I'd wanted to kiss her awake. She pouted her lips, her face expressive even as she slept. I'd lightly kissed her soft cheek before I'd left her, admiring her thick dark hair that was a riot against the white pillowcase. Now, she was behind me, her breasts pushing into my back, talking about me making her scream with her hands close to my dick, and my need to have her was becoming a distraction. She was going to pay for those comments.

She clung tight as we crossed the river and followed a trail up the side of the mountain that wound its way through the forest, before coming out into a clearing that sat above paddocks of apple trees. Aside from my neighbour Martin, who was in town at that moment, no one knew of this place. The afternoon sun was warm, and you could see mountains rising tall in the distance. When the wind blew, the blossom petals floated around like gently falling snow.

"Wow," she said after I helped her dismount, then followed. She took off my jumper and handed it to me to stow on the horse, as I tied Cora to a tree branch.

"It's beautiful, right?" I asked, pulling out a blanket and the food.

"It's more than that."

We laid out the blanked and Kate opened up the food packages. I poured her some wine, which she accepted and we lay on our sides, looking at each other.

"Thanks for bringing me here," she said giving me a small, private smile.

"It's nice to share it with someone," I told her and her cheeks went pink. "How was Alma?"

"Alma was, well, Alma. It's been getting easier to talk to her, but part of me is torn between betraying my mother and learning more about what made her give up all this," she said, looking around like *this* was worth something. I smiled. I'm sure she didn't find it easy in the beginning, but I was more than pleased she liked it here. "It's nice to have family again too. I haven't called her Nanna yet, and I feel bad about that. I don't know how to get there. She wants me to, but it feels too personal, intimate, and I haven't earned the right."

"You don't need to earn anything. When it comes to family, love is unconditional."

"I think you have an unusual family. Most people don't have the relationship you have with your mum and sisters. The way you talk about them tells me you respect them and would do anything for them. Very few people are like that."

I thought about what she was saying, and I supposed we weren't like everyone else. I never contemplated us being any different.

"Maybe you're right. I only know that if I love someone, they get all of me and I want to do what I can to make them happy. People call me a "nice guy" and I hate it. It's an apathetic word to begin with, and it makes me seem like a pleaser, or that I'm trying to be nice. I don't know how to explain it, but it doesn't cross my mind. If I care about you, I've got your back."

"You're selfless in a world where most people aren't," she said, looking at me with intense emotions.

"You are too. Did you move up because of Alma?" I asked her.

"Yes, but that was through a sense of duty and wanting to do the right thing. Sometimes it's responsibility that drives us," she said again, demonstrating how mature she was. "Sadly, a lot of the time people don't do the right thing in return for good deeds either. I found that with Cleo and Layla, who only took from me. I bet you know plenty of people who take from you but don't give back," she said.

"That's true, but I don't do it to get something in return," I added.

"Of course not, but that doesn't mean they shouldn't still do it." She was right again. I didn't mind normally; I wanted to help with no thought of gain. But, I also wanted someone who cared if I was happy. I wanted that someone to be Kate. When she'd given me a present, and told me she thought I was sexy, it was the first time I'd felt cherished. Sheridan had never done anything personal or thoughtful. This realisation was unsettling; I didn't like to think I needed anything, let alone praise or gifts.

"What has you frowning?" Kate asked as she touched my hand lightly.

"Nothing worth dwelling on," I said, looking into her big, grey eyes, remarking again how thick and long her lashes were. She dropped her gaze to my mouth, her eyes going hooded. Turning on a dime, my mood lifted. I took her mouth, driving a hand into her hair, feeling the thick, silky strands move through my fingers. She was eager for my touch, and with a slight nudge, I rolled her to her back and moved partially over her. We kissed as the sun warmed our skin, and the breeze dropped petals over us. Soon, our hands began roaming as we let go of the world and focused on each other.

I lifted up her shirt, and pulled the cups of her bra down, unable to stifle my groan at her full, soft breasts on display, her brown nipples hardening in the cool air. I took one in my mouth, and palmed the other as I moved between her legs. She shifted beneath me, her hips rolling, wanting attention. Good thing I would give her whatever she wanted, I moved down lower, unzipping her jeans and sliding them down her legs. I looked up her body, her grey eyes hooded and on me, her breasts moving with her deep breaths, her smooth skin covered with little white petals. It was magnificent. I pulled her panties down and she gasped as cool air hit her soft flesh.

"Are you sure no one will see?" she asked, but it didn't sound like she actually cared.

"I'm sure. Kate, I won't share you with anyone," I vowed as I lowered my mouth to her. I started slow, unsure if she'd done this before. She was tense at first, but when I looked at her and got a shy smile, I returned to licking and sucking at her most sensitive parts. Before long, she relaxed, and her knees dropped to the side, giving me full access. I took her trust as a gift and made sure she knew I appreciated it. Kate didn't take long to get there, and when I sucked her clit into my mouth, she detonated, crying out my name. I watched her come down, and she reached for me, pulling me close so my arms were around her, protecting her while she was vulnerable.

"Ben, you are a man who keeps his promises. That counts way more than being *nice.*"

Chapter Fourteen

After our horse ride and my orgasm, I'd done my best to get my hands on him, although he was adamant that I was under no pressure to return the favour. But he was missing the point: I *wanted* to give him pleasure. We'd spent the rest of the afternoon on his farm, and after a quick tour of the work shed, and the shed he lived in, we were out feeding animals and planting vegetables.

I was not a natural, and Ben had to show me how do everything, including use a shovel. At least he found me amusing, not ridiculous. Erik had called and asked us to dinner with him and Annie. I'd agreed to go because it meant more time with Ben, and these people were important to him. Besides, Annie was funny in a scary sort of way, and this time, she had another friend with her, Fleur. Fleur knew Ben and Erik; they had grown up together. Fleur was beautiful, but I wasn't jealous. It was obvious she only saw Ben as a friend, and she was so kind to me that I didn't have a bad word to say about her. I thought she was sad in a way I could relate to. She reminded me that there had been a time when I'd thought the world was not my oyster—more like a leaden anchor holding me to the seafloor as the relentless, rough sea, pounded me.

But I didn't feel like that anymore, and partly it was because of Ben, and partly because I'd allowed people in. People like Mia and Viv, Hannah, Leslie and Carol, Alma and now Erik, Annie and Fleur. As we cuddled in bed that night, Ben asked me to have dinner with his family. I'd said yes because it was the right thing to do, but by Sunday afternoon, I was regretting my decision. I was getting used to the idea of not being alone, but meeting Mrs. McTavish and her beautiful daughters was next level, and I didn't feel ready. Ben adored these women, and I knew that compared to them, I'd come up short.

Needing to get the lay of the land, I visited Alma before we were due to visit. She was more than pleased with the news I was going to the McTavishes for dinner. She told me a little about Ben's family, but there was nothing she said that extinguished my fears. Ben's mother was a strong, hardworking woman who raised her children on her own, working two jobs when she had to. Her daughter Melanie McTavish was once a drama queen, but after moving to the city for university and returning to Bright, she had mellowed and matured. Evelyn McTavish, or Evie, was a wild child. She did what she wanted, when she wanted. Both girls were known for being at the pulse of town gossip, and probably knew all about me already.

My mind turned to Frank. No one had ever mentioned seeing us, but I was sure someone would've noticed me walking out of the pub with him. Ben knew him, but I had no reason to bring him up, and I certainly didn't want to share what he'd done. The rational part of my brain knew it wasn't my fault, but that didn't stop me feeling tainted, and even more unworthy of someone like Ben.

I'd left Alma's more nervous than ever, and went to the bottle shop to buy wine to take for dinner. As if knowing I'd been thinking about him, Frank was parked a few spaces down from me. When our eyes locked, I could see he hadn't forgotten what had happened. He looked at me with malice and a hint of enjoyment at my obvious distress. He held my gaze for a long time, and while I desperately wanted to look away, I couldn't. He had some sort of power over me, leaving me immobilised.

Eventually a car drove past and someone called out to Frank, and he looked away. Panicked, I got in the car, my hands shaking as I tried to control my breathing. I needed to get away, but starting the car seemed difficult, and the key wouldn't fit. My phone buzzed with a text message, and it was enough of a distraction to get me to look at it and stop scratching the ignition.

The text was from Ben, giving me the address of his mum's place, and signing off with "xx." Ben. I needed to see Ben. I needed that. He would make me feel safe. With that in mind, I started my car, pulled out and drove to the address Ben had given me, not thinking about his mum or sisters. No. I just needed Ben.

I headed up the long drive in the small foothills of Harrietville, which was lined with deciduous trees covered in blossom, glowing white in the dusk. I tried to pay attention, but I was too anxious. I did notice some horses, lots of paddocks and then a garden as I neared the house. I pulled up, undid my seatbelt, ready to throw myself at

Ben, when I looked at his family home more closely. It was a two-story country cottage with a wraparound veranda painted in heritage colours of cream, maroon and white. The windows were lit with warm light, smoke rose from the chimney, and potted flowers covered the big steps leading to the leadlight front door. Nestled amongst old trees and the mountains, it was idyllic—something I expected from a Hallmark movie. It was perfect.

Tears prickled my eyes as I sat in my old car, staring at this warm, inviting home. I couldn't go in. I didn't belong. Being with Ben on my own was one thing, but seeing a real family full of love? I was too damaged, had done too many terrible things, like got drunk for a year and wasted all my money, like let Frank Mancini touch me. I didn't belong. I wanted to, with a desire that burned my throat. But I didn't.

"Kate, you okay?" Ben said, sounding a long way away. Then his face appeared in my window and I jumped. He opened my door and knelt in front of me, concerned.

"I'm fine," I sniffed as I wiped at the tears.

"Beautiful, what happened?" he asked taking my hand in his. It was warm and strong.

"Nothing."

"Baby, you're sitting in your car, looking at my house, crying," he said, wiping a tear from my cheek tenderly. I let out another sob, then leant into him. He wrapped his arms around me, tucked my face into his neck and held me close. He smelled good like he always did but now mixed with delicious-smelling food. He was warm, and his shirt was soft against me.

"Tell me. Let me help," he said. But he couldn't help, not with all of it.

"It's perfect."

"What is?"

"You. This house, this place. I don't belong here; it's too good, too right." I wanted to say I wouldn't recover if I lost it, lost him. But I didn't.

"Shhh. Kate. You belong next to me." His words meant a lot to me, because even while I was being difficult and weird, he still wanted me next to him. I loved this man. No question. That was why there was no way I was telling him about Frank. He'd been accepting so far, but everyone had their limits. I drew in a deep breath and he released me from his embrace, then helped me out of the car.

"It's going to be okay," I said as I tried to wipe the mascara from my face.

"I got it," he said, pulling out a hanky and wiping my tears.

"You're not going to lick it first are you, like my dad did?"

"No, but you can call me 'big daddy' if you like. I can assure you, you won't be crying after," he said, using a phone-sex-operator voice. I laughed then hugged him.

"Thanks," I said.

"For what?"

"For being awesome," I said. He didn't say anything, only gave me a small smile then walked me to the front door.

Ben's mother looked exactly like his sisters, but with thick black hair and brilliant denim-blue eyes like Ben. They were all tall and slender, like *willowy* was their natural body shape. I fidgeted, trying to hide my natural *billowy* body shape as introductions were made. I was uncomfortable and I needed to put a lid on it.

"Kate, let's get a drink. I have some things I want to show you," Christine McTavish said as she put an arm around me and lead me to the lounge room. I wanted Ben to come with me, but he gave me an encouraging smile, so I took in a deep breath and went with his mum.

The lounge was comfortable, with big tan leather couches surrounding a low, square coffee table. The fire was burning bright, making the room glow. The walls were a soft white, with photos and prints on every surface. She had a few big antique pieces, and a colourful silk rug, alongside signs of everyday life like a wood bucket, and a plastic tub full of wool and knitting needles. It felt lived in and safe, and I started to relax as we sat on the couch and she poured me some wine.

"Here, this is for you, thanks for having me," I said, handing her the bottle I'd bought.

"You didn't need to, but thanks," she said as she inspected the label then put it down beside some old photo albums.

"I have some pictures here of your mother, grandmother and even your Uncle Luca. Would you like to see them?" she asked before taking a sip, eyeing me cautiously.

"I'd love to," I said honestly. I was nervous and out of place because a stranger was telling me about my own family. But my need to learn about my mother before I knew her won out.

"Your mother and I were only a few years apart in age, and we both played netball. These photos are from the year we won the grand final," she said as she opened the album and showed me fading colour photos. I instantly recognised my mother; she had the same body shape and hair as I did now. She even had a similar haircut back then. She'd kept it short and perfect since then, but here it looked wild and free. There were pictures of Mum in her uniform on the court, and with Alma and Uncle Luca after a game. Christine was there too, and she grinned as she told a few stories of how they used to train after school, and that when Alma took them to the games, she would always pack the best egg and lettuce sandwiches. I found myself smiling, relieved to know my mother wasn't always distant and cold.

"Thanks for sharing this with me. My memories are different. She wasn't like that with me. She loved me and was a good mother, but she was always removed," I said.

"I don't know what made her leave, but Alma was heartbroken," Christine said.

"Alma hasn't told me yet, but she said she would. I want to understand what happened."

"Your Nan was devastated when Luca died. He was such a beautiful boy, funny and sweet like his sister. Then Jennifer left and we all worried for her and Alma."

"Mum loved Luca. She kept photos of him at home," I told her and she nodded.

"It must've been hard for you, being on your own for so long," she said as she patted my hand. I looked at her, knowing that she too had lost.

"It was. I didn't know what I was doing really, and I made a lot of mistakes, did things I regret. I'd like to think I've learned from them," I said my voice wavering.

"That's normal. We all make mistakes, especially when we're young. You've met Evie; she's a walking disaster. Even Ben made mistakes."

"I can't imagine that." I grinned and she smiled wickedly.

"He has everyone fooled except me. He has had more than a few clangers. When he was seventeen, he was supposed to be minding his sisters, but instead took my car for a drive and crashed it. He was okay, but he had caused significant damage reversing into a tree at the dredge hole. I was furious with him, and he did his best to charm me out of my poor humour, but it didn't work. He spent the next year weeding my garden as punishment."

I smiled, imagining Ben at seventeen. "I bet it was hard being angry at him."

"It was, but I blame Sheridan too. She could make Ben do anything," she said as she drank more wine.

"Who is Sheridan?" I asked and she looked at me, eyes wide, before swallowing hard. "An old girlfriend? It's fine, Christine. You can't be as gorgeous as Ben and not have women chasing you." She smiled at this, but gave me a strange look. I didn't know who Sheridan was, but something about her reaction let me know that I needed to find out.

***

"Ben, I need to talk to you for a minute." Kate had left dinner, and I was about to follow her home when Mum called out.

"About what?" I asked standing with my keys in my hands. I needed to get going so I could check on my girl.

"About how your new girlfriend is too nice for you!" Evie said and I rolled my eyes.

"Or about why you made her cry before she even entered the house," Mel added but I glared at her.

"Ah, no, it's about the chat I had with her. She doesn't know about Sheridan?" Mum asked and I went still.

"Geez, Ben, everyone knows about Sheridan," Evie added unhelpfully.

"What did you tell her?" I asked, trying not to lose my temper. I didn't do it very often, but fucking Sheridan was at it again.

"I was telling her about you growing up, and I made a comment about Sheridan being to blame for some of your scrapes. She said that it was fine, that she knew you had had girlfriends in the past, but my reaction, I'm sorry to say, might have confused her."

"Confused her?"

"Ben, Sheridan wasn't just your girlfriend. She was your fiancée."

"Shit," I muttered.

"Shit isn't the half of it. Ben, everyone in town knows this story, except for Kate. I can see you're into her, so you better tell her before someone else does," Mel gritted out.

"It shouldn't matter," I said. "It's in the past." I didn't want to tell Kate, because Sheridan wasn't solely to blame, and the fact was, I hated how Sheridan made me. She'd made me lose control, pushed me almost too far. I did not like reliving that and I didn't want to scare Kate off.

"Be serious," Evie said. "Of course it matters. She's looking at you with love in her eyes, and no doubt, *no doubt*, you will want to marry her next week. When she finds out she wasn't the first girl you loved, she might not like it." I was about to tell her to pull her head in when Mum spoke again.

"It's new, I get it. No one wants to share their past hurts if they don't have to. But the girls are right; she needs to hear it from you. Ben, she has been alone for a long time, and I can see by the way she is with you, she's in deep. I bet you're the first person she has loved, and while you can't help it, you've loved someone enough to propose. She's got a lot going on emotionally, but don't wait too long. That's all I'm saying." Mum spoke gently, and my sisters at least had the sense to back down and nod thoughtfully.

"Fine. I'll tell her. Anything else I need to know?"

"I saw her talking to Frank Mancini ages ago," Mel said, and I sighed. "You better keep her safe from that arsehole." Frank was a little shit, and there was something shady about his entire family. They loved making money and didn't seem the charitable type, but they had dumped heaps of money into the Hub. And the foster kids? Sure, they were well dressed but none of them looked happy to me.

"Noted," I said as I walked to the door. "Thanks for dinner, Mum," I said giving her a hug. The night had started rough with Kate arriving in tears, but it had been awesome after that. The girls had included her, Mum had shown her photos and we'd laughed at my expense.

"Ben, she's a great girl," Mum said. "Tough and capable given all she has endured."

"And she's hot," Evie added, waggling her eyebrows. I smiled.

"Thanks, I really like her."

"Well, let her like you back," Mel added.

"What's that supposed to mean?"

"You always go overboard, doing everything for the women in your life. Don't forget, she can stand on her own two feet, and she might want to spoil you in return. So, let her."

"Mel. That's freaking deep, and beautiful. I need to learn to love myself first…" I said, wiping away non-existent tears. She punched me in the arm.

I left and drove to Kate's with too much on my mind. I could see how she felt about me. It's one of the things I loved about her. She telegraphed her emotions clearly, without any pretense. But the look on her face when she said she didn't belong almost broke me. Mum was right; she'd survived a lot, and I was in awe of her strength, and her willingness to be open. When it came to Sheridan, though, I didn't know how to explain what had happened and what I'd done. My sisters didn't even know—only Mum. I'd reacted poorly, and lost myself. I'd also lost my cool and said awful, hurtful things. I wanted us to be on more solid footing before I rocked the boat. I didn't want her to leave me. She may love me, but I wasn't sure she knew it herself yet. And Sheridan had said she loved me, but when it came to commitment, she'd run. My thoughts were heavy as I walked to Kate's door to find her waiting for me, a sexy, wicked look on her face. She was a vixen without knowing it.

"Hey," she said, her cheeks flushing as I gave her a hot, hard kiss.

"Hey yourself. Dinner okay?"

"Your family are wonderful, I can see why you love them," she said as she took my hand and led me to the bedroom. She was planning something and I was down with that. I loved that she wanted me like this, like I wanted her. But I wanted to lay down foundations that would last, so she would know me, want to be with me—not only want the physical aspect. When Sheridan and I first were together, we had fucked liked rabbits, but later, when I'd started to build the life we could have together, there was no substance to what we were. I needed to wait to make sure she was all in with *me*. We would have plenty of time for love making—the rest of our lives if I had my way. That didn't mean we couldn't test the waters a little.

"Are you tired?" I asked her as we stopped at the foot of the bed. I gripped her arse and pulled her into my now hardening cock, almost growling with satisfaction. Her arse was magnificent; full, soft and deliciously pear shaped. She was trying to get fit, and I appreciated that, but I hoped she never lost this.

"A little," she said, running her hands into my hair. "But, I wanted to try something."

"Yeah? What did you have in mind?"

"Nothing kinky," she said seriously and I laughed.

"I better put my cable ties back in the truck," I said. She shook her head. "This body is yours, Kate, do with it what you will," I said as I held my arms out.

"You mean that?" she asked excitedly.

"Well, I'm not up for home surgery or anything with animals but..."

"You know what I mean."

"Beautiful, you touching me makes me want to come. Proceed at your own risk."

"Risk of what? Getting shot in the eye?" she said cheekily and I barked out a laugh. I loved it when she was crass and then blushed afterwards—another reason why she was it for me. She refocused back on me, slipping my jacket off, then my shirt. She spent time exploring my chest and stomach, her eyes hungry and hot. She planted kisses everywhere, and I had to dig my nails into my hands to distract myself. My dick was painfully hard, and she was toying with me unknowingly. Next she moved to my belt, and knowing what she wanted, I slipped out of my shoes.

"Eager, are we?" she asked and I grinned.

"What do you think?" I asked looking pointedly at my crotch. She blushed as she licked her lips, her pink tongue darting out and along her soft pout. This look made my dick jerk, needing attention. She didn't delay, unzipping my jeans and pushing them down my legs, leaving me in my underwear. Her eyes went wide and I smiled.

"Something changed since last night?"

"Have you grown even bigger?" she asked honestly and I chuckled.

"I don't think so."

"I hope it fits in my mouth," she muttered.

"Baby, you're killing me here," I ground out as she smoothed her palm over my cock, driving me closer to the edge.

"Lie on the bed please, handsome," she said as she climbed on and patted the space next to her. I crawled on all fours to her, kissing her before I lay down on my back. She looked a little nervous but determined as she wrapped her hand around me and pulled me free. I hissed at the contact. I was so hard precum was beading at the top. This would be a quick show if I didn't rein it in. Then she licked her lips again. Fuck.

"Your cock is very attractive. I haven't seen many, but I doubt any of them would beat this," she said right before she licked me from base to tip. I wanted to respond but I couldn't manage a coherent thought. Her tongue and mouth lavished attention on me, and eventually she found her rhythm and my orgasm started to build.

"Beautiful, I'm close. Be careful or I'll come in your mouth," I told her arching my back, my hands in her hair as she sucked me deep. So, fucking, deep.

"Will you come in my mouth?" she asked and I looked at her, to find her parted lips swollen and wet and I nodded. She smiled again, then resumed and within a minute, I was having the orgasm of my life.

"Fuck," I breathed when I finally opened my eyes again. She was beside me now, looking down at me both proud and jazzed. "You like doing that?" I asked, my voice gruff.

"Yes, I do."

"Well, that's a relief, because I fucking loved it."

"Even better," she said as she kissed me. I slipped my hands into her panties to find her dripping wet.

"Baby, you're so wet. Is that from having me in your mouth?" I whispered as I nipped at her ear.

"Yes…" she breathed as I started rubbing circles at her clit. She was quivering within seconds and in the next minute, she came. She held me tight as she came down, using me as an anchor to reality. I understood the feeling.

"Let's sleep," I told her and she nodded, climbing up the bed and under the covers. I joined her and wrapped myself around her back. She yawned and snuggled in before saying, "One day, you're going to have sex with me."

Chapter Fifteen

I could not wipe the smile off my face as I walked into work. The weekend had been life changing, and there was no going back to the old Kate. New Kate was here to stay. Ben had left before I woke as usual, but when I woke, his side of the bed was still warm. I had offered to stay at his place so he didn't have to leave early, but he said it wasn't good enough. I didn't care but clearly he did. I wanted him to be able to sleep longer, and if I stayed, I could help.

"Look at you! That right there is the look of a woman who has a handsome man's boots under her bed," Mia said as I sat down at my desk with a coffee. I had nothing to say. She was absolutely correct.

"I take it you took my advice?" Hannah asked, coming up to my desk.

"What advice was that?" Viv asked, joining the conversation.

"That I need to communicate clearly," I said, my cheeks going pink.

"Well, it fucking worked!" Mia said and we all laughed.

We got on with our work, but I often found myself smiling and when Ben texted, I almost giggled. It was fortunate that we were about to undertake accreditation, so there was a boatload of work, or else I'd be constantly daydreaming. The week continued in the same vein. The nights I didn't see Alma, Ben and I walked. After promising we would go to the top of Bungalow Spur on the weekend, I allowed myself to try some new tracks. We had dinner together, and I learned that Ben could really cook.

I now looked forward to my visits with Alma, and her commentary on life in the nursing home were funny, especially about Barbara who, without fail, managed to bring up my work, the Hub's progressive policies and Alma's displeasure with the food every time I walked in the door. We were sitting together watching the last newscast when I broached the topic of her return.

"When will you be able to come home? Should I organise a bed for me now?" I asked and she smiled.

"Home. I like the idea of it being your home," she said quietly, and I squeezed her hand. "I'm not coming home yet. The physio is making great gains, but I still need help with showering and getting in and out of bed. We need to update the house first."

"Are you feeling better?"

"Yes, love, I'll be dancing again soon enough."

Leaving Alma's on my way home to Ben who was already there cooking dinner, I wondered how it would work with Alma in the house. I didn't want her to be at Rosella Lodge longer than she had to, but I was unsure about living with my seventy-eight-year-old grandmother. Then there was Ben. When we were together, I was… well… loud, and I couldn't keep my hands off him, but there was no way I could give him up. When I got home, I told Ben about the potential of Alma returning and he went very quiet.

"Ben?" I asked, not sure what this meant. He wouldn't give up—would he?

"Beautiful, get that look off your face. We'll find a way. I'm thinking through the options. I could rent in town. Erik's old place is probably available."

"Why? We can be together at your place," I said and he grimaced.

"We'll see."

On my way to work on Friday, I walked past the real estate agent to see what it would cost to rent somewhere, but it was a ridiculous notion, given Ben had somewhere to stay. I wasn't going to let him waste money like that. With my newfound funds gaining interest, I could afford to build the house he'd talked about. The possibility that maybe one day it would our house made my stomach drop with nerves and excitement. The feeling dimmed as soon as I entered the office.

"What's going on?" I whispered to Viv when I saw Hannah, Carol and Leslie along with serious-looking people in suits and the foster care coordinator walk into our meeting room, all looking grim.

"I don't know, but it's big. Hannah, Carol and Leslie were here over the weekend and the State Department people arrived before nine this morning," Mia said, walking over. "They aren't the auditors. I think something has happened with the one of the foster kids."

"Can you imagine if something happened to one of those kids? I helped place them, and I vet the volunteers," Viv said sounding sick and Mia gave her a hug.

"We don't know that. And if something like that did happen, you are certainly not to blame. We follow guidelines," Mia tried to reassure her.

The incident cast a shadow over the end of the week, but until I learned more about what happened, it wouldn't help to worry about it. At least I hadn't seen Frank again, and Ben and I had big plans for the weekend.

***

"Ben, how're you travelling?" Jeremy asked as he wandered around my work shed. I did not want him to be here, but when the bank came calling I had no choice. Jeremy was a slimy, miserable motherfucker and I loathed the fact it was his bank that had leant me money for the farm.

"I've had better weeks," I lied. I hadn't had a better week. My time with Kate had been superb and no amount of money worry was going to change that. But now, I had to face the music.

"I heard. Drainage can be a real money pit," he said, and didn't I know it. We'd had heavy rain yesterday, and it had brought down fencing along the river. I'd had to extend my account at the hardware to fix the fences so I could keep agisting horses.

"Sure can, but that's sorted now," I said as I pulled out the bag of chicken feed and walked out, Jeremy trailing behind me.

"That's good to know. I heard you've got tractor issues," he said. I could almost hear him smiling. He'd leant me money, telling me he was doing a favour—and he was. I had enough for down payment, but my income wasn't regular, so banks were concerned about how I would repay the debt. Once I had accommodation and a range of income streams, it wouldn't be as risky.

"I can manage without it," I lied, partially. I would struggle without it.

"You are resourceful. I'll give you that."

"Thanks for the vote of confidence," I muttered as I hefted the feed down.

"I do have confidence, but it's hard when you hear things, especially from Mick at the hardware store," he said, playing his trump card. Fuck. I hated small towns.

"I'm pretty sure my dealings with Mick are confidential," I said and Jeremy had the sense to look a little worried. But only a little.

"He mentioned your chickens here eat a lot, that's all." He was lying and we both knew it. But then, his point was made.

"Is there anything else I can help you with?"

"Nope, just a friendly visit to remind you that your repayment is due next week," he said.

"It's in the diary, Jeremy. But if you don't mind, I need to be somewhere."

"Somewhere with Alma's granddaughter. She's a looker all right, but I hope she isn't as feisty as Alma. You'd be signing up for a headache." He laughed, but nothing about what he said was funny.

"You'd do well not to talk about Kate or Alma that way," I said, letting him know that his bullshit was not welcome here.

"Now now, I meant no harm," he laughed, his fat gut moving as he did.

"Good," I said as I walked by him and into the shed to get ready for dinner with Erik, Annie and Kate. I didn't look back, too furious with his underhanded visit and with myself for finding myself in this position. Inside I surveyed the scene and my mood didn't budge. I'd insulated the walls and put in chipboard to make it warmer in winter. I'd put in a woodfire and an air conditioner, small bathroom and kitchenette. On the back wall near the fire was my king-size bed, another purchase to try to make the place livable, then there was a couch, TV and coffee table and a dining room table that served as my desk.

It wasn't terrible; there was some natural light, large carpet rugs covering most of the floor, and a makeshift closet. It was bigger than most studio apartments, but it didn't feel like home. I had plans ready for a four-bedroom, energy-efficient house that would have views of the mountains and river. But I didn't have the cash. I'd planned on getting the accommodation cabins happening first, to get their income. But then I'd met Kate and now I wanted to give her a place that showed her how I felt about her, and the future we would have together. This shed did not say that.

I took a shower to wash off my shitty mood before dinner. I was looking forward to the weekend; tomorrow we would both visit Alma, and Sunday we would hit the top of Bungalow Spur. I was getting dressed when my phone rang with an unfamiliar number.

"Hello, Ben McTavish speaking," I said.

"Hi Ben, it's Lindy Watts from AidLine. I have a job offer for you," she said and I deflated. It would be in Melbourne, and given Jeremy's visit, I would have to take it.

"When do you need me?" I asked, resigned.

"Monday."

I tried to be positive when I drove into town to meet Kate, and when I saw her, I did feel better. She was waiting for me outside of the Hub, talking to Mia, Viv and Carol. She looked cute and fuckable in a green knitted dress that clung her to curves, and heeled boots that one day, I would get her to leave on while I was inside her. She had been pushing for that all week, and I knew she'd been concocting ways to get me to relent. But she was it for me, and I had to make sure she was all the way in.

"Hey," she said as she smiled and skipped over to me, almost tripping into my arms and landing with an oomph.

"Hey yourself," I said, smiling before I kissed her. She was flushed after, both from the kiss and almost tripping but at least now she could see the funny side of things. I held her close a moment, reminding myself that she made everything worth it. When I managed to get my farm operational, I would be able to provide for her in a way she would deserve. We headed to the brewery for a drink before dinner while we waited for Annie and Erik. Mia, Viv, Carol and Leslie joined us and while we made a motley crew, it was a good time.

"Ben, ladies," sounded another voice I didn't want to hear today from behind me. Frank fucking Mancini. I looked at Kate to see her frozen solid, and noticed Carol and Leslie looking alert.

"Frank, we're kind of busy here," I said, moving so he couldn't see the women behind me. It was a caveman move but I didn't want him anywhere near these people. My sister's comment about Kate and Frank sharing a drink rocketed into my mind. Something must've happened; she looked like she'd seen a ghost.

"I'm only being friendly. I know Kate and the girls from the Hub. It's all good," he said, peering around me and giving a charming smile.

"Frank," Carol said, her face now blank.

"Looking forward to the AGM," he said. She looked a bit confused, then nodded.

"It'll be good," Leslie added as something passed between her and Carol. Kate, who was directly behind me, said nothing, but Mia smiled smugly as she looked from me to Frank. Something was going on here, but I didn't know what.

"As I said, we're busy here," I told the little shit as I towered over him. I took a step towards him and he put his hands up in surrender.

"All right, calm down, McTavish. I meant no harm. I'll see you ladies later, enjoy your evening," he said before he turned and walked out.

"What was that about?" Mia asked as I pulled Kate close and she wrapped an arm around my waist instinctively.

"He's a little shit. Always has been," I said.

"He was in high school," Viv added. She knew the Mancinis as well as I did given she and Evie were in Frank's high school class.

"His father and mother told him he could do no wrong and now he's an entitled arsehole with too much money and no fucking brains," I added. Mia's eyes went big.

"You don't like him then?" she asked dryly.

"Not so much," I said with a smirk. At the small amount of levity, everyone seemed to relax a little. Kate was still shaken, but I couldn't ask her about it here.

"What about you, Viv?" Mia asked.

"He didn't really notice me," Viv said quietly. I didn't know why he didn't—she was beautiful and far less irritating than her brothers and sisters.

"That's a good fucking thing," I said and Viv nodded, giving a small smile.

We went to dinner with Annie and Erik, and Kate continued to mellow. Annie still picked up on it and watched her closely. Erik, the big lug, didn't see a thing other than Annie, but perhaps that was a good thing. I wanted to beat the shit out of Frank, and if Erik thought anything was amiss, there would be no stopping us. I'd told

Kate that I had to go to Melbourne when we got back to Alma's, and her disappointment echoed mine.

"It's too good an opportunity to pass up, and it'll help get the tractor fixed, and us into our own place."

"We don't need our own place, I can stay with you at the shed, when we, you know," she said nodding her head in an effort to communicate what *you know* was. Oh, I knew what she was talking about; ask the steel rod in my damned pants.

"Then we will be living at the shed because we 'you know' all the time." At this, she laughed.

"Let me pay for the rental then," she asked but I shut that down.

"No chance," I said.

"Ben, I can contribute and I want to," she said.

"That may be true, but it isn't happening."

Later that night, Kate brought up getting the rental again, and I once again ended the conversation, doing my best not to be a dick. When I asked her about Frank she didn't shut me down, just agreed with me that he was an arsehole. I sensed there was more to it, and I wanted to ask, but she was clearly communicating that she did not want to discuss it. I couldn't argue; that was how I felt about the rental, and about Sheridan.

Having all this between us was getting under my skin, which was already chockablock full of frustration with my financial situation and my dislike of Jeremy and Frank. I didn't want to fight. Instead I focused on stopping her trying to finagle me into having sex with her. I needed all my resolve, because when she told me she was having a bath, and led me out to the back deck and lit candles, I almost caved.

The next day, we visited Alma together. As usual, she was a smartarse and rolled her eyes at me when I walked in. She and Kate seemed comfortable in each other's presence and I knew before long, they would see themselves as family. I was happy for them, although I was not looking forward to visiting Kate with Alma there. I couldn't imagine touching Kate with Alma in the next room. At least it made my decision to spend the next month working in Melbourne seem like the right one.

"Are you ready?" I asked Kate as she fiddled with her backpack. It was Sunday morning and the sun was shining but the air was still cool. It was the middle of spring, so the days were perfect but the mornings and evenings still held a chill.

"I think so." Kate seemed not quite distracted, but like she was carrying something heavy with her.

"Why wouldn't you be?" I tipped her chin up to look into those arresting grey eyes.

"When I came here, and saw this track, I thought of my mother. I have mixed feelings about her now, but after being here and spending time with Alma, I think it must have been something significant that made her leave her family. And that makes me sad. Sad for her and sad for me. I feel like this walk brings me close to her, and reconnects her with this place. That sounds ridiculous—I know. But I feel like I'm reconnecting *for* her."

"I get it, and the good thing is, this walk will always be here. You can do this, think of her, visit with her, whenever you want. Like when I use my dad's tools. It really doesn't matter why she left or why she didn't want you to come to Italy. She was still your mum, and in her own way, she loved you."

"You're pretty clever, you know that?" she asked, giving me a watery smile before kissing me.

"You too," I said and kissed her again.

We started up the track, and after all our preparation, we set a good pace. When we got to Picture Point, we took photos and had something to eat before heading on. At Federation Hut, we had lunch and a makeout session that had me looking for a quiet space to show Kate what I thought of her spandex. Unluckily for me, we were interrupted by a group of over-sixty-five bushwalkers who gave us coy smiles.

From there, in the midday sunshine we walked to the summit. I'd forgotten how beautiful it was; walking across exposed ridges in the alpine mountains, seeing for miles. It was spring and the grass was vibrant and dotted with an array of native flowers, the sky a bright blue without a cloud in sight.

"It's amazing," she said as we reached the summit point and sat down. "We're on top of the world."

"We are."

We sat quietly as she looked over the mountain range and valleys below, tears in her eyes as she remembered her mother. I pulled her between my legs and she rested back against me, and I held her while she said her goodbye and hello. When the sun started to drop a little, I reminded her we had to go and she kissed me like she was desperate to.

"Thank you for this," she said, her look intense.

"For what?"

"Being here with me," she whispered and my heart clenched.

"Always."

We walked down in the shade, the afternoon a cold reminder that this week was going to be hard because we would be apart. It served to strengthen my resolve to find a way to get my finances back on track, so we would have golden weekends all the time. Together.

Chapter Sixteen

It was difficult with Ben being away, even though I was used to loneliness. I definitely missed him, but it was more than that; I'd come to rely on him. It was clear last Friday when I'd seen Frank at the bar. Ben didn't know how much he was doing when he protected me from him. I would never tell him, but I was eternally grateful he was the way he was, because seeing Frank had almost brought me unstuck.

We spoke every morning and evening, and we texted, but it wasn't the same because I missed touching him. Sure, hearing his sexy, deep voice while using my own hand had been great, but when I was actually with Ben, it was earth shattering.

Mia and Viv teased me whenever he texted because apparently I had "kissy face." I'd laughed because they were probably right. It was the only laughing happening at work, with all the managers looking serious all the time. We assumed it was due to accreditation and the auditors coming, and I felt sorry for Hannah who was having her engagement party that weekend. We were all invited, and Mia, Viv and I were going all out. With some urgent ordering online, my lingerie, dress and heels were on their way. I'd even booked in to have my hair done on Saturday morning. I wanted to surprise Ben; he wouldn't be home until Saturday afternoon, and for some reason I liked the idea of meeting him at the party.

I'd seen Alma on Tuesday, and it had been as always, continuous news watching, eating and social commentary. She'd seemed more tired than usual, but she assured me it was only because her therapy was hard. I wanted to believe her, but it made me consider yet again, what I would do if something really happened. Little did I know, the following day it would become a reality.

"Hello, Kate Bloomington speaking, how can I help you?" I said, answering my desk phone.

"Kate, it's Barbara, you know, from Rosella Lodge, where your grandmother Alma is?" she asked and I wanted to assure her I knew who she was and where Alma was given I'd seen her three times a week for months now. But there was something about her tone that had me sitting down.

"Is Alma okay?"

"Well, dear, I'm not sure. She's in an ambulance on the way to the hospital. She had a fall, I think it's a stroke. She's coherent, but they had the lights on so it must be serious."

"Where are they taking her?" I whispered.

"Albury Base. That's where they usually take people when it's a big—" she said but I hung up on her, looking at my desk blankly.

"Kate?" Mia asked, coming over to my desk. "Everything okay?"

I didn't answer. I grabbed my bag and stood, trying to get my jacket on.

"What's happened?" Carol asked coming out of her office.

"It's Alma, they think she had a stroke," I muttered, rummaging for my keys.

"Kate." Carol's voice held authority and I looked at her. But she wasn't mad, she was concerned. "You need to show me you're okay before you go."

"I am. I—don't want to lose her. Last time they called me it was a false alarm, but this time is different and I need to get there, speak to her while I still can. I haven't told her I love her. I need to," I said looking her in the eye, trying to communicate that I *had* to do this.

"Can Ben go with you?" Carol asked.

"He's in Melbourne," I told them, wishing more than anything he was here. "I'll be okay, true. She's conscious; I'm only… worried. I was a mess after my parents and I need to see she is okay. My car doesn't go above fourth gear anyway," I said giving a small smile as I tried to control my panic. I must've succeeded because they let me leave as long as I promised to tell them as soon as I arrived. Then Mia, Viv and Carol gave me a hug and their support warmed me in a way that was there to stay. I wasn't alone.

I called Ben as I pulled out of town and left him a voicemail. I knew he was in meetings all day and would call when he could. I didn't want him to panic either; if this was nothing then he didn't need to worry on my behalf. I got to the hospital and navigated my way to the emergency department.

"What's your relationship to Alma?" the triage nurse asked.

"She's my Nan," I said, liking the sound of it on my lips.

I was instructed to wait as she was being assessed. I'd been sitting for a few hours when Ben called. As I expected, he said he would come for me but I told him to wait until I knew more. He didn't like it, but I insisted and he relented, assuring me he was on standby. I felt his support down to my bones. Eventually they called me and told me she was being admitted and gave me a room number where I could see her in an hour.

"Can she eat?" I asked.

"She can, but we provide food here," the nurse said, affronted. I hid a smile, knowing exactly what Alma would think about that.

"Of course," I said before driving into town and buying sushi.

I returned to her room and knocked hesitantly on her door, nervous. I knew that given she could eat, she wasn't dying. But I was still afraid.

"Come in," she said, her voice sounding weak.

"Hey, Nan," I said softly, walking in. She had her own room with a window that allowed the pink dusk to come in and make the room glow. She looked older than usual propped up in bed with tubes attached everywhere. "I'm not sure if you're hungry but they tell me you can eat; I got some sushi. How are you feeling?" I said sitting on the bed, taking her hand, needing to feel her. When she didn't respond, I looked up to see her with tears in her eyes.

"I have to have a stroke to get a Nan out of you," she said grinning and I rolled my eyes, which were filling with tears, then I hugged her.

"It was a good motivator," I said and we both laughed, hugged and cried a bit more. Then we ate sushi and watched the news. Nan told me between segments that she'd had a very mild stroke, and they were observing her, and doing more tests. I was relieved, and told Ben and the girls, so everyone would stop worrying. When it was getting late, and I was getting ready to leave, Nan held my hand and asked me to sit. I looked at her confused but she only gave me a sad smile.

"I need to tell you a few things Kate. Now is as good as time as any."

"You've had a big day, Nan, and…"

"I need to tell you. Please." At this, I nodded and sat down. This was it. She was worried enough to tell me what happened with my mother. Despite being exhausted, I needed to hear it.

"I married your grandfather when I was young. We were close friends and I knew that he didn't like women, and he knew I didn't like any of the local men in town, but that I needed to stay close to look after my dad. We thought getting married would be a good way for us both to get what we wanted, and it started off fine," she said eyeing me warily. "You don't seem surprised."

"I found out when I visited the lawyer's a few weeks ago. I wasn't sure you knew," I said. She shook her head.

"Believe me, I knew. We were two misfits; Peter because he liked men in a time and place where that didn't happen, and me because I was a woman and I believed my opinion mattered."

"That must have been hard," I said trying to imagine how limiting life would have been.

"It was, but we were friends and even managed to have a child, your mother—after many bottles of wine. But, I yearned for another child, and your grandfather had met someone in Sydney and it didn't feel right for us to try again. We agreed that I could fall pregnant from another man, and I had a secret affair with Tulio Mancini."

"That's extraordinary."

"It was, and Luca was a beautiful boy and your mother loved him. She was still the apple of her dad's eye, but it did something to your grandfather. He couldn't connect to Luca, and couldn't accept the child as his. It made him bitter and twisted. That was the start of the end really, and after a few years he left us. Then, three years later, he died of cancer. Your mother took it very badly.

"I was a single mother trying to do the best I could, and I can tell you I got it wrong a lot of the time. It was a difficult few years as we adjusted, but Jennifer and I didn't part ways until she was about to turn eighteen and Luca died after coming off a motor bike at a friend's place. That's when she found out he had a different father. Your mother blamed me for Peter leaving, for turning him gay, and I think even his sickness. She didn't know how to feel about Luca; she loved him, but I had betrayed Peter by being with Tulio. She was angry, and confused I think, and she just up and left. I tried to reach out, going to Melbourne to see her, but she either refused to see me or told me she hated me. I knew she was hurting and angry; I was too. I'd had enough loss to last a lifetime, and her bitterness was something I couldn't take as I mourned Luca. Tulio was no help. Our affair had been mutual and romantic in a way, but there was no way he would upset his wife, and their position in the town. When Peter left, I supported the children on my own, and when I lost them both, I grieved on my own, while he ignored me, pretending I didn't exist. It's part of the reason I hate them."

"You have every right to," I said. My insides shrunk at the thought of Frank's family causing more pain to mine.

"When I finally had myself back together, I went to see her again but she'd met your father and said she was happier without memories of the past. In a way, I could understand that, so I let her be. Other than the one time she visited when you were little, we never spoke."

I was quiet a long moment, not sure what to think. This was one of the saddest stories I'd ever heard, and I realised that we shared more than blood; we shared grief, regret and the ability to survive.

"I'm sorry to hear that, Alma, I never knew."

"I know you didn't, and I never blamed your mother. She was young and trying to make sense of the world. She never recovered from your grandfather dying, and he never got over his bitterness."

"You paid the price for that."

"I did, but I had to let it go. They each had their reasons and dwelling on it would only make life unbearable."

"Do people in the community know about this?" I asked. Maybe Ben already knew.

"No, just your mother and me."

"That's a big burden, Alma," I said, and she nodded. "Thanks for sharing it with me."

***

The call from Kate was exactly the reason I didn't want to be in Melbourne. She needed me, and I wasn't there for her. Well, she didn't need me, not really. I supposed I wanted to be needed by her, wanted to think I added value, and could help with what she had to face. That made me narcissistic but it was the truth. She helped give me purpose. And here I was stuck I Melbourne feeling like an arsehole.

Instead of being supportive to the woman I loved, I was trying to sort out a clusterfuck of an international aid program that had slid so far sideways it wasn't funny. They wanted to send me to Timor-Leste but I did not want to go. I was already asking Mum and Kate to help with the farm more than I wanted to. Months away would be impossible. I'd spoken to Kate as she'd driven home from the hospital, and as bad as it was for Alma to have a minor stroke, Kate had told me she'd learned what had cause her mother to split from Alma, and that she finally called her Nan. It was such a small thing to me who had family close, but for Kate, it had been monumental. Her excitement was contagious, and I went into Friday not dreading work because Saturday morning I'd drive home to see Kate. The reprieve was short lived, however, when Mum called.

"Hey Mum, everything okay?"

"Well, yes. Sort of. Actually, not really."

"What is it? Are you okay? The girls?"

"Yes honey, we're fine. It's about the chickens."

"The chickens?'

"Yeah. Some of them are missing. I can't see any place that they have escaped, and you have clipped their wings; I figure someone must have stolen them," she said.

"Fuck. How many?" I hissed. I did not need this.

"Maybe ten or twenty," mum said.

"Who would do that?"

"Someone who wanted chickens but didn't want to pay. We are going to do more drive-bys and Evie will sleep at your place tonight. If anyone decides to come back for more, they'll have her to deal with." Despite it all, I had to smile. Evie was fierce if not unhinged. They would get more than they bargained for. "I haven't told Kate. Given all that's happened with Alma, she has enough on."

"Thanks, Mum. You're all helping so much. I couldn't do it without you. I'll make it up to you," I said, hating she was having to sort my problems.

"You will not. You do a lot for everyone; let people help you."

"Yeah, yeah," I said not wanting to go down this road. I wasn't a martyr, but I needed to be able to manage on my own.

"Don't give me that. You're like a duck on the pond, acting like it's all good while your legs are motoring. It makes you more of a man to ask for help when you need it," she said and I chuckled.

"I know that, Mum, I don't need it."

"You let me know if that changes."

"Of course."

I loved my mum but she didn't have to worry. Ten chickens weren't going to kill me, but I would have to do something about the pen this weekend to make sure I didn't lose any more. After work on Friday, I spoke to Kate who was seeing Alma in Albury then turning in early. She said she had things planned with Mia and Viv on Saturday, and would meet me at the party. I wanted to see her as soon as I got in, but the reality was, I needed to spend time at the farm to assess any damage. I'd waited a week to see her; I could wait a few more hours.

Next, Erik called me as he often did after work and ear-bashed me about Annie, how great she was and asked if I was free to help him finish her deck. When all that was out of the way, he laid the bad news on me.

"I checked about my old place—it's already been let out."

"Shit," I muttered. Most rentals were out of my price range. I'd been hoping Erik's would be available for when Alma got home.

"Why keen to rent man? You have the shed and Alma's."

"You want Alma in the next room while you're with your girl?" I asked.

"Fuck no," he said.

"And the shed is no place for a woman, especially not Kate."

"Is she precious or something?" Erik asked, disbelieving.

"She is precious to me," I said.

"All right, Gollum," he said. I huffed a laugh.

"So you *can* read."

"Read? I watched the movie, dickhead. Annie has an almighty thirst for action and violence," he said.

"Good for you."

"And Kate? What does she have an almighty thirst for, other than you? She looks at you like you are the bee's knees."

"See? This is why I need a new place. I can't be the bee's knees and get her to live in the shed," I said.

"That's exactly the reason you can. You don't need to impress her. I reckon you're in. She digs you in all the right ways. Let her love you as you are." He spoke seriously, but I couldn't contain my laughter.

"That. Was. Fucking. Priceless. You should start writing a *Dear Erik* column in the local paper. I'm proud of you," I said, and now he was laughing.

"Think about it," he said. "She isn't looking at anyone else, don't worry." I was reminded, again, of Frank, that little fucker.

"Frank Mancini wanted her. They had a drink but she says he's an arsehole."

"She's smart, that's good," Erik said. He hated Frank as much as I did.

"It's more than that. He did something to make her think that. I don't know what but if I ever find out, I'll give the little shit a visit."

"Count me in."

Chapter Seventeen

"Kate, your hair is amazing," Mia said as I followed her into her house. She lived in Bright, within walking distance of the main street. Viv was there, seeming a little more lost than usual. I loved both girls, and could finally feel safe in the fact I had friends that valued me. Another gift from Ben: he'd given me the opportunity to put my past with Cleo and Layla to bed, and here I was living for the future.

"Thanks," I said as I took a seat at her kitchen table, admiring her space. It was a little red brick house, but Mia had serious home-decorating skills. Her furniture was comfortable but modern, and she had great art on the walls, fresh flowers on the table and cute patterned tableware laid out for us.

"Here they are," I said as I put the hot pies on the large ceramic serving plate.

"I want to fit into my dress, but I want to eat pies more," Mia said and we all laughed. Then Mia opened a bottle of wine and we ate and drank while we discussed our dresses for tonight. Viv was going in a slinky black number that would no doubt set off her long auburn hair and pale skin. Mia had taken my route and scoured online sales, landing a lace midi dress from Ted Baker in emerald green. Hers had a high neckline unlike mine that was low cut at the bust. With the corset push-up bra I'd purchased, my enormous boobs would be on display and Ben would not be able to put it off any longer. I was taking the gloves off and he was going to take me all the way no matter what.

"Do you think there will be any eligible men there?" I asked as we sipped on coffee.

"What for? You already have Ben of the glorious ginger locks," Mia said.

"Not for me, but for you two?"

"I've about given up. I had considered chasing after your Frank, Kate, but when I mentioned it, Leslie told me to steer clear."

"He was always up himself in high school," Viv said.

"Well, for some reason, Leslie and Carol want me to steer clear too."

I said nothing, my heart racing as they talked about that vile creature. I thought about telling them what happened. They would understand, and it would stop people, good people like Mia, ending up in the same situation I was in. I should say something, but I was too selfish, wanting it all behind me. Life was as good as it had ever been—why mess it up?

"He's a douche who is self-centered and only wants sex," I said, trying to sound casual. "He was a dick about it. I wouldn't waste your time."

"I'm sorry he was a dick," Viv said softly and I smiled at her.

"Good thing though, because now you've got Ben and he's the shit," Mia said.

"Speaking of shit, what is going on with the managers?" I asked, keen to be on a different topic.

"I don't know," Viv said. "It's all very confidential but I haven't seen them like this. It has something to do with our foster care program. It's tightly regulated but nothing seemed amiss with the reports I prepared. It was a mess when we took it over but I thought we were through that."

"Well, you don't meet with Child Services more than once if everything is fine," Mia said. "There was a new woman with them this week. She looked very serious; I hope everything is okay."

"It will be," I said. "Hannah, Leslie and Carol have this. The least we can do is make sure Hannah enjoys her night." Everyone agreed.

Ben texted me when he got home, but he sounded like he had a lot on his mind and was busy with the farm, so I left him to it. I took the time to get ready. I showered, shaved and moisturised my entire body. Then I pulled on my sexy new lingerie thanks to Dita Von Teese, who knew a few things about fuller-figured women. It was a black lace, strapless push-up bra with purple silk paneling, high-waisted panties with a slight French cut, exposing a hint of my bottom, and lacy, thigh-high, back-seam stockings. This was the last weapon in my arsenal for getting Ben to sleep with me.

I slipped into my strapless purple dress that hit me right below the knee and was a fitted sheath with a light ruching from the bust to waist that showed my curves. The sweetheart-cut top barely covered my bra, but was tight enough to give me some added lift. I wore my hair out, giving it a slight curl then pulled back one side, allowing the rest to fall over one shoulder. I did smoky eyes, glossy lips and wore my mother's diamond earrings. As I looked in the mirror, I knew I looked sexy. During all my time in Melbourne going out with Layla and Cleo, only wearing black baggy outfits that they suggested, I never felt an iota of what I felt now. I felt powerful and beautiful; there was no going back.

Ready to go, I slipped into my ridiculously high heels, grabbed my overnight bag and headed out the door. Ben didn't know it yet, but I was staying at the shed no matter what. He needed to get his head around the fact that I was more than happy there with him because it was *his*. I was contemplating telling him about my newfound money. I'd heard him mention a tractor once or twice, and knew he had to work in Melbourne to make sure he could get it all going while he found his feet. I wanted to help because he showed me I was worth it. He would fight me, but surely he would understand I wanted to give.

I drove to Hannah's friend Molly's winery for the party, to find I was perfectly late. I'd wanted to make an entrance and surprise Ben. This would keep him off balance for later when I planned on seducing him. I parked on the road and walked up the drive, the trees leading to the entrance lit up with small lanterns. I could hear people talking and laughing, along with live music coming from two huge open barn doors. I entered the brick building to find it full of people who were dressed up, sipping champagne and eating food that smelled amazing. I looked for Ben, peering around massive bunches of flowers resting on high-top tables but to no avail.

"Holy shit, Kate!" I heard Mia say as she came to me.

"Whoa," Viv said following, a big smile on her face.

"Ben is a lucky man," Carol said joining the group and I blushed, hard.

"You all look lovely," I said, taking them in. Carol looked sharp as ever wearing a tuxedo, Viv an ethereal vision and Mia a goddess in green.

"Ben stepped out with Thor for a moment," Mia said. "I saw them head towards the cellars. While you wait, I have to tell you there *are* eligible bachelors here." Her eyes twinkled excitedly.

"I think you need to calm down," Viv huffed but Mia rolled her eyes.

"One of Howard's colleagues is here and he's gorgeous. And Viv here has been unable to take her eyes off Molly's new wine maker, although he looks about as happy as a man facing the hangman's noose," Mia said identifying a handsome blond man who was standing beside Howard, and a dark-haired, older-looking gentleman holding a glass of wine in the corner, looking like he was plotting his escape.

"You're in luck then," I said but everyone's attention was focused over my shoulder.

"No, you are," Mia said, grinning and I turned around to see Ben walking towards me, his eyes flashing fire.

***

My day hadn't been great. I'd got up early to leave Melbourne to find I had a parking ticket. Of course I fucking did. Then on the way home Evie asked me to drop by to help her with her computer. She was dead set the worst young person ever to use a laptop. I wanted to be home and sort out what was going on with the farm. I needed to take in the views, smell the fresh air, feel the dirt to remind myself that my struggle was worth it. Instead, I spent an hour at her place, listening to her tell me why I needed to tell Kate about Sheridan, and that I should bring her around more so they could get to know her. I wasn't in the mood for this.

"Isn't it enough that I'm here helping you when I need to get home? Do I have to hear a lecture as well?" I snapped and regretted it instantly because Evie looked hurt. "Shit, Evie, I'm sorry. Just a rough start to the day." She nodded, but she looked down, her cheeks pink.

"I'm sorry, Ben, I know you have better things to do."

"Not better, but *other* things."

I wanted to give her a hug but she moved away to the kitchen and started cleaning. I sighed; the rest of my apology would have to wait. When I eventually got home, I spent time checking fences, counting my other animals, watering the vegetables I'd planted and inspecting the chicken run, before adding a damned lock. That's right. A lock to a fucking chicken run. As the afternoon got late, I headed inside to get ready before Fleur picked me up. Kate had driven to the winery, and I was going to drive her death trap home. I had a quick shower then donned a white shirt and my navy suit. I added a pocket square, to annoy the shit out of Erik who reckoned they were ridiculous, and put my shoes on right as Fleur arrived.

"You look handsome as always, Ben," she said when I got in the car.

"Well, you're looking rather snazzy yourself. You might meet a prince charming tonight in that dress," I said and she smiled. Fleur did look lovely in a dusty pink dress with her soft blond curls piled on her head. But despite her outfit, she looked sad. "Are you okay?" I asked.

"I'm fine," she said doing her best to make her smile genuine. I wanted to ask her about it, but selfishly, I didn't think my brain could take any more burdens. When we arrived, the party was barely getting started, and I headed inside with Fleur to find Erik, Annie, Hannah and Howard enjoying a drink. Desperate for one, I took a beer off the first server that came past.

"You okay, mate?" Erik asked.

"Yeah, why?"

"You look like something heavy is on your mind," he said. I nodded. I was thinking about Kate, excited to see her again, but the farm, money and my fight with Evie were weighing me down.

"It's all good," I said, forcing a smile, but he didn't believe me.

Molly rushed over, looking irritated.

"Erik, Ben, would you mind bringing up another two cases of the limited release Shiraz?" she asked. "The caterers got the wrong one."

Happy for something to do, we headed off. When we returned, I put the box down and as I stood up, I heard someone say Kate's name. Then I saw her.

Her back was to me, giving me a moment to catch my breath as I took in the sexiest dress I had ever seen. Her shoulders were bare, all that lovely soft skin on display, but that dress. THAT DRESS. Fuck me, but it hugged her curves and her sweet, full arse in a way that made my dick grow hard in an instant. She was wearing black heels that I knew at some point, I would have to fuck her in.

I started to walk towards her when she turned around and gifted me with her ten-thousand-kilowatt smile, and I was done. D.O.N.E. I needed to feel her, touch her, taste her. A week was too long to be apart from her, and the closer I got to her, the less my other worries seemed to matter.

"Ben," she breathed as I reached her, and not giving the first shit who was watching, I took her mouth and wrapped my arms around her, pulling her close, wanting contact in as many places as possible. She kissed me back, letting me know she felt some of what I did. Our kiss was cut short when I heard someone say, "I think my ovaries exploded." I pulled back a few inches to look into her grey eyes that were hooded and hazy.

"Hey, beautiful," I whispered.

"Hey…" she sighed then kissed me, as the people around us started to laugh.

The rest of the party was an absolute blast and exactly what I needed. Being with Kate again, and having her openly show how she felt about me did wonders for my shitty mood. We ate and drank, and when the band really got going, I was on the dance floor with Kate. We danced through a lengthy Bruce Springsteen playlist, to some more modern hits. When "Dancing in the Moonlight" came on, I had her in hysterics as I spun her in and out, dipped her and twirled her around the floor. She was loosening up, but when "Mr. Brightside" came on, I saw a different side of her. She jumped, rocked and sang every word with Mia and Viv like it was their anthem. Watching her jump in THAT DRESS, I decided I could live with that. As the night wore on, more and more people joined the dance floor. Erik, Howard and his new architect Ethan were strictly fringe dwellers, but Hannah, Fleur, Molly, Dave, Leslie, Carol and Annie were up to the challenge and soon enough we had a dance off. I pulled out the worm, and I think I won. As we passed midnight, it'd been hours since I'd had an alcoholic drink and I was ready to go. Kate's dress and hair had kept me in a prolonged state of arousal—I couldn't take any more.

"I need you to take me home," she whispered in my ear after I'd migrated us to the edge of the dance floor, clearly reading my mind. She gave me her keys and we headed to her car, arm in arm.

"Are you tired?" she asked and I shook my head. "Good. I have plans."

"Plans?" I was curious and a little afraid. It would be hard to say no tonight.

"Plans," she grinned and I smiled back. I was looking forward to what she had in store. "But, you need to do something for me."

"Anything," I said as I opened her door and she got in.

"Anything?" she said in a way that had me thinking of some qualifiers as I got behind the wheel.

"I think so. What do you need?"

"I need to stay at your place tonight," she said and I sighed.

"My place isn't…good enough, Kate. It's makeshift."

"Ben, it's perfect. I want to wake up with you in the morning, not an empty bed. I want to help check the animals or whatever it is you do."

"Look, I appreciate that. I don't need help though."

"I want to help. And besides, I don't want to be in my grandmother's bed for what I have planned for you tonight," she said, and at this, thinking of what she might want to do with me, and what I wanted to do to her in return, I could see her point. I put my foot down and took us home.

The evening had cooled, so once inside I lit the fire while Kate sat on the bed watching me. She had a devious look on her face that had my heart racing.

"I've got to get some wood for the evening," I said as I removed my jacket and headed outside. When I returned, I almost dropped it all on my foot. The lights were off and she'd lit a dozen candles. She stood by the fire in nothing but her underwear and heels. Her long hair partially covered one breast, but the rest of her body was on display for me. The firelight flickered across her skin and she looked at me with lust, and a hint of vulnerability that undid me.

"Ben," she said and I looked at her, unable to move. I was too enthralled by all she was offering me. I could see she was worried I would reject her, but I couldn't. I'd never been looked at like this, like I was everything.

"I'm bringing out the big guns," she murmured as she smoothed her hands up her body to cup her breasts over her bra.

"Fuck," I hissed as I prowled to her, and she smiled, a little nervously.

When I reached her, I held her face in my hands and looked into her eyes.

"You amaze me, Kate. You're so fucking brave, and strong, and sexy," I said right before I kissed her.

Chapter Eighteen

I loved this man. I loved him because he made me want to do better, be better. I loved him because whenever we were together, I was free and hopeful. And now I loved him because his words reminded me that I deserved the best life could offer—including physical love. I kissed him, needing him to understand I *had* to have all of him, and he had to have all of me. I unbuttoned his shirt with trembling hands. Adrenaline and arousal coursed through my veins as our tongues dueled and his hands roamed my body. Once his shirt was undone, he pulled it off his shoulders then removed his pants and underwear before returning to grip my arse and hold me against his hard length.

"Ben, don't hold back tonight. I need all of you," I said against his mouth as I rubbed against him.

"There'll be no holding back," he growled as he lifted me so my legs went around his waist. Turning, he took us to the bed and put me in the middle. I lay back, looking up at his silhouetted form and I almost came apart. His thick, muscular shoulders stood out in stark relief with the fire at his back. My eyes travelled down to his narrow hips and his erection that was bobbing under its own weight.

"Oh my god," I breathed as I looked at this man who was the stuff of fantasies.

"Yes, my child," he said in a silly voice and I laughed, loving how we could be both intense and light. He threw a row of condoms on the pillow, then bent and spread my legs wide as he crawled up between them, running his fingers from my ankles all the way up to the edge of my panties.

"I'm glad I didn't know you were wearing this at the party. If I had, I would have fucked you right there on the dance floor," he murmured as he looked at me, exposed before him.

"You like it?" I asked, rolling my hips into his touch.

"I do. I'm going to love taking it off you more, but first, I need you to come for me."

He moved his fingers over the lace, rubbing against my clit. "Beautiful, you're so wet," he murmured and my hips jerked up, needing the pressure. "I like it when you're greedy," he said before he started to gradually make his strokes harder and more directed at where I needed them. "Kate, come for me," he said, increasing the pressure and that was all it took for me to fall over the edge.

He continued to apply pressure, and I tried to hold his hot, covetous gaze while writhing, calling out his name over and over. When I was eventually able to focus, I noticed he was now no longer only touching me. Now he was gripping his erection, stroking slowly as he watched me. Watching him touch himself as he watched me made my belly quiver. My eyes were glued to the muscles in his forearm that flexed with each stroke, and the thick head disappeared behind his fist.

"Baby, you keep looking at me like that and I'll come before I get inside you," he murmured, releasing himself and shuffling back enough to remove my underwear.

"These are staying on," he said, running his hands over my stockings before tapping my shoes. "When I walked in and saw you in that dress with these shoes, I wanted to steal you away and hole up somewhere with you for a month."

"That sounds good," I murmured. He moved up my body again but only as far as my hips. Then he lavished attention on my core with his mouth, while reaching an arm to my breast to palm it before rolling my nipple between his fingers.

"Ben," I said as I ran my hands through his hair, before gripping tight and holding him to me. He moaned against my skin and I almost came from the vibrations. He kept at me, driving me harder and higher and words came tumbling out.

"I need you. God, I need all of it, everything, Ben. Fuck. Ben. Please baby. Please." I wasn't making sense, I was feeling too much. He growled again and I screamed his name as I orgasmed, my back arching off the bed.

"Fucking beautiful," he said as he kissed his way up my body, before nuzzling my neck. "Let's take this off," he said as he undid my bra. Then I wrapped my arms around him, my legs around his hips, and kissed his mouth. He was doing his best to be gentle, and after two body-wracking orgasms, maybe that was a good idea. But I wanted to give him pleasure. I reached between us to hold his hard cock in my palm.

"Kate, baby, careful with that. I'm close already," he murmured at my mouth but I didn't listen. I held him in my hand as I rubbed my slick, hot sex against him. He growled as his hips started to roll of their own volition. "You feel good. So fucking good."

"I want you inside me," I said, after he kissed me senseless. He rolled off to the side, and put on a condom then came back to me, cradled between my thighs, and resumed kissing me. I started to shift restlessly beneath him, wanting him to move, but he didn't.

"What do you want, Kate?" his voice was deep and rough as he baited me.

"You," I breathed.

"Me?"

"Yes, you. Now," I pleaded.

"Where? Where do you want me?" he teased.

"In me," I heard myself whimper.

"Deep inside you?"

"Deep, Ben, please." I was going crazy as he lay on top of me, his erection against my clit, but not moving. He pushed up to look down at me, and his eyes were ablaze with desire and intent. He was making me pay for all the times I'd tried to seduce him. I smiled a little because clearly, it had worked.

"Okay, baby. I'll give you what you want," he said giving me a smirk.

"Need," I said.

"What?"

"It's what I need. I need you. I love you," I said, the words coming without any finesse or design. Once I realised what I'd said, I froze. It had not been my intention, and while it was true, I didn't want to scare him off. But I should've known better. This was Ben.

"Kate," he moaned as he kissed me before he sat back on his knees. He positioned himself at my entrance and drove in.

"Ben," I breathed as he filled me and I became accustomed to him inside me, and the feeling of completeness. He didn't move and when I opened my eyes, I found him looking down at me, his face on the verge of pleasure and pain.

"You love me?" he whispered, a tremor in his voice.

"Yes, I do," I told him, overwhelmed as my eyes filled with tears.

"Good, because I love you too," he said as he started to glide in and out of me, his eyes never leaving mine.

"I love everything about you, Kate. Every. Little. Thing," he said as he started to stroke faster, harder. He remained upright as he gripped my hips and drove into me, his eyes intense on mine as my body shook with each thrust.

"You're so fucking beautiful. Fuck, I could watch this all day, every day."

"Ben," I moaned as I got close.

"Wait for me, Kate," he said and I bit my lip, trying to stop the orgasm that was barreling at me like a freight train.

"Ben," I pleaded, on the edge. He moved faster, moving his hands beside my head as he dropped his face close to mine, his blue eyes going hazy.

"Come, Kate. Come with me," he hissed and I did. I came so hard my hips left the bed before I clenched around him. He followed suit, his eyes unseeing as pleasure stole over his features and he emptied himself into me. He slowed his movements to long, leisurely glides as we both came down from the intense emotional high. He lowered his body to mine and I wrapped my arms and legs around him, holding him close as he breathed heavily into my neck.

"That was fucking awesome," he murmured into my skin.

"Yeah, it was. Now I've had a taste though..." I trailed off and he laughed.

"Let me take care of this condom, and I'll give you another," he said as he pulled out and got off the bed.

And as was his way, Ben was true to his word.

***

It was right before six a.m. when I extracted myself from Kate and slipped out of bed. I added wood to the fire, used the bathroom, threw on some clothes and headed outside to let the chickens out and feed my other animals before Kate woke up. In the fresh spring morning, Kate in my bed, I was at peace again, like things were as they should be. I smiled as I worked, remembering last night. As I went to get water for the chooks, I noticed Kate standing in the doorway of the work shed, holding two cups of coffee. My heart stopped. If I'd thought she looked beautiful last night, then I was mistaken because seeing her with her hair a wild mess on her head, wearing one of my thick jumpers that hung to her knees and my gumboots made my chest ache. She smiled sleepily at me as she walked over and I grinned as I noticed her smudged mascara and kiss-swollen lips.

"Need a hand?" she asked, her voice rough from sleep.

"You should've stayed in bed," I murmured as I took my coffee, then leant in and kissed her.

"I wanted to know what you get up to at this hour," she said, and together, we fed the animals. When we returned to the work shed, I saw her eyes stray to a pile of hay and I chuckled.

"Fancy a roll?" I asked and she grinned, then leaned down and pulled off a gumboot. I was confused only for a moment, because she pulled out a condom and smiled at me.

"I came prepared," she said, blushing, and I laughed so hard, I had to hold my stomach.

"You're my kind of Girl Scout," I said, pulling her close, wrapping her in my arms.

"I think I'm addicted," she said.

"Addicted to what?" I asked still chuckling.

"You," she said as she leant up on her toes and kissed me. I knew exactly how she felt. I kissed her back, taking charge and feeling a high as she let me. I edged us back to the hay pile where I took off my shirt and lay it out over a bale before sitting down on it, and pulling her down to straddle me. Hungrily, my hands touched her skin. It was warm and soft despite the cool air around us. I slid my hands up her thighs around to her bottom, ready to dive into her panties, when I felt none.

"Holy shit, Kate, you were prepared."

"As I said, addicted," she said right before she removed the jumper and bared herself to me.

"You're not too cold?" I asked before I took a nipple into my mouth, and palmed her other generous breast.

"You'll think of something," she said sucking in a breath as she threw her head back, offering more of herself to me. My dick was painfully hard in my jeans, and as I sucked and rolled her nipples, she started to rock her hot, wet core against me.

"Fuck baby, I need to be inside of you," I murmured at her lips and she nodded in agreement as she rose up on her knees and handed me the condom. I undid my jeans and my cock sprang free. I rolled the condom on, my eyes returning to her hazy, grey ones as she looked down at me. Then she licked her bottom lip and I was done for. I slammed her down on me and we both moaned as we reconnected. I loved that she was unguarded in her lovemaking too.

I gripped her hips and started to move her up and down my shaft, trying to keep the pace from accelerating, wanting to savour it. But Kate had other ideas. She gripped my hair tight and held on as she started to move herself up and down. Her beautiful, fulsome breasts started to bounce with her and I leant forward to nuzzle them as I slammed her down harder and harder, needing more and more. Kate liked this, because she took over. Holding me to her chest, she drove herself up and down, moaning and saying my name each time she took me to the hilt. It was almost too much for me to hang on to my release. It was fucking hot.

"Ben, baby, I'm going to come," she said as she threw her head back, drove down hard and pulsed around my cock.

"Beautiful," I ground out right before I followed her.

We stayed joined as we came down from the high, our breathing slowing, our hold loosening to an embrace then a cuddle as I wrapped my arms around her and she burrowed into me. I was about to get her jumper when her stomach growled loudly and she laughed.

"I need to make my girl some breakfast," I said.

"Yep, we both need our energy."

"For what?"

"For more."

"More?" I asked.

"More everything," she said, wiggling her hips, and my dick twitched back to life as I chuckled. I absolutely wanted more everything with Kate.

We spent the rest of the morning in bed, making love. Kate was insatiable, and it seemed I'd unlocked some sex goddess because she was all about me, my cock and getting her hands on it. Needless to say, there were no complaints. As we neared lunchtime, we decided to take a walk around the property. I wanted to check everything before I headed to Melbourne, and Kate was happy to come. In fact, she had planned on being here the whole day, as evidenced by the endless supply of clothes that came out of her bag.

I realised quickly that having her here was completely fine. She wasn't worried about the fact it was a modified shed, or that there were farm duties. In fact, I think she liked it. She begged me to tell my mother she was off egg duty, because Kate was going to do it while I was in Melbourne. I was still shitted off I had to go, but knowing Kate would be here, in my place, somehow made me feel better. I wanted her to get used to it, because eventually, I would build her a house that we could start a family in. The thought had me smiling as we walked along the fence line near the river.

"What is it?" she asked, giving my hand a squeeze. I looked down at her, and my smile widened. She looked the part in jeans, boots and a flannel shirt that was barely containing her magnificent breasts.

"I was thinking about how much being here suits you," I said and she nodded.

"I didn't realise I was a country girl."

"You don't miss the city?"

"Not at all. I feel sorry for you having to go to Melbourne," she said.

"It has to be done. I need to get a few things sorted, like buying the tractor mower, and keep pushing to get the accommodation built, then the house." She looked at me like she had something to say but was holding back.

"What's on your mind, beautiful?" I asked, pulling her close, wrapping an arm around her shoulder.

"I have some money that you could—" she started but I interrupted her.

"Kate, stop right there. I am not taking your money to do this. I bought the farm knowing it was a mess and now I am going to fix it. I'll be working my butt off to make it happen, especially because I don't want you to have to spend any more time in the shed than you have to. But don't worry, I have this," I did my best to assure her, but she looked like she wanted to argue, so I kissed her.

We kept walking before returning to the shed for lunch and a long afternoon nap. Kate was exhausted, but I was used to less sleep so I was up and about getting my bags ready for the week while she rested. Remembering I had clothes in the washing machine, I went to the makeshift laundry—only to find water everywhere. Fuck. I had neither the time or the money to get this fixed, because I wasn't even sure I could make my mortgage repayment. I'd already had to ask for an advance on my pay and Linda had said she would try but didn't promise anything.

"Fuck," I ground out, wanting to hit something. Everywhere I turned, something else broke. I ran my hands through my hair then gave it a tug, frustrated. "You have got to be fucking kidding me. The fences, the chicken run, the tractor and now this. FUCK." I was taking a moment to be absorbed by my anger when I heard Kate.

"Ben?"

I took in a deep breath before I turned around. "Hey, beautiful, be careful," I said trying to school my features as I walked to her. She was in my shirt, her cheeks pink with warmth after lying in our bed, her oversized sleep socks slouching around her ankles. She looked cute, but I had a hard time focusing on that while I tried to put my frustration away.

"What happened?" she asked looking at the water.

"Not sure, I'll take a look now," I said.

"I can help," she said but I shook my head.

"I've got his, but do you think you can order pizza?" I asked.

This seemed to distract her enough, and after giving the washing machine another long look she walked into the kitchen and grabbed her phone. I used the time to pull my clothes out, rinse them in the sink and use the dryer while I tried to figure out what the fuck I was going to do.

Chapter Nineteen

I walked into work Monday morning bursting with happiness. I'd always rolled my eyes at people who were eternally cheerful because I'd been so unhappy myself and couldn't imagine ever feeling that. But now I got it. Those people must have had the best sex on the history of the planet, all weekend. Like I had. Turning on my computer, I remembered back to the barn, the bed, the couch and the kitchen bench where Ben and I had made love yesterday. Well, a few times were making love, but there was some straight-up hot sex in there too. I'd gone from a nonexistent sex life to having it on demand, thanks to Ben.

The weekend had been utterly perfect, except for two things. One, Ben had to work in Melbourne and I had to wait until Saturday for my fix, and two, he had financial troubles. He thought he was hiding it, but he wasn't. I'd seen the overdue bills on his desk, noticed him noting down all the things he had to fix around the farm as well as the frustration verging on despair at the broken washing machine. I'd lived so frugally after I'd almost wasted my inheritance that I knew how much life cost.

But Ben was proud, and wanted to be a provider. It wasn't because he was a man; I think it was in his DNA. That said, he still needed help and he was too focused on everyone else, being Saint McT, that he'd forgotten how to accept it. But I needed to do something, because he had given me so much. I decided to see about the shares I had, and speak to someone who knew something about business.

"Looks like things are ramping up," Mia said as she wheeled her chair over to me and we watched another suit walk into a meeting with the managers.

"It doesn't look good," Viv said, joining us.

While the managers were taking a break from meetings, I asked Hannah if Howard had time for a quick chat. She'd seemed confused, but I explained that I wanted to ask him about what I could do with my inheritance, given he had lots of money and knew how to keep it. She laughed at my bluntness but invited me around after work. I followed her home and while she walked her dogs, Howard and I discussed what I could do with my newfound money that would set both Ben and I up for our future. He'd given me a wry smile when we first sat down; clearly Hannah had shared my reasoning for asking him. But, after that, in his quietly spoken way, he talked me through my options. When Hannah came home, she made dinner for all of us and we had a chat.

"Is everything okay?" I asked her as we finished dessert.

"Of course, why?"

"I mean at work," I said, and she paled.

"Honestly, no. Not even close, but it's not what you think. It's nothing we've done, so don't worry about that. I think we will bring you all in tomorrow and explain because it's about to get worse," she said.

Tuesday morning I saw there was a two-hour meeting booked in all of our calendars. At ten a.m. we trudged into the meeting room with three other people looking as grim as Hannah, Carol and Leslie. We took a seat and Carol started talking, focusing on Mia, Viv and me.

"Thanks for coming. Let me introduce everyone: Francesca DeBortoli, senior detective with Victoria police, May Dodge, from the Department of Child Services and Jennifer Pascale, who is a lawyer. Ladies, this is Mia, Kate and Vivienne. This is now the entire team." Mia, Viv and I smiled awkwardly as the women we met gave us sad, tired grimaces.

"We're bringing you into this now as we are about to be hit by a shitstorm and you need to be aware," Carol said. "That said, everything in this room is confidential, and I'd like you to sign the agreement in front of you before we begin." I looked down at the paper in front of me: a nondisclosure agreement. We all signed, then looked at her in anticipation.

"A little while ago, two young women who had been fostered here through the program before we took over went to the police and reported that they had been sexually assaulted while with one of our families," Leslie said, her voice shaking. We all sucked in a breath.

"The department and police investigated and spoke to us about it. They have since interviewed other young people involved with this family, including one who was still placed with them. They have all confirmed that they were approached by the son of the foster parent, lured into being alone with them under false pretenses, given alcohol and sexually assaulted. They didn't speak up because they were scared, because alcohol had been involved and because they thought no one would believe them. Now the investigation has been concluded, charges are going to be laid. But it involves us because the family are major supporters of the Hub and the program, and are well known here." When Leslie finished speaking, my mouth went dry and I started to feel sick.

"The alleged perpetrator is well resourced, so we wanted to get as much evidence as we could before we started the process," the detective said. "These cases are not easy on anyone, let alone the victims, and we wanted to see if you had anything to add before we take it further."

"Who is it?" Mia asked but before anyone could answer, I did.

"Frank. Frank Mancini," I whispered.

"Sorry, Kate?" Leslie asked, not having heard me.

"It's Frank Mancini." The room fell silent as all eyes were on me. "You'll get a conviction. I'll help you."

At my statement, everyone spoke at once, asking me what had happened and what I had seen. Eventually, Carol intervened, and everyone else stared. Her look was the gravest of all.

"Kate, do you want some of us to leave?" she asked and I looked at her, seeing only concern, and no judgment. I started to speak.

"It's fine. I know it's Frank Mancini because I've had a similar experience."

I told them my story, leaving none of it out, being clear about the part of why I went home with him in the first place. The detective took notes madly, seeking clarification along the way because she didn't want me to repeat myself later, and I appreciated that. At the end, Mia gave me a hug and everyone had tears in their eyes, just as I did.

"I regret my decision not to come forward, more than you'll ever know. He might have hurt more people because I was selfish," I sobbed into Mia's neck and she patted my hair, telling me it was going to be okay.

"No Kate, none of this is your fault, and you're allowed to do whatever you want with what happened," Hannah said. I pulled out of Mia's hold and gave her a watery smile.

"Not really. I kept silent not only because of how it looked; I'd been drinking, been seen talking to him, had said words to the effect of wanting him and because his family members are pillars of the community. I did it because I wanted to belong here. I was alone, and had decided to restart my life here. Selfishly, I knew if I reported it, I would never be able to do that, that I would lose any hope of having a life and family. I didn't speak up because I was afraid," I said, taking in a deep breath.

"Does anyone else know?" the lawyer asked.

"No."

"Not even Ben or Alma?" Mia asked and I swallowed hard. I hadn't told Alma because I knew she hated the Mancinis, and Ben? Well, I didn't want it to change how he looked at me, how he loved me. But I couldn't let Frank walk. I couldn't. I shook my head.

"They're going to find out if you proceed," Carol said and I nodded.

"I know. It's the right thing to do," I said and she smiled sadly at me.

After spending the day with the detective, going over what had happened, I went home and got the clothing I had worn that day which had blood stains on it. I got the photo I'd taken out of my cloud storage and emailed it. Then I went to Nan's.

"Kate, what on earth is wrong?" she asked as I sat opposite her and put dinner between us. Looking at the food, my stomach turned. She would be eating alone tonight.

"We need some wine for this," I said, pouring two healthy glasses. Nan turned the news off, but I stared at the TV, wishing we were going to have our news-athon—anything other than the conversation we were about to have.

"Tell me, darling; it will be all right." I looked into her wise, loving eyes. She'd already seen a lot of tragedy in her life. I didn't want to burden her, but she was going to find out soon enough, so better she heard it from me.

"It's about Frank Mancini," I said and she went stock still. She remained this way as I told her what had happened in the lead up to that evening, including my interactions with Frank at the home and down the street, how I'd willingly gone home with him, and what had happened and the investigation that was underway. We both shed more tears as she looked at me.

"Kate, I am sorry that this happened to you. You came here to help me and this happened. I wasn't there for you when you needed it and I couldn't protect you," she said as tears ran down her face.

"Nan, shhh. It isn't anyone's fault but Frank's. I know that because I've had time to think about it, and because I've had a ton of good since then. Good with you, with Ben, my friends. But all this is going to come out in the public, no way around it, and Frank Mancini will get what's coming to him." She nodded, but remained distraught.

"Nan, it will be okay," I told her.

"Frank is like his father and grandfather. Rotten."

"His father? I thought you and his grandfather…" I trailed off because she sighed heavily.

"Luca and Frank's father were friends. It wasn't what I intended, but it happened because it's a small community. Frank's father was always up to no good, and when Luca died while they were together, I always wondered if it wasn't an accident. I'd convinced myself it was punishment for having a baby with another man, and ruining my marriage and my relationship with my daughter, but maybe it was because the whole family is like that."

"Alma, you don't and can't know that. Don't torture yourself."

"It's hard not to. Tulio had pretended to care about me, but after Luca died, he left me alone to suffer in my grief. It seems they're all bad," she said. I hugged her as she continued, "And they have a lot to answer for."

"They do, and this time, they're going to pay."

I'd left Nan's with mixed feelings. I was relieved to have told her, but I knew she would worry. I was dreading telling Ben. When I'd told the detectives he'd driven me home *that* night, and seen me upset without a jacket, they'd wanted to speak to him. But I'd insisted that they let me tell him myself first, in person that weekend. They agreed, saying that because they were compiling evidence, and all children had been removed, it was safe to do so, but on Monday, they would be getting Ben's statement and then an arrest warrant.

I had a few days to prepare, but keeping it from him on the phone that night was hard. He knew something was up, and I couldn't seem to act normally. I didn't know how to lie and it was making him worry. I reassured him that I was fine, but he was now coming home on Friday night to see me, despite it being a late drive for him. I spent days feeling sick, practicing how I would tell him.

But I needn't have bothered rehearsing; on Thursday morning, as I got my coffee, Frank Mancini stormed into the café, staring me down with a feral gaze.

"You'll pay for this. You think you can do that to me? Me? Accuse me? You wanted me to fuck you, you little tease, and you got what sluts like you deserve. To bleed," he screamed. I thought I was going to be sick. I wanted to defend myself, but I was immobile, terrified despite being in a crowd of people. He was so angry, so wild that he couldn't see anything but me. In fact, neither of us saw the barista come around and manhandle a spitting, unhinged Frank Mancini out the doors. He was yelling abuse at me through the window even when the police came and took him away. Shaking, with everyone staring at me, I ran to the Hub, needing the protection and support of my friends. As soon as I passed the security doors, and everyone took one look at me, they rushed forward, enfolding me in a hug.

When I told them what happened, Carol nearly hit the roof and the detective arrived not long after. Frank wasn't supposed to know about any of this yet, not until next week. The detective said she'd spoken to local police about another woman who had accused Frank of assault because she had to, but not given any names. Clearly, Frank and his family had hooks in the police department, which didn't surprise me. I guessed that when they had spoken to Frank he'd assumed the woman they were asking after was me.

"I'm sorry, Kate," Carol said bringing me tea in an attempt to calm my nerves.

"I'm thankful Ben isn't in town. I don't know how I'm going to face him. He won't look at me the same. No one will, and we'd just started—you know—and now he is going to see Frank when he looks at me," I said as a new wave of fear and nausea rolled over me. I'd thought I was on top of my emotions, but after today, I knew I wasn't. It felt like Frank's hands had been on me only yesterday.

"I never wanted Ben to know, and since Tuesday, I'd been fixating on telling him how Frank had hit me, knowing he would find it hard to hear. I still have no idea how to tell him what Frank did sexually and I can't imagine how he will take it. Given all that Frank had done and tried to do to my body, Ben might not want it," I said, my head a mess, and I started to understand what this becoming public would mean for Ben. He was respected in this town and now his name was going to be dragged into the mud. Because of me.

"Don't sell him short," Carol said.

"I'm not. He'll be great, but it will be the end of us. He hates Frank, and when he sees me, he will see him," I said, letting out a long sob.

"Do you want to go home?" Carol asked gently, but I shook my head, afraid of what more time on my own might mean for my mental health.

"No, I'd prefer to keep busy and stay here for the afternoon. It's safe."

"If you need anything, you let me know," Carol said. I nodded, knowing she couldn't do anything for me. But I was wrong. I needed her sooner than I thought.

***

"Fuck," I said as I threw my phone against the passenger window. Why wasn't she answering her phone?

Doing my best not to speed, I drove home nonstop, not giving the first shit that I walked out of the office, leaving a meeting without a word. When my sister had called and said she'd heard Frank had accosted Kate, I was already on my way out the door. But now that I knew more, that Frank was being charged with sexual assault, and Kate was among the victims, I would stop at nothing until I got to her. I spent the whole drive trying to wrap my head around what was happening. That motherfucker, that filthy, conniving cunt, had put his hands on Kate, my beautiful, precious Kate. I was sick with worry and angry, so damned angry, I didn't know how to contain it. If I'd thought I'd lost control with Sheridan, that was nothing. I was at breaking point, and if it wasn't that I wanted to be there for her, I would've shattered into a thousand pieces. I took deep breaths and drove, trying to piece together any information I had. That night I picked up Kate, with her in tears and asking me to stay because she was scared? Fuck. He'd hurt her, violated her, and I didn't know. I could have done something. Shit, I could have stopped it. If I'd been nicer, made sure she knew I was interested, maybe she wouldn't even have had a drink with him. Now, it had happened and I needed to find a way to fix it.

The only thing I felt other than anger and worry was confusion. Why didn't she feel she could tell me? I would have listened; I would've kicked his arse, gone with her to the police, the hospital, the lawyer, whatever she needed. But she didn't want to tell me. I needed to let it go and not be selfish, but I'd tried hard to be there for her, be open and support her. I wished she felt she could have told me. Now, I was crazy with fear, worry and love for Kate and she wasn't answering her damned phone. When I made it into town in the early afternoon, I went straight to the Hub to be greeted by my mother, Evie and Erik.

"Not now," I growled as I walked past them.

"Ben, this is not the place," Mum said.

"Mum. I need to see her. I love her," I said as reached to the automatic doors to find them shut.

"I know, Ben, but you need to tread carefully," she said, following me.

"I will, once I see her. I need to know she's okay," I said, banging on the doors.

"Hello? Anyone there? Kate?" I called out, not understanding why I couldn't get inside the fucking doors.

"Mate, take it easy," Erik said at my back.

"I don't need to take it easy, I need to see Kate. Then I'm going to go to Frank and—" I started to say before Erik got in my face.

"I get it man, I really do. But do not threaten him out here. People are watching and I know you don't care, but do not make this any more public and sure as shit do not threaten him."

"You get it? Really? What if this was Annie?" I laughed incredulously, sounding like a stranger to my own ears. Erik sucked in a breath, and shook his head.

"I would be doing exactly what you are, but I would also expect you to try to help me, like I'm trying to help you."

"Help me? I need to see her, make sure she's okay," I said my voice getting thick. The doors opened and our heads turned, but it wasn't Kate. It was Carol, and I was more frustrated than ever.

"Ben—"

"Where is she?" My voice was loud and rough.

"I'm not going to tell you that," she said.

"Why? I'm her boyfriend and I need to make this right," I said running a hand through my hair. This was surreal, why was it hard to see her?

"She doesn't want to see you right now."

"What?"

"You heard me. She needs time," Carol said quietly. But I didn't want to be quiet; I wanted to howl.

"But I love her, and I can do something, anything," I pleaded.

"It's up to Kate, not me."

"I only want to be there for her. I love her," I repeated.

"Then you need to give her time."

"I can't. I'm going crazy here. I hear from my sister that that... I can't even think of a word that fits him, put his hands on her, assaulted her, twice, and I couldn't protect her. And now, I still can't. I need to see her." I was unravelling fast, and I didn't know how to stop.

"Ben, you're making this about you."

"What?" I choked.

"You're making it about you. You want to see her because it's what you need. If you love her, you need to do what she wants," she said, almost apologetically. This took the wind out of my sails. I leant against the wall and looked at the ceiling.

"Is she okay?" I asked, my voice gruff as tears stung my eyes.

"She will be."

"Will you tell her I love her?" I asked, looking at her. She didn't show me pity, only understanding.

"I think she knows."

"Does she? She won't let me see her."

"Think about it from her perspective. Think about how she might think you might be feeling about her," she said as she turned to leave.

"But I love her; this doesn't change that," I called out to her retreating back.

"I hope not. And she needs time to come to that on her own," she said stopping to look at me for a beat before heading back inside, leaving me with family close, and the rest of Bright a few meters away.

"Let's get out of here," Erik said. I nodded, unable to make sense of what was happening.

"I'll see you at home," Mum said and I walked to my car, feeling like I was giving up, like I was losing her. When I got to my truck, I saw Evie sitting in the front seat. "I'm not very good company," I said as I got in. Erik climbed in back quietly.

"I know," she said and buckled up. We drove to Mum's in silence, and I appreciated what she was trying to do, and that she didn't make me talk. It must have been a struggle for Evie, but she managed. At Mum's I walked out the back to the woodpile and proceeded to pick up the splitter.

"I'll chop, you stack," Erik said. I grunted in response, and for the next hour we worked side by side, as I exerted as much energy as I could. When all the logs were done, Erik looked at me.

"Enough?" he said, breathing hard. I nodded, the exhaustion setting in. "Good, now go shower and get out of that damned suit."

I smiled faintly as I took in my ragged, filthy suit before I headed inside, showered and got changed. When I came out everyone was out on the deck, with a drink in hand. I sat and Erik held out a beer.

"What happened?" I asked the collective as calmly as I could. Between them, they told me what they knew, which confirmed my suspicions. But no one could tell me what had physically happened to Kate. And I didn't know if I was thankful for that or not. The only pleasing thing was that after Frank abused Kate in town, admitting his guilt, he was in custody and unlikely to get out. At least there was that.

Chapter Twenty

That night, I lay in bed cradled between Mia and Viv, and cried all night. They said nothing other than words of endearment and comfort as I shed tears. I shed tears for Ben. He must be confused and hurt, but I couldn't bear to see him yet, to know he was looking at me differently, looking at me like someone who had been sullied by the likes of Frank Mancini. One day, I would tell him what happened, but right then I was too afraid. Now I knew what it was like to be with him, like we were meant to be together, the idea that he might not want me anymore was too big, too frightening to consider. I shed tears for Ben.

I shed tears for Nan, that she was dragged through the mud again because I'd been stupid enough to trust Frank, against her advice. He was a predator, but that didn't mean my heart and mind didn't blame me for being so lonely, so desperate, that I took him up on an offer that I didn't understand. And now, Nan had to think about Frank's family and all that those memories made her feel again. I shed tears for her too.

Lastly, I shed tears for the girls who'd been fostered with the Mancinis. It turns out that the girl was abused before I was, but my selfishness and desperation to put it behind me could have led to another girl being violated. I shed tears for all the girls out there who suffered this fate. Needless to say, it was a lot of tears. In the morning, we sat up in bed and Mia brought in coffee and toast.

"What are you going do, Kate?" Viv asked.

"About what?"

"About Ben," she said quietly. We had all heard him call for me yesterday.

"I need to explain why I didn't tell him," I said with dread.

"You don't need to explain anything to him," Mia said.

"I do, because I love him and I need to trust him to take it the right way."

"What about work? Can you face it?" Viv asked.

"I'm going to keep on working. I want to be over this. I want to get past it because despite how bad it is now, the last few months have been the best of my life. It was how I was able to put it behind me before, and will be how I do it again." I gripped their hands and they smiled at me as we all shed yet more tears before going into the office. The media were outside, and I had cameras in my face, but I figured that it was a small price to pay so that the other girls would be left alone. The cat was out of the bag. Frank had made sure of that yesterday. I ignored it as best I could.

The managers were supportive, and we tried to make sense of what this might mean for our programs and the Hub more broadly. While the criminal case had nothing to do with us, we were doing damage control because of the negative media we had received inadvertently. We developed a communications plan that had us being supportive and positive of our volunteers, and assured people we were reviewing everything to make sure these things didn't happen on our watch. To our surprise, after Carol had a press conference, all the troublesome, difficult volunteers called and emailed, offering their full support of us.

At the end of the day, we'd had fifty people from the community stand with us publicly and this only served to fill a few more cracks in my heart. But there was one major crack remaining, and I needed to do something about it. First, I visited Nan. On the way in, Barbara was there, but instead of talking my ear off, she looked at me, torn. She'd seen how Frank had looked at me, come on to me. She knew and looked sick with guilt.

"Barbara, it's not my fault, and it's not yours either," I said and she nodded, getting a little teary but at least biting her tongue. I walked into Nan's room to find her in the chair, waiting for me.

"Kate, baby, come here," she said and held me close.

"I'll be okay," I told her as I held her back.

"I know you will, darling. You've survived a lot already, and done it in a way that not many people could."

"How's that?" I sighed, not feeling like I was managing at all.

"Coming out stronger because of it. Doing the right thing despite how it makes you feel. That's what's important."

"I'm not sure anymore. I need to see Ben; I refused to see him yesterday and he must be going crazy." I took a seat beside her and held her hand.

"Why didn't you want to see him?" she asked.

"I don't want him to look at me and see someone Frank has touched. I love him, Nan, but he's a man and I'm a woman who has had someone touch me in a way that he can't tolerate. I'm terrified he won't be able to see past that," I admitted.

"You need to give him the benefit of the doubt."

"I know, but I'm afraid."

"I bet you are, but have faith. If you love him, you need to believe in him," she said and I nodded. Then we watched the news and drank wine, our hands remaining connected.

I left Nan's and headed straight to Ben's farm. I could still hear the sound of him calling my name at the office yesterday. It had almost killed me, but I needed time to face him, to prepare what I was going to say and harden myself in case he rejected me. I wasn't ready but I couldn't stand the thought of him suffering because of me. It was dark when I pulled up beside his Land Rover. He was home. I didn't know if that was a relief or not. I looked inside the shed and the lights were on, but no one was inside, I headed into the work shed to find it empty too. Lastly I headed to the chicken run to see him walking towards me. He faltered a little when he saw me, but kept coming, his face blank. He stopped a few feet away from me and my resolve faltered.

***

I was on the edge and I didn't know what to do about it. All night, and all day, Kate had been on my mind. Was she okay? What had Frank done to her? Did she need a lawyer? What could I do? What could I have done? It was eating at me, and it took every ounce of strength not to go to her. Carol's words played in my mind, and it was only the fact that this was what she wanted that kept me away. I was hurt, but I needed to respect it.

My phone had been ringing incessantly but I ignored most calls. Linda from the AidLink left me a voicemail, and as expected, I wasn't getting an advance. In fact, because I'd left and hadn't fulfilled my contract, my salary was forfeit. The other voicemail I couldn't ignore was Jeremy, telling me that my payment was now late. My contract was strict, and two late payments meant I would lose everything. That was the price of borrowing money from an arsehole.

Unable to do anything about my money situation in that moment, other than sell my bike and the watch my father had given me, which I was seriously considering, I focused on the farm. I worked like a Trojan, seeing to the animals, using a hand mower to mow the lawn, building netting around the vegetables. I even cleaned the work shed, but the memory of Kate and I on the hay had me getting out of there as quick as I could. It was a great memory, but I wondered if I would ever make more with her.

Mum and Erik had checked in, and both seemed satisfied that I wasn't going to break down Kate's door or try and kill Frank Mancini. I wanted to do both, but I was refraining. Barely. I'd lost it once before, at Sheridan, and it had changed me. It had been close to the end, and she had been giving me the silent treatment for days because I hadn't included her enough at a social gathering. Instead of apologizing or talking it out as I would usually have done, I went out of my way to be around her, but not talk to her. I needed her to know I was pissed. But when she started crying and told me I didn't love her, I lost it. It had been months of us arguing, and I couldn't understand why she was going out of her way to upset me. Instead of comforting her, I'd yelled at her. She'd been shocked, and that pissed me off more. What did she expect?

Then I started to do more than just yell. I flipped over a table, broke a lamp against the wall, needing her to understand my rage. I wouldn't have hit her—she wasn't even in the room I was wrecking—but she watched me unravel, watched me make my words about loving her a lie. I trashed the room, and after, I felt no relief. Instead, I was ashamed and afraid that I could do that, become an angry, aggressive animal. That was when I ended it. Since then, I'd always remembered that I hadn't handled it like a man, like the good person people thought I was. I'd been a monster, breaking furniture, smashing a TV. It still disgusted me.

I was working hard to control my rage, because I didn't want to become that person again, a person who couldn't be rational, a person who wasn't there for the woman I loved. I didn't share this with Mum or Erik—which made me miss Kate more. I missed chatting to her about my day, the farm, her crazy volunteers. I missed how she looked at me, like I was everything to her. Did her absence mean she didn't want to look at me like that anymore?

Near exhaustion, I was walking back from locking up the chickens, ready to shower and fall into bed when I looked up and saw her. My heart stopped, then beat so hard it hurt as I took her in. She looked tired, and worried, but still the same beautiful woman I'd come to know. But she wasn't smiling; her face seemed wary and I hated that she was worried about what I would say. Surely she wouldn't think I'd hurt or judge her, would she? And if she did, what did that say about us?

"Hey," I said as I stopped a few feet from her, not sure if she wanted contact or not. I was itching to touch her but I didn't know what to do.

"Ben..." she started but stopped. Tears filled her eyes and I couldn't hold back. I wrapped my arms around her and held her tight. Her arms rounded my waist and she squeezed.

"Are you okay?" I asked as I kissed the top of her head.

"I am sorry," she said sobbing into me.

"Nothing to be sorry for," I said and she sighed heavily.

"I was going to tell you this weekend. But only after I knew I had to do something about it. Before the other girls came forward, I was going to bury it and never think of him again. I didn't want anyone to know. I'd taken the coward's way, but right now, I'm not sure fighting is any better," she said. I cupped her face, looking into her tired, tortured eyes.

"Kate, whatever you choose to do is fine. There is no right answer here," I said and she smiled.

"I've missed you," she sniffed. I wanted to ask why had she kept me away, but I didn't. I tried my best to be supportive, but it was hard because now I had her, and I could see and touch her, the rest of my questions were buzzing in my head so loud, it was hard to think of anything else.

"I've missed you too. Come on, let's go inside," I said, pulling her close but remaining silent as we walked.

"Do you want to know what happened?" she asked, her voice shaking.

"Do you want to tell me?" My throat was clogged with emotion.

"Honestly, I don't," she said and I tried not to wince. She had told me other secrets, but she wouldn't tell me this, and I didn't like how that felt.

"Okay," I said keeping my face blank while inside a war raged. I needed to know if he raped her. I don't know why, I just needed to know. It wouldn't change how I felt about her, but I had to know. But if I wanted to keep her with me, I needed to let her take the lead. I would wait.

"What's on your mind?" she asked as we walked to the feed shed to drop my tools.

"A lot," I admitted.

"Is everything okay?"

"Yeah, nothing to worry about," I lied.

"Look, before this all happened…" She paused and I wanted to tell her it happened months ago, but I didn't because I was trying not to be a dick. "I'd been thinking about the money my grandfather left me."

"He left you money?" I asked.

"Yes, that's what I learned in Melbourne from the lawyers," she said. I knew the meeting was about her grandfather's estate, but this was something else she didn't tell me.

"Well, that's good right?" I asked as we walked inside.

"It is, and I want to put it to good use. I spoke briefly to Howard and I was thinking that I could give you a loan or…"

"Wait, what?" I was sure I didn't hear her correctly.

"Give you a loan so we—I mean you—could start the accommodation or get the tractor fixed."

I did my best to school my features but I couldn't stop the words: "You spoke to Howard?"

"Yes, I asked him for help with my inheritance."

"And you didn't ask me because…?"

"I—well…" She didn't seem to have an answer. But I did.

"Because I don't have a lot of money."

"No, I wanted to come to you with options you would say yes to," she said. She wasn't getting how this might be hard for me.

"Say yes to? Options?'

"Yes, Ben, I have a shitload of money, and I want to help you with this."

"And you shared my business with Howard?"

"Not specifically; it was about my money," she said and I wanted to believe her because I didn't want Howard up in my shit.

"I don't need help," I said, my frustration leaking into my words.

"Yes you do. And we both know it," she said, that backbone going straight.

"No I don't. I have it sorted."

"Why are you hell bent on helping everyone else, but not accepting it in return?" she accused. My grasp on my temper slipped.

"Because I need to fix problems; it's what I do," I spat.

"Is that what *I* am? A problem to fix? Is that why you have been helpful, because you want to fix me?" She sounded hurt and I realised my mistake too late. I didn't want to fix her, but I did want to help.

"Kate, it's not—"

"No I get it. I can't offer you help, but I have to accept yours. Because I'm broken. This shit with Frank must give you something new to focus on. Is that why you wanted to see me? To fix me?" she asked. I couldn't take it anymore.

"No. I wanted to see you because I love you and because I do want to help you. In any way I can." I reached for her but she stepped back.

"Why can't I do it too?" She crossed her arms and tilted her chin up.

"Do what?" I needed this conversation to be over.

"Help."

"I don't want your help," I said losing my cool. Yet again, I was becoming a man I didn't want to be.

"I see," she said looking down, and I knew she was about to cry.

"Kate, I didn't mean it like that," I said softly.

"That's exactly how you meant it. You could absolutely use some help, it's obvious. But you don't want *my* help. No, you're all about saving me. Well you know what? I want to think I can save my damned self. But given your need to fix problems, I'll never know."

"Kate, please, it's not like that."

"Yes it is. And I can't live with a double standard. I need to give as much as I take but you won't let me." She was getting angry now and I didn't know what to say.

"Why are we talking about this? There are more important things—"

"More important to you. This is important to me but you won't even discuss it, yet you expect me to tell you everything. So you can help me. So you can fix me."

"Christ, Kate, he touched you. Hurt you. Did god knows what, and I am trying to be there for you because I wasn't before."

"You can't be there for me all the time. It's physically impossible. You can't control everything, fix everything, make it all good all the time. You can't, no one can. And your blindness and focus on everyone else is heavy-handed and one-sided. I can't live like that. You cannot make me the victim all the time. I already know what that feels like, and I don't want to feel that way anymore. Goodnight, Ben," she said before turning and walking out.

And just like that, my heart broke into a thousand pieces.

Chapter Twenty-One

"Kate, can I talk to you a moment?" Carol asked. I stood from my desk and followed her into her office. It had been a week since it had all come out about Frank, and the Department had assured us we weren't responsible, but that we needed to demonstrate tighter regulation. Although that was firmly in Leslie and Viv's domain, we decided to review all policies and procedures. As a result, we were flat-out reviewing, evaluating and re-writing.

Unsurprisingly with another two girls coming forward about Frank, the hearings were going to be a non-event. He was guilty and everyone knew it. There was lots of talk in town about what sort of sentence he would get, but I'd switched off. I'd fallen apart after my parents died, but learned that life had gone on and eventually I rejoined it. Now, I was trying to skip the desolation. I was speaking to a psychologist, spending time with friends and family and exercising. The assault was being managed. What hurt more than anything I'd experienced, though, was my split with Ben. I meant what I'd said to him, despite it not being my intention. But not having him in my life, after all that promise, was more than I could take.

"Carol, what can I do for you?" I asked as I took a seat. She turned to me, looking serious, intent and a little uncomfortable.

"I wanted to check in with you, see how you're doing."

"I'm okay, I suppose. I think because it's being resolved now and I have people at my back, it isn't as daunting. I'm glad I spoke up," I said honestly.

"But it came at a great cost," she said, giving me a sad smile. I bit my lip so I wouldn't cry.

"Yeah, it did."

"I want to tell you something, and it isn't my place, and it might be wrong, so you can take it or leave it. But I'm telling you because I've learned a little about love over the years, and how it can make you do things you didn't think you could, both for good and for evil. I've seen people fall in love and get hurt, and as an observer, things look different." She paused and looked at me dead in the eye, seeking permission to continue. I nodded.

"When Hannah met Howard, they shared something when they looked at each other, talked about each other. You've seen it, haven't you?" she asked. I thought about Hannah and Howard when they came to my rescue in Melbourne, and at their house over a week ago. They shared a deep love and sense of togetherness that you could feel all around them.

"Yes," I said quietly.

"You and Ben have your own brand of that, a connection that is strong and pure and visible. That's rare."

"But—" I started to speak but she cut me off.

"There is no need to respond. It just is. You know Annie and Erik, right?" I nodded again and she smiled wryly.

"Well, Erik was a bit of a dick, with reason, but Annie defended him because she knew him, and held onto that—not his words said in anger. It was brave of her, and it showed Erik and everyone that when she loves, she loves completely. Now look at them: bickering like a couple who have been together for decades."

We were silent a long while as I thought about her words. I knew what she was talking about, and what she was suggesting, but those couples were on even footing. Ben thought I was broken. He'd said as much. He'd rejected my help, knowing that my parents had done the same thing.

"Think on it," she said. I nodded and returned to my desk.

Carol's words dogged me all week, making me consider Ben and what we had before this all came out. I had to admit that I was happy with Ben, and felt safe and valued with him. But now, would he see me as I was, or would he see me as the person Frank had put his hands on? On Friday night, I took fish and chips in to see Nan. I took in a DVD player and a copy of her favourite movie, *Out of Africa*. Exhaustion, heartache and a few glasses of wine later, it was clear this was a mistake; like Carol, Nan had words to share with me that were hard to hear.

"How are you really doing?" she asked, eyeing me suspiciously.

"I told you, Nan, I'm fine," I said, fidgeting with the blanket covering our legs.

"No you're not. You will be, but right now you are putting on a front."

"Well, I can't be crying all the time, can I?" I sounded defensive, and I hated that.

"You miss him?" she asked, her tone getting softer and I slouched in my chair.

"Yes. But I don't know if we can go back. We had an argument and he said he wanted to fix me."

"Are you broken?" she asked, but it was an honest question.

"A little," I admitted.

"Even though he helped you doesn't mean he fixed you. Ben is the kind of person who wants to step in or stand up when needed. It's better that than some people who leave you adrift when they could help."

I hadn't thought about it that way, but she was right. I'd had both, and I knew I would take a Ben any day of the week.

"I can't imagine what he must have gone through," she continued.

"He was devastated," I said, thinking about him looking at me with despair when we'd fought, hearing him call for me at the office. "I suppose I haven't really thought about it other than knowing it was hard for him."

"It would be hard for any person. But for Ben? Saint McT who protects his mother and sisters? Who has fought for vulnerable people in his work overseas? Who has loved his community since he was a boy? Well, it must have shaken his foundations to think of you, someone he loved, being hurt this way."

I didn't respond, because again, Nan was right. Ben wasn't just any person; he was a protector who acted based on his morals and tried to live his life in a way that was right and good. It made me ashamed, not of what happened, but that I didn't give him a voice.

"Does he know what actually happened with Frank?" she asked and I shook my head.

"No, I told him I didn't want to tell him what happened," I muttered, wishing I'd responded differently.

"That is absolutely your right, but you might want to tell him what *didn't* happen."

"What do you mean?"

"He might be thinking all manner of things. All of them bad. Kate, what happened to you was wrong, and terrible, but put yourself in his shoes. The love of his life was abused, but he doesn't know how badly."

I left Nan's and drove home, not sure what to think. The sick feeling I'd felt as I heard desperation in Ben's voice outside the council door returned. He was thinking the worst and I was letting him suffer. I tossed and turned all night, but I didn't know what to do because two questions remained: Could he see past Frank, to me? And would he let me help?

Saturday morning, I headed into town early to meet Mia, Viv, Hannah, Leslie and Annie. Once Annie had heard about my newfound love of hiking, she had arranged a group hike. Mia had joined begrudgingly and Viv had simply said she had nowhere else to be. We met at Mount Buffalo, ready to hike for the morning. I was glad that Erik and Howard were picking us up at the top; while I liked hiking, I was still a klutz.

We started out early, the sun not yet warming us. It was going to be a brilliant spring day, with the low cloud burning off by mid-morning. The hike was perfect, because as a group, we talked about everything and nothing, without one mention of me, Ben or Frank. It was refreshing and recharging. When Mia started sharing some of her brilliant dating stories, I was laughing again and feeling normal for a brief moment. Then Annie started to talk about Erik's impending birthday and Christmas, and that she wanted to make sure he could spend time with his sister and mother in Sweden.

"He won't commit. He knows it's the bloody right thing to do, and I will go with him, but he is pussyfooting around," she said, exasperated. I chuckled, because I couldn't imagine Erik, who looked like a bronzed, blond-haired mountain of muscle, *pussyfooting*.

"What are you going to do?" Hannah asked.

"I've already done what I had to. I bought tickets, booked a hotel and have spoken with his mother," Annie said.

"How is he going to take it?" Viv asked, concerned, but Annie shrugged.

"Not sure, he'll no doubt get all macho about paying for the airfares, but he'll get over it because he loves me."

I was a little in awe of both Hannah and Annie; they both seemed to stick by their actions and not worry about what was going to happen. When we reached the summit, Mia ungracefully hugged Howard and Erik, sweating all over them while telling them they were a sight for sore eyes. When Howard pulled out coffees and cake for everyone, we all wanted to throw ourselves at him. Sitting at the edge of the lookout, we relaxed in the sun. I knew Erik was watching me and would report back to Ben. I was about to ask for an update of my own when Howard came over and handed me an envelope.

"What's this?" I asked.

"It's some paperwork I had prepared in case you need it," he said quietly.

"Paperwork?" I was confused.

"For your business deal. My accountant and legal team have included instructions should you wish to proceed. I too would like to invest, although that might not be well received at present," he said, giving me a small, quiet smile. I nodded, remembering our conversation about Ben's farm.

"Thanks, Howard, but I don't think it'll be well received from me, either," I said and he nodded thoughtfully.

"I'm sure everyone is giving you advice; it's what happens when people care about you. So, here is mine. Sometimes you need to fight, and if you want to win, play dirty," he said, tapping the envelope.

"Thanks, Howard," I said, giving him a genuine smile that actually made me feel better. As he walked off, I could see Hannah watching him, admiration, respect and pride clear on her face. That's how I felt about Ben.

We finished our drinks and started to pack up and head to the cars. I sought out Erik. I wanted to know how Ben was, but I didn't know if Erik would tell me. My heart started to race as I tried to imagine what he might say, and if Erik would be pleased that I asked, or blame me for hurting his friend. I started to panic, because I probably deserved it.

"Kate, are you okay?" a deep voice said and I snapped my head up to look up into Erik's extraordinary blue eyes.

"Ben," I said, sounding strange, but he was the only thing on my mind.

"Ben?" Erik seemed confused.

"How is he?" I blurted then held my breath, afraid of the answer. Erik looked at me for a long time, clearly unsure how to answer. "Sorry, I'm putting you in a difficult position. You don't have to answer that," I muttered.

"I want to answer, but I don't know how you are going to take it," he said quietly.

"It's that bad?"

"It isn't good. But you were right when you told him he has a double standard when it comes to accepting help," he said. I deflated.

"I wasn't too kind when I said it," I admitted.

"He's a big boy, he can take it. And to answer your question, he's battling some old demons, and trying to keep an even keel. He's worried about you. Like it or not, that's how he is." Erik gave me a sad smile and I returned it. Before I could ask about the demons Ben was fighting, Mia was yelling at me out of the window of Howard's car.

"Kate, you have to check out this sweet ride—there are TVs in the back, no shit."

Erik laughed then looked at me.

"It'll be okay," he said and gave my shoulder a squeeze.

"I hope so," I said before I hurried over and made Mia sit in the middle seat.

***

I was on autopilot. Every day was the same. Get up, work on the farm, eat, go to sleep. Every now and then I changed it up and helped Mum at her place or applied for jobs, but that was it. I was in a rut of my own making, and I fucking hated it.

I regretted losing my cool with Kate. Even though I *was* worried about her, and didn't want her to have to give up her money for my problem, I shouldn't have lost it at her like that. Memories of Sheridan tortured me, and Carol's words replayed again and again: *it's not about you, it's about her*. I hated that I'd been selfish, let my own needs come above hers especially at a time like this when she should have had my faith and support, not the frustration and disrespect I'd shown her. I wanted to apologise but I wondered if that would make it worse. And the fact remained: I didn't want her money.

The sadness and resignation in her face right before she left made me think that all of my brooding was for naught. She had seen that we had come to an impasse and so had I. I think that was why I'd been angry and let it show. It didn't make me proud, but she was prepared to give up on me and not try to find a way forward. It was history repeating itself.

"Ben," Erik called out and I snapped my head around.

"When did you get here?" I asked as I turned from the work bench where I must have been standing for at least thirty minutes.

"A few minutes ago. I've been calling your name, you arse-hat," Erik said. I shook my head, trying to clear the fog of melancholy.

"Sorry, I've got a bit on my mind."

"I bet you do," he said as he reached me.

"You're here to be my Dr. Phil? Is that it?" I huffed and he shook his head.

"No, I'm here to kick your arse into next week," he said.

"Thanks, I'm managing that on my own," I told him.

"I can see. But I want to join the action because you borrowed money from Jeremy Styles. Are you fucking kidding me? That guy is a scumbag." Erik was fuming, but I dropped my head. The truth always came out, didn't it?

"It wasn't a decision I made lightly," I muttered.

"Tell me," he said as he shoved a beer in my hand. We walked out of the shed and sat on the fence railing.

"Please tell me you brought food too?" I asked, realising it was four p.m. on Saturday and I hadn't had lunch.

"Of course." He rolled his eyes then threw me a burger. We ate in silence, but when we were done, Erik opened another beer and looked at me. "Now tell me why the fuck you took his money."

"Because I had to."

"You had to?"

"Yeah, I had too. This farm had been on the market and I was interested, but others were too. I went to all the other banks, but because I'd worked overseas they had a hard time verifying my employment. Then there was the issue that I do project work, so my income isn't regular. My deposit was fine, but my ability to repay was a problem."

"Why didn't you say anything?" Erik asked, looking at me without judgment.

"What? What would I say? I need money? I didn't at the time," I said, knowing I sounded defensive.

"Well, Jeremy has been saying this farm is practically his."

"He is a scumbag," I said taking a pull of beer.

"Ben, why is he saying that?" Erik was getting frustrated but he had to know I did not want to talk about this.

"Don't worry, I'm sorting something."

"Fuck that, I am allowed to worry. If this is the bullshit you said to Kate, then I get why she is pissed with you."

"Have you seen her?" I asked, needing to know. Erik grimaced. "Is she okay?"

"Yeah, she is. She isn't great, don't get me wrong, but she has people around her," he said.

"That's good," I said but it hurt, because I wanted to be around her too.

"Ben, I have been your best friend since we were kids. We have done everything together, and I told you all of my dirty laundry with Annie. It's your turn to unburden. Why is Jeremy saying that?" His voice was quiet but ticked. I bit the bullet.

"I've missed a loan repayment. Our contract is ironclad. If I miss another, I'm fucked. The farm is costing a lot right now, my washing machine broke, I needed to fix fences and the tractor is wrecked—shit like that. I've taken work in Melbourne but I've had to pay for fuel and accommodation down there, which eats into it. Then last week when I heard about Kate, I walked out of a job, needing to see her. My employer who was going to give me an advance to cover the repayment reneged because I didn't finish the job."

"Fuck, Ben, I would have loaned you the money—so would your mum or sisters."

"I didn't want to be a burden."

"Burden? We're family."

"I know, but Mum is working hard, and I've been helping Evie and Mel financially for years," I said.

"Wait, what?" Erik had gone from ticked to livid.

"I've been paying for their car registration and phone bills. I set it up ages ago and never stopped."

"Evie and Mel can pay their own way, Ben. Enough of this savior shit."

"It hasn't been a problem until now, but I have a plan."

"What? Selling the watch your dad gave you? I saw it on the bench when I was looking for you, along with a card for a bike dealership."

"I don't really need them."

"No fucking way. You love that watch, and your bike. I won't let you," he said.

"You're not the boss of me," I said with a harsh laugh. Erik scoffed.

"I am now. And we are starting with getting that motherfucker off your back then fixing shit with Kate."

"I'm not sure that can happen. I was an arsehole," I said, appreciating his efforts.

"You can't have been worse than I was to Annie," he said.

"I'd be a close second. It's like it was with Sheridan."

"What? Kate is nothing like Sheridan." Erik sounded irritated.

"No, *I* am like I was with Sheridan. It brings out the worst in me, and I can't make things right."

"Stop trying. There is no such thing as right. You need to make it better," he said as he finished his beer.

"That's deep; have you been rehearsing that?" I said, nudging him.

"You're a dickhead, you know that?"

"Yeah, you're not the first person to mention it."

Chapter Twenty-Two

By Monday morning, my mind was a mess because I was starting to realise I was full of shit. I didn't want Ben to think I was broken, but after everything with Frank, I was—and that was okay. I'd thought that would be all Ben would see when he looked at me, but he was the best person I knew, so how could he? Something was very wrong here, and I couldn't make sense of it.

Erik, Carol and Nan had all pointed out that Ben loved me and had my best interests at heart. Deep down, I knew that, and wasn't that what I'd always wanted? Someone to love and be loved in return? What was wrong with me? Now, I had a chance to fight for the man I loved, and not take no for an answer. With my parents, I'd taken their desire not to have me come on the trip as a reflection on me and it had hurt. With Cleo and Layla, I took their bullshit. But I wasn't that girl anymore, so why couldn't I go there and talk to him? I was still trying to figure out the answer when I received call at my desk from Ben's mum.

"Hi, Christine, how are you?" I asked, dreading what she might say to me.

"I'm doing okay, how about you darling?" She sounded genuinely concerned and it made my chest tight. I shouldn't have been surprised.

"I'm getting there," I answered honestly.

"You don't need to go any faster than you can. Whatever you're feeling is right. Remember that," she said and I smiled.

"Thanks."

"I wasn't only calling to see how you are doing," she said, hesitating.

"No?" Now I was afraid.

"No. I need you to come around after work. It's about Ben, and I need your help," she said.

"I'll be there," I answered without hesitation.

I spent the rest of the day worrying about what Christine wanted to say. I didn't think she was going to berate me for hurting her son. She sounded genuinely interested in my wellbeing. But that left the other option, that something was seriously wrong with Ben, and guilt that I might've caused it threatened to crush me.

"I'm sure it's not that bad," Mia said as I packed up my desk.

"What if something terrible has happened?" I asked, dropping my purse as I clumsily got ready to leave.

"I get that you've had more than your fair share of heartache, but Kate, the world isn't all bad. You'll see that soon enough," she said and I closed my eyes, sighing.

"You're right, Mia. God, I am sick of the drama, the tragedy, these intense situations that I try to survive. I want to have some happy, some peace, some safety."

"Then do something about it," she said, giving my arm a squeeze.

"What can I do?"

"Build a life that gives you that. One where you can be your best you. What do you need to have that?" she asked. I didn't need to think about it. I'd been my best me, my most peaceful, safe and happy version of Kate Bloomington, when I was with Ben. Now, I had to find a way to break down the barriers that stood in my way to get back to that. I needed to get Ben to accept help, and trust him to want me after all that had happened. It wasn't going to be easy, but tonight was the start, and somehow, Christine was going to help.

I picked up some wine and drove to the McTavish family home. As I parked, I was once again reminded how Ben had been there for me when I'd fallen apart, and how he had gifted me with family and more memories of my mother. It made my resolve stronger so when I walked into the house, wine in hand, I was ready to do whatever it took to win him back. But when Christine led me into the living room, I stopped, confused. I saw Mel and Evie sitting with an attractive, blond woman who looked like she wanted to be anywhere but here. I handed the bottle to Christine as she spoke.

"Kate, this is Sheridan, Ben's ex-fiancée." *What on earth?*

"I bought two," I said numbly, pulling the other bottle of wine I'd bought as part of the deal and handed it to her. I heard Evie chuckle but my eyes were locked on Sheridan, who looked about to pass out.

"I'll get the glasses," Christine said and I took a seat next to Mel.

"Well, this is awkward," Evie said with thinly veiled animosity. I looked at her, only to see her glare fixed firmly on Sheridan.

"Evie," Mel warned. Evie huffed then looked back to me.

"How are you holding up in this fishbowl of a town?" Evie asked. I found myself smiling.

"I've had better weeks," I understated.

"Ain't that the truth." She huffed a laugh.

Christine came back and took a seat on the other side of me, and poured everyone a glass of wine. I took a sip but Sheridan practically drank the glass in two large gulps.

"Nothing has changed," Evie muttered and her mother gave her a searing glare. She had the sense to sit up a little straighter.

"Kate, I wanted to you here so Sheridan can talk to you about Ben, and what happened between them. It's in the past, and she isn't here to drive a wedge, but she might shed light on Ben and why he is the way he is," she said, giving me a reassuring smile, before looking at Sheridan and saying, "You better get this out while you can still drive." And on that note, Sheridan started.

"Ben and I were friends through high school, and started dating in our last year. We were together while he studied and I started working and we got engaged when we were twenty-two. Back then, I was completely besotted with Ben. It's hard not to love him because he is such a... great guy. I knew I was lucky, but being with him, my own shortcomings became obvious. Everyone loves Ben, and it was hard. It makes me sound pathetic, but I felt inferior, and instead of doing better, I started to resent him.

"Ben would do anything for me, I knew that. I loved it at first, felt like a princess. But, the more time passed, the more I learned that I wasn't special, that he did this for everyone. He was a do-gooder, and that is why people loved him.

"As we neared the wedding, Ben was planning a big party that was going to be the talk of the town. I'd become negative, feeling inferior and hating that he was naturally *good*, so I started to do things to see if I could get him to lose his cool, not be so great." She paused to have big gulp of wine. She looked around and paled when she saw that all of us were looking at her like she was from another planet.

"Let's finish the story," Christine said kindly. I was amazed, because Christine had welcomed her as a daughter, only to hear how Sheridan had set out to sabotage her own wedding. I didn't want to hear any more, but I needed to know how this ended.

"I was young and clearly not right—" she started.

"Clearly." Evie was staring daggers.

Sheridan swallowed and I almost felt sorry for her.

"I know now I was in the wrong, but I had it all twisted in my head and had been pushing him. I'd be difficult, Ben would try to fix it, and then I'd freeze him out. Eventually it came to a head and he lost it and came undone. I mean, he was really *mad*. I'd never seen him like that. When he calmed down, he told me the wedding was off. He'd looked so broken and it caught me off guard because I'd been focused on how I compared to him, that I forgot he loved me, and I'd said yes to marrying him. The truth was, I didn't want to marry him and was too weak to say so. Instead, as Ben put it, I'd made him do things he wasn't proud of, be a person he didn't want to be, forcing his hand to call it off. But even in his fury he did the right thing by telling people, and returning engagement gifts, before he went overseas." Sheridan let out a deep sigh and sat back looking shattered. I was glad she'd finished; I couldn't take anymore.

"Have you learned?" I asked her, and she looked at me.

"Learned what?"

"How to value yourself on your own." She shook her head in confusion. "You lost the best man to ever walk this earth," I said quietly. "Men like Ben are a gift; I've learned firsthand there are a lot of arseholes out there. Your mess had nothing to do with Ben, not really. It was about you, and the fact that you didn't like how people looked at you. Have you learned how to value yourself?"

"I'm starting to," she said. She looked ready to cry. I gave a small smile.

"I hope you do, because that's what is important," I said, and she sighed before looking at Christine.

"Can I go now?" she asked like a child. Hiding a smile, Christine nodded. In a flash, Sheridan was out the door and driving down the driveway. I sucked in a big breath. Ben was engaged. He hadn't said anything. I wanted to be hurt, but then, I remembered why I was here in the first place. I hadn't wanted to share and I expected him to love me still. I was not going to fail this test, although I was going to question what on earth he was thinking.

"Gah! I don't hate her anymore. She is… sad," Evie said, pulling me back into the room.

"At least she can admit it. How did you get her to come here of all places, Mum?" Mel asked.

"I told her it was for Ben, and she agreed immediately," Christine said and huffed a laugh.

"You're a badass, you know that?" I said the words before I could stop them.

"Damn fucking straight," Evie said.

"Evie," Christine reprimanded.

"A straight-laced badass," Mel muttered and we laughed.

"Kate, I organised this because I want you to be with Ben. He told me what you fought about, and… you're right. He has double standards and is so blinded by his need to be there for others, that he misses the point. He's been blaming himself for years that he couldn't save their relationship. He can't get his head around the fact that it was on her, not on him. I wanted you to understand how that shaped him. I wanted to tell you something else about Ben, and how he was when his dad died," she said and I sucked in a breath. This was going to break my heart all over again.

"My husband was an amazing man and father, and Ben looked up to him. But as a fifteen-year-old, Ben couldn't understand why he couldn't stop his dad's sickness. Ben couldn't beat the cancer, and since then, I think he has been driven to make sure everyone is all right all the time, because we were broken after he died.

"It's not an excuse, but he doesn't see things the way most people do. He isn't wired that way. While you're right to be upset with him, I want you to consider what drives him. To Ben, it doesn't matter what has happened to anyone that makes them need help. He is focused on what it will take to make them happy again. No one likes feeling helpless, and Ben has had two situations where he did and he hated how he felt. He has done everything in his power to prevent it from happening to himself and people he loves. But as he is learning, he can't control everything."

I drew in a deep breath, trying to take all she had said on board. Guilt washed over me because I hadn't thought enough about Ben, and what he might need. But that ended now.

"I have a plan, but I need your help," I said. All the women leant forward as I laid out what I was going to do.

***

I knew it was a bit melodramatic, sitting in my shed, lights off on a Monday night drinking whisky on my own. But it seemed like the right thing to do, because I was completely miserable. After Erik's visit on Saturday, and Fleur bringing me food on Sunday and reminding me that I wasn't alone, I'd felt unsettled. Thoughts, wants and needs swirled around my brain, making it hard to see clearly, so I'd written it all down. My thoughts were about Sheridan, and my own actions towards Kate. I had been trying to do right by both of them, and I would not apologise for that. It was a good thing to do something nice for someone else, and if you cared about someone, you should let it show. But I had lost control, and that was something I needed to atone for.

Then there were my wants. I wanted to keep my farm, so I'd been tossing up how I managed that. I could sell some things, hold the debt off while communicating to everyone my situation. I hated the idea of that, and the watch I held in my hand, which I got for my last birthday before Dad died, would fetch a good price, but I was sick at the thought of not having it. I could ask for money, and people would help me. That idea made my skin crawl. I didn't want to be vulnerable and fess up that I wasn't managing. But I wanted my farm, so something had to give.

My needs were more straightforward. I needed money to live. That was why I took a job for a few days with a mate who had a landscaping business a few hours away. I would camp, work for him and get paid cash. I needed to do that. I also needed Kate. There was no other option; I needed her because how things were now would kill me. Slowly and painfully, I would cease to be myself. She was *it* for me. To torture myself, I would think about her living here in the shed with me, riding horses, helping build our house, then putting children in it and decorating a Christmas tree.

To get her back was going to be hard because I couldn't unsay what I'd said—and I still meant it. I wanted to help her, be relied upon by her. The sticking point for me was accepting her money, and I didn't know how to feel okay about that. I put it aside, packed up my truck, and drove away from everything I loved for the sake of a couple of hundred bucks. It wasn't until I was on my way home that my mood started to lift, and that was not because I'd finished a week grueling week of manual labour. It started when Alma called, needing a chat.

"What can I do for you, Alma? Everything okay?"

"This is about what I can do for you," she said, sounding amused and grouchy. I sighed, knowing where she was going. I appreciated that she wanted to help but I needed to do this on my own.

"Alma, if this is about Kate—"

"It's about you, Saint McT." I could imagine her squinting her eyes and pointing.

"Honestly, and no disrespect, but I don't need another lecture about double standards and accepting help," I said.

"Well, you're in luck. This lecture is about choice."

"Choice," I repeated.

"Well, you'd make a good-looking parrot. Yes, choice. Ben, some things you can choose. I chose to marry Peter, who turned out to be a grumpy gay man who hated me for wanting more children," she said.

"Wait, what?" I asked, flabbergasted.

"Don't mind that. Kate will fill you in. The point is, I chose that and I lived with the consequences. It wasn't all great, but I had beautiful years with two children, and a granddaughter I am proud of. But I chose that. What I didn't choose was that Luca died, and that Kate was hurt in a way that still makes my heart sore," she said. At the mention of Kate being hurt, I sucked in a breath.

"I'm sorry, Alma."

"Not your fault. My point is, some things you choose and they don't turn out how you expect. Some things you can't choose; you just have to roll with it."

"Okay, what does that have to do with me?"

"You don't have a choice about how you are. You want to give all the time. It's part of you. You can't turn it off, and Kate doesn't get a choice about that, it's how you come. Fact."

"Alma—"

"Here is another fact. Kate has money. You have no control over it, and she didn't choose it either."

"I know but—"

"Kate can choose to be with you if she wants, knowing full well you come with being Saint McT."

"Will she choose that?" I asked, afraid of the answer.

"I don't know. It depends on you what you choose."

"What's that?"

"If you choose her, you can't choose to have her without her money. It comes with her, as does her right to spend it."

"It's not that simple."

"Isn't it? Are you really prepared to miss out on my granddaughter, because of how she chooses to spend her money? It *is* that simple. You take her as she is, or you miss out."

I said nothing, because she was right.

The second thing that helped was a text from Kate, asking me if I would be home the following day. She said nothing else, and I didn't know what that meant. Did she want to see me because she wanted me? Or was she going to set me straight about being a dick? Either way, it was promising because I needed to apologise. I assured her I would be home all day, hoping my text didn't sound too eager. In reality, I would be waiting at the front gate with a cut lunch at seven a.m.

When I got to the farm, despite how tired I was, I couldn't relax. Alma's words teased me, another note from Jeremy saying he'd dropped by ate away at my confidence, and the emptiness of my bed crushed me. I was up and out on the farm early, determined to get as much work done as I could before I thought Kate would come, so I could shower and be ready to win her back. I needed to be there for her in any way she needed. I needed to make sure she knew that I was still in love with her, and that what Frank did didn't change that. That was my truth and she needed to believe it.

By eight-thirty I was coming in for a coffee when a truck arrived. I walked out to see it reversing in, a tractor-mower on the flat bed. It came to a halt and the driver lowered the ramps then came around to meet me.

"You Ben McTavish?" he asked, looking none too impressed with working on a Saturday.

"That's right," I said, about to tell him he had the wrong address when he grunted.

"Well, you need to drive it off so I can be on my way," he said, holding out keys.

"I didn't order this," I said but he shrugged.

"Not my problem. I had to deliver this to Ben McTavish and the order was confirmed yesterday. Give me a hand, yeah?"

The set of his weathered jaw had me taking the keys and driving it down the ramp. Old mate didn't hang around to talk to me about the order, but before I got a chance to call the store, I heard I another truck honking its horn on the road. I walked up the driveway to see a small cattle truck reversing down the drive, with six Highland cattle cows looking at me. What in the actual fuck? When the truck came to a halt, a man and woman got out and walked to me.

"Ben McTavish?" the woman asked as the man looked around the fences.

"Yes," I said.

"What paddock are Bella, Alice, Renee, Esme, Renesme and Rosalie to go into?" she asked, smirking.

"They come with names?" I asked at a loss.

"Well, the woman who ordered them suggested these. I didn't have the heart to tell her that I didn't think they were pets but she thought it was what you had to do," she said.

"Did the woman give her name?" I asked, wanting to confirm my suspicions.

"Yeah, but I think you already know it. If you want sperm, let us know. She said she drew the line at *bull spunk*," she said and I laughed.

I showed them a paddock that could hold cattle, at least for a little while as my mind raced. It was Kate; it had to be, right? The knowledge that she was doing this had my heart beating too hard, too loud. Did she want me back? Without me apologising? How could that be? I needed to speak to her, but I got the feeling she had a plan and I could not afford to put a foot wrong.

When Ethan, Howard's architect, arrived at the shed, a quiet smile on his face, I knew that Kate was behind this, and she was making her statement. I'd only met Ethan the once at Howard and Hannah's engagement, but I knew he headed up Howard's commercial and residential design team, that he was an architect and that he was a nice guy, but possibly even quieter than Howard.

"Ben," he said, grinning outright when he took me in and I rolled my eyes. We shook hands and I led him into the shed.

"Beer?" I asked and he nodded. "Good, because I sure as shit need one." He laughed at this, nodding agreement.

"I'm here to revisit your house and accommodation plans. I've been commissioned to get them ready to submit to planning."

"Okay, but…"

"There are no buts. I'm paid up and on the clock. Give me what you have and talk me through what you envisage. My advice, for what it's worth, is to get the house done first. Women love new houses," he said tiredly, like he knew all about that. I didn't ask because I figured we needed more than one beer under our belt.

Instead, I pulled out my concepts, and we went through them before going out and looking at the farm and where I thought things needed to be. Ethan listened, took notes and only asked questions at the end. He made a few initial suggestions that let me know he knew his shit, and I, or should I say *we*, were in safe hands. When he left, I sat down on the couch and thought about Kate, and what I would say to her when she arrived. The cows and the tractor I could handle. I would pay her back of course. She would hate it but I would do it. The house though? I didn't see how I could cop that. I desperately wanted to give her a home, but having her pay? I didn't know if I could.

But before we crossed that bridge, I needed her back with me. The thought that she would forgive me had my heart and mind racing. I'd began to hope we would be an us, and that settled deep in my chest, so deep it would break me if it didn't work out. With my nerves shot and my mind scrambling, I took care of my animals before it got too late, then came inside to wash up and prepare for whatever was going to happen next.

Chapter Twenty-Three

When I arrived at Ben's, everything became frighteningly real. It was one thing to make calls from the safety of Nan's, and be buoyed by Ben's family and my friends. It was entirely another to put myself completely out there with the man I loved, and who I wanted to be with forever. And I had put myself out there in a big way today, taking the gamble of my life. But it wasn't how he would react to the money that had me worried. He had to find a way to deal with it. I was feeling sick because I was going to tell Ben all about what happened with Frank, and why I'd cut him out. I wanted to tell him once, and be done with it. Everyone said he would be accepting, that he wasn't the kind of person to love me less because I'd been hurt. I wanted to believe them, and for the most part I did. But there was always that chance that he couldn't get over it, couldn't see me without Frank. He hated him, and I was worried I would be a reminder. But, I was in the lap of the gods now.

It was late afternoon as I drove in and parked next to him. My little green car looked out of place on the farm. It was time for a change, but perhaps Ben could help me with that. I didn't know the first thing about cars, and after talking cows and sperm with some farming goddess, and given what I was about to tell Ben, I will have had enough time outside my comfort zone for a while.

I couldn't see him outside, so I knocked, and entered the shed to find the lights on, but no Ben. When I heard the shower click off, my hands started to shake, and I swallowed nervously. This was it. I wiped my hands on my jeans, then paced. As I passed the mirror, I checked my hair, which was out and didn't have any major kinks in it, straightened my shirt, and reapplied lip gloss. I hadn't dressed up necessarily, but I had made an effort with my appearance. I hadn't seen him in days and I didn't want to make a mistake.

When he walked out of the bathroom, his eyes landed on me and he stopped dead. He hungrily took in my body as I devoured his. My heart raced at the sight of him in jeans and a henley, his hair still a little wet but his gorgeous face clean shaven. He was beautiful; my fingers itched to touch him. But when my perusal made it to his face, I drew in a long, deep breath because his eyes let me know he was worried. Well, it made two of us.

"Hey," he said coming to me, a small smile on his lips.

"Hey, Ben," I said as he wrapped his arms around me and pulled me into a hug. The fact he made the first move, and it was to hold me, released the trigger on my emotions that I'd barely been holding.

"I've missed you," I said as my eyes filled with tears. I was overwhelmed by the comfort of being back in his arms, his big, warm body against me.

"Hey, beautiful, don't cry. It's going to be okay," he said, planting a kiss on the top of my head.

"I really hope so," I added.

"It will, but we have a lot to talk about," he said, pulling back to look down at me. He gazed into my eyes as he cradled my face in his hands, his thumbs moving slowly over my cheeks.

"Can we take a walk? I need to tell you about what happened, but I don't want to do it in here," I murmured as I held his eyes. I did not want to tell him, but he needed to know if it was going to be put behind us. It was still sunny outside, and I wanted him to hear it in the light of day, when things looked golden.

"Beautiful, you don't have to tell me."

"I want to," I said as I moved away and grabbed my cardigan. Ben put on boots and we walked outside, then down along the paddock fence.

"Have you met our girls?" he asked as we walked past the Highland cattle.

"Not yet," I said, feeling shy for some reason.

"Thank you," he said and I assessed him.

"Do you mean it?"

"Of course."

"Can you accept them?" I pushed and he smiled.

"Yeah, I can. This is the start of our herd, and it's exciting. I'm grateful, but it's more than that, I love that you thought of *me*. It feels good to be thought about like that," he said. I looked into his denim-blue eyes for a long moment, seeing he meant what he said.

"Good," I sighed, relieved. We were quiet again and Ben found my hand, linking his fingers with mine as we walked towards the river in the late afternoon. I shivered a little as the cool breeze came up, and Ben put his arm around my waist and pulled me close.

"Let's sit," I said when we reached the river, and we both sat down on a big fallen tree as the river bubbled in the background. "I want to tell you what happened, and why I didn't confide in you. I'm afraid to, because I think it could change things between us for the worse, but I don't want to hide things from you. I love you, Ben, with everything I am, and I need that from you in return if we are going to work. So, let me tell you. Then you can think about it, and let me know how you feel."

"Kate—" he started but I cut him off.

"Please, I need to know you've thought about it, that you are okay with it, really okay with it," I insisted. He nodded, but pulled me so I was sitting in his lap, my head on his shoulder while I faced the river.

"When I first moved here, I didn't want to let anyone in. My friends had hurt me and my parents had turned me away. But as I began to get to know people, like the girls at work, Nan and you, my defenses started to crumble because people were good here, and good to me in a way that I'd forgotten was possible. I liked you, from that first moment of Sauce-gate..." I said, laughing a little at myself.

"Sauce-gate?" Ben sounded amused and held me closer.

"That's what I've been calling it. Or do you prefer the sauce-capades?" I asked and he shook with laughter.

"I like both." We both took a moment to enjoy how we were, before I started again.

"I thought you were handsome way back then, and every time after, even when you were a bit of a dick," I continued, and he sighed, amused.

"I was, wasn't I?"

"Yep. Not a complete dick though. The point is when I got over myself and realised that you weren't being awful, things changed. Then I heard people like Nan talk about you. I started to see you were exactly what a man should be and I wanted you. But, I thought you would be out of my reach. You're a man, with a sense of *right*, who is loved by many people, and I was a girl who had been living a fake life, who wasted all her money when she fell apart and had no one to care about her. I felt like an imposter, but this place wore me down enough to consider the possibility. I gave in. It was huge for me, and I'd started to hope that I would actually belong somewhere.

"That's how I ended up out for drinks one Friday night with Mia and Viv. We'd had a few, not copious amounts, but enough to be buzzed. Then Frank came in. He'd been flirting with me and while I'd been avoiding him because I wanted you, for some reason that night, I thought maybe he was low enough down the food chain for me." I paused because Ben stiffened.

"I'm fine," he said quietly. "I don't like hearing you talk about yourself that way, but tell me the rest so we can get it done." I took a big breath and continued.

"He was attentive, and after Mia and Viv left, he invited me back for a coffee. They'd seemed encouraging, and given Frank's involvement with the Hub, I thought he must be okay. I was wrong about that. We walked to his apartment in town, and I enjoyed being flattered. Then he started to kiss me, and I was okay with that. I had little experience but it seemed natural. Then he started to get more forceful, laying me down, touching me over my clothes, then over my underwear. I let him know I wasn't entirely down with it, but he asked if I liked him, if I wanted him and I felt like I should say yes, given I was willing up to that point. The moment I said yes, things changed and he became violent. He didn't get his hands between my legs, but he tried hard, and he had his hands up my shirt. He relished that I was struggling and even bit my shoulder—hard enough to draw blood. But I fought back and managed to hit him where it hurts and escape. He was furious, in a scary, malevolent way that even now, makes me feel sick.

"I ran out before he could recover but he threatened that I would pay. I tidied myself up as best I could and waited for a cab when you stopped. You drove me home and were so safe, and kind and good that I felt worse, dirtier, more tainted, but I needed you to stay because I was terrified." I stopped and Ben said nothing, but I could feel him taking in deep breaths as he fought his emotions. It was understandable but I was too afraid to look at him, so I plowed ahead.

"After that, I thought about going to the police, but I didn't, and I regret it," I said, my eyes filling with tears. "I thought that it was a he-said, she-said situation, and no one knew me in town, but everyone knew Frank and his family. I thought about the fact I'd been drinking and willing to a point, that I'd said yes, I wanted him. I thought about Nan, and what this might do to her. Lastly, and selfishly, I'd started to make real friends here, and if I could bury what had happened, I might have been happy for the first time in a long time. I said nothing. Then things changed with you, and I realised I had a chance of actually being *with* you. But I didn't want to make you dirty too, or tell you and have you only see Frank, not me. I couldn't risk it.

"Then I heard other girls had experienced worse than me and I couldn't remain silent. I'd begged the detectives to let me tell you in person that weekend, but somehow, Frank found out and in trying to intimidate me, incriminated himself. But then my secret was out, and that afternoon you came for me. I heard you outside my office and it almost killed me. I was sitting on the other side in tears. I wanted you to hold me, to tell me it was going to be okay, but I couldn't. I could not let you see me, to think about what Frank had done to me, to see the disgust in your face, or for you to not care for me, not love me. I was ashamed. Ashamed at what had happened and that I lied to you. I was afraid that it would be the end."

"But you came to see me," he said, his voice rough.

"I did. I decided that I should believe in both of us, and fight for what I wanted. But when I wanted to help you, and you got frustrated and I took the easy way out, running because the risk of rejection was still there; it wasn't resolved. I was indebted, and knew it would only get worse."

"Kate…"

"I know, it sounds wrong, but that's where I got to. I got pissed, because I need to be able to give back. That's part of my healing, and my new life here. I need to be able to reciprocate," I said, standing up so I could turn and look at him. I sucked in a deep breath when I saw angry tears in his eyes, his jaw clenched and his lips drawn tight as he tried to keep his hurt from spilling out. "Are you going to be okay with any of this?"

***

I was going to be okay. Eventually. All she had said cut me deep, and it would take me time to stop hurting. I would never stop wanting to beat the ever-loving shit out of Frank. The only thing balancing my need for vengeance, was the fact that she needed assurances that I still loved her and that I still wanted her. It was making her cry, and for the first time since my dad died, I was too.

I closed my eyes briefly, remembering her tear-soaked face the night I'd picked her up, and when she'd asked me to stay. Fuck, if I'd known what had happened, I would have done anything to make her feel better. But I couldn't have done anything at the time. This was going to be hard for me, not to wonder what I could have done, or if I had pulled my head out of my arse earlier, if I could have prevented it.

"Ben," Kate whispered. I opened my eyes, hoping I was looking at her with all the love I had in my heart.

"You are strong and brave, it floors me. I have no words. You are able to be honest and open, and optimistic about the future—it's awe-inspiring. You don't see it that way, maybe you never will, but from where I'm sitting, you have struggled through many challenges in life, and still remained a beautiful, generous and brave person. Lots of other people don't bounce back from that. I had one bad breakup and I moved overseas for years. But you? You're incredible," I said as I pulled her close and squeezed her.

"About that," she said, chewing her lip.

"About what?"

"Your breakup with Sheridan," she said. Hearing that name had my stomach dropping. "Ben, no. It's fine. I get why you didn't tell me about her."

'I was going to, I just wanted the right time. But then there was never a good time to explain how I'd lost it and disgraced myself."

"It sounds like she is the one that disgraced herself. She admitted as much," she said but I didn't understand. "Your mum made her explain to me what happened between you."

"You know?" I asked, searching her face for judgment.

"Only that she pushed you beyond your tipping point."

"It was more than that. Kate, I was so mad at her, so backed into a corner that I lashed out. I trashed a room, threw things, caused thousands of dollars of damage. I was an animal." I couldn't look at her yet, not wanting to know if it was too much.

"Ben, look at me," she said softly, putting a hand to my cheek, "No one is perfect. I'm sorry she pushed you and I'm even sorrier you didn't handle it how you wanted to. I know all about how it feels to act in a way that isn't who you want to be. But it's done; you need to let it go," she said, her grey eyes intense and glittering from yet more unshed tears.

"Let's leave all this behind us," I said, my voice harsh.

"What about Frank, and what he did?" she said, her voice cracking. I hated her feeling vulnerable, but she deserved the truth.

"Honestly, I am relieved he didn't get very far with you, for your sake. It should not have happened at all, but I think I would have completely lost my mind if he did *that* to you. As it is now, I am always going to want to kill him. It's going to take some time for me to stop wondering what I could have done differently. I wanted you from Sauce-gate too, and when I saw you after that, and kept putting my foot in it, I nearly knocked on your door and made you see I wasn't trying to offend you. Instead, I waited. I wished I hadn't; maybe things would be different. But I'm logical enough to know that hindsight isn't reality."

"This isn't your fault," she sobbed. "I know it isn't mine either, but—"

"Baby, shhh. You had it right. It isn't anyone's fault other than Frank's. We both need to help each other to get there. I want to move on, with you," I murmured as I rocked back and forth.

"You still want me? Like that?" she asked, peering up at me, her eyes red and puffy, looking as gorgeous as ever.

"Of course. Kate, that hasn't even entered my mind. I will always want you, in all ways," I said, but she seemed unconvinced. "My feelings on this, my emotions are geared towards anger that he hurt you, and regret I couldn't have done something to protect you. That's it. It will change us, but eventually, not for the worse. It will make us stronger."

"What about me not telling you?" She was pushing and I got she needed to *know* I was there.

"It hurt at the time, because I wanted to be what you needed. But it was selfish. I can see why you wanted to bury it. When it all came out, I couldn't fathom why you wouldn't let me in, but seeing you now, hearing why, I do. I hate all of it, but I understand why. To do my part, I'm going to make sure you know that I love you, from now until, all things going to plan, until we die of old age side by side."

She gave me a watery smile and nodded.

"We can do this," she croaked.

"We are going to do this," I told her and I kissed her, starting slow and sweet, tasting the salt on her lips, a reminder of what we had overcome. I took my time and she wrapped herself around me, and I her, as we reconnected. Before long, we started to get more passionate, and there was nothing I wanted to do more than to be her with her in every way. But before that, I needed to find out what she intended to do with her money. I ended our kiss and stood.

"It's getting dark, but we need to talk about this money. It's a lot and I might not ever be able to repay you. You won't want it, but I don't know how I can handle feeling indebted to you in this way. It's my pride, sure, but I can't switch it off. I should be providing for you, not the other way around."

"I'm the one who owes you a debt I cannot ever repay," she said cupping my face in her hands. I leant in to kiss her palm.

"What debt?"

"All I am offering you is money, but you have done infinitely more. You gave me my mother back—we walked that Bungalow Spur track and talked about her, making her real again, and I came to terms with how I felt about her. You gave me a family, pushing me about Nan, telling me about her so I could see her as I should have when I was young. I can't make old memories, but sharing yours helped me cross that abyss. I have your mum and sisters, who helped me with my master plan. You made me feel strong, being in my corner with Cleo and Layla, so I could reclaim my confidence and pride. You showed me that I was sexy, desirable and powerful. I hadn't thought it would be possible after everything, but being with you made me want to look forward, not back, and do it feeling like I deserved it. You didn't even know you were doing it, but by being you, and making love the way you do, meant I could want you, and be wanted in return. I could be touched by you, feel you inside me, thinking *only* of you. And you gave me hope. I had been alone, and I thought I was going to be okay with that. Then I met you, and you showed me how it could be. I won't hear about your debt because without realising it, you have given me more than I could ever repay."

"Kate," I breathed, trying to take in what she said.

"Don't. You need to accept it. I love you, and your openness and desire to make me happy has helped me find myself, find happy, find family and find you. You need to accept it. It's a non-negotiable," she said, kissing me before I could argue.

"I love you," I whispered at her lips.

"I love you too." Hearing her say those words, I knew it was going to be fine. I kissed her, worshiping her mouth with mine, wanting her to fully comprehend how much I loved her. Eventually, as night came in, I broke the kiss.

"Can we move on now? I don't want to talk about debts. It's too negative, and I don't feel like that at all," I said and she nodded.

"Okay, how about we talk about gifts? You have given me gifts," she said and I smiled, liking the sound of gifts better than debts.

"Speaking of gifts, tell me about this spending spree you've been on," I said as I grabbed her hand and started walking her to the shed.

"Well, the cows and tractor are gifts. You need to accept them."

"I'm working on that, but the designs for the home and accommodation? I can't let you do that."

"I know you can't. When I spoke to Howard, he suggested we start a business where we are equal shareholders, to start the accommodation side. If I contribute what we value the land at, then we can start building a few units. Would you be open to a joint venture?"

"You want to do that with your money?" I asked, not hating the idea.

"Yes, I believe in this idea. Howard does too and wanted to invest, but I didn't think that was what we wanted," she said.

"You really believe in it?" I stopped to look at her..

"I do. It's a good way to start our future, and the profits can fund our house. You know… if we go there," she said. Blushing. I kissed her hot and hard.

"Beautiful, we're going there," I assured her and she grinned.

"Good, because I don't want to have you making me scream your name with Nan next door."

"Fuck—don't ever mention that again. I won't be able to look at Alma now," I teased and she laughed as we started to walk again.

"It's going to be fun, building something with you. If you are happy to share your dream with me."

"You are the dream, Kate," I said, pulling her under my arm. "And I like the *we*. I want to do all of this with you, if that is what you want."

"I don't know much about farming, but I can give it a go."

"You named our cows," I chuckled and held her close.

"You bet. That way, you won't eat them."

ABOUT THE AUTHOR

As a girl growing up in Australia, Laura was lost in the world of *Anne of Green Gables* and *Little Women*. During high school, volleyball dominated her life. There had to be something positive about being 6'1" with red hair. Representing Australia from a young age she eventually took a scholarship at the University of Iowa. Living in America and being a full time athlete in a college town was an eye-opening experience and lots of fun (from what she can remember). #gohawkeyes

Returning from the States, her career took a different turn as she started working at the Red Cross and completed her Masters of Law in Human Rights. As one of the few non-lawyers in the class, her essays were far more floral than the rest, something that caused the discerning professors to shake their heads. Through working and studying, she realised there are other ways to win hearts and minds.

While she's spent the last 14 years as an advocate against poverty and homelessness, the desire to change the world through storytelling has only got stronger. She now lives in the Alpine Valley of North East Victoria, Australia with her husband, daughter, son, two dogs and seven chooks. When she's not doing the whole mum thing, working at a homelessness agency, renovating her farmhouse, or trying to do laundry bleary-eyed at midnight, she is writing.

Say G'day to Laura:
website: www.lsimpsonauthor.com
facebook: facebook.com/l.simpson.romance
twitter: @ladyporepunkah
instagram: @lsimpsonauthor
linkedin: linkedin.com/in/laura-simpson-47278971

OTHER BOOKS BY L. SIMPSON

Love Sabre
Beyond Today
Good Trouble

www.BOROUGHSPUBLISHINGGROUP.com

If you enjoyed this book, please write a review. Our authors appreciate the feedback, and it helps future readers find books they love. We welcome your comments and invite you to send them to info@boroughspublishinggroup.com. Follow us on Facebook, Twitter and Instagram, and be sure to sign up for our newsletter for surprises and new releases from your favorite authors.

Are you an aspiring writer? Check out www.boroughspublishinggroup.com/submit and see if we can help you make your dreams come true.

www.ingramcontent.com/pod-product-compliance
Lightning Source LLC
Chambersburg PA
CBHW031309120626
46554CB00001BA/347